PUT ON
THE ARMOUR
of
LIGHT

PUT ON
THE ARMOUR
of
LIGHT

CATHERINE MACDONALD

DUNDURN
TORONTO

Editor: Laura Harris
Design: Colleen Wormald
Cover design: Jesse Hooper
Cover image: © Alex Belomlinsky/iStockphoto
Printer: Webcom

Library and Archives Canada Cataloguing in Publication

Macdonald, Catherine, 1949-, author

  Put on the armour of light / author: Catherine Macdonald.

Issued in print and electronic formats.

ISBN 978-1-4597-1549-3 (pbk.).--ISBN 978-1-4597-1550-9 (pdf).--ISBN 978-1-4597-1551-6 (epub)

  I. Title.

PS8625.D626P87 2014   C813'.6   C2014-901027-3   C2014-901028-1

1 2 3 4 5   18 17 16 15 14

 Conseil des Arts du Canada **Canada Council for the Arts** Canada ONTARIO ARTS COUNCIL / CONSEIL DES ARTS DE L'ONTARIO / an Ontario government agency / un organisme du gouvernement de l'Ontario

We acknowledge the support of the **Canada Council for the Arts** and the **Ontario Arts Council** for our publishing program. We also acknowledge the financial support of the **Government of Canada** through the **Canada Book Fund** and **Livres Canada Books**, and the **Government of Ontario** through the **Ontario Book Publishing Tax Credit** and the **Ontario Media Development Corporation**.

Care has been taken to trace the ownership of copyright material used in this book. The author and the publisher welcome any information enabling them to rectify any references or credits in subsequent editions.

J. Kirk Howard, President

The publisher is not responsible for websites or their content unless they are owned by the publisher.

Printed and bound in Canada.

Visit us at
Dundurn.com | @dundurnpress | Facebook.com/dundurnpress | Pinterest.com/Dundurnpress

Dundurn
3 Church Street, Suite 500
Toronto, Ontario, Canada
M5E 1M2

 MIX / Paper from responsible sources / FSC® C004071

For GKM

1.

June 4, 1899

"Sergeant, if you want me to take a photograph of his head you'll have to get out of the way."

Setter, startled by the sound of her voice, sprang up from the crouching position that he had been holding too long for the comfort of his knees. They had not spoken for almost twenty minutes and she had spent most of that time huddled underneath the black cloth that covered the back of her camera, doing mystifying things with its finely calibrated dials and settings.

"Sorry." His voice sounded loud in his own ears. "I was thinking about the blood. Not much here, even though it's a scalp wound. Can you take the head from several angles?"

She emerged from under the black cloth, stretching gingerly. "Of course; still lifes are rather a specialty of mine — oh, mercy!" She clapped a hand to her mouth and stifled a giggle.

Setter gave her a tired smile. "It's all right, Mrs. Cliffe. A little lightness actually helps in these situations."

He was relieved that it was only lightness she was indulging in. Rosetta Cliffe had a steadiness that was, in his opinion, unusual for her sex. If she had been prone to female histrionics, he would not have hired her for this kind of job. As it was, he had been stepping carefully around the room with his gloved hands for two hours; writing in his notebook, directing Rosetta to photograph the open safe, the desk top, the upset waste paper basket, the papers strewn on the floor, the chair on its side, confident that he could do his work while she did hers. They had only just gotten to the prostrate figure lying in front of the fireplace, his — its — head cocked at an odd angle over the fender.

If Rosetta was unnerved by the earthly remains of Joseph Asseltine, she was refusing to show it. She ducked under the cloth to recheck the focus against the ground-glass viewfinder, made a last adjustment to the stand on which the flash lamp was fastened, and pressed the shutter release. There was a loud *whump* and everything was frozen in white light, including Inspector Crossin, who had entered the room just as the flash lamp exploded.

"For God's sake, Setter. How long are you going to be at this? — Whew!" Crossin wrinkled his nose and waved his hands to clear the smoke from the spent flash powder. "I thought I told you. A few photographs to record the position of the body. Not a damned portfolio."

"Yes, I know, sir," Setter said. "But I felt we needed a few pictures of the rest of the room. And Mrs. Cliffe does such excellent work."

Crossin shot an embarrassed look at Rosetta and touched the brim of his hat to her. "Mrs. Cliffe, pardon my language. Now look, Setter. I've told you before — these extras of yours are well outside our standard practice."

"Yes, sir, but it's just extremely useful to be able to record what the murderer — if that's what he is — left for us to see."

"What do you mean, 'if that's what he is'? Look at this poor sod." Crossin pointed to the unfortunate deceased. "He didn't do this to himself, you know."

"Well, with respect, sir, we don't know that for certain and that's why I would hate to miss something. It's too late after the room has been cleared and cleaned and all the details obliterated."

"Look — my other detectives could follow your example in the way of effort and we'd all be better off." He dropped his voice and turned Setter slightly to the side. "But most likely we've got our man in custody already and — blast it." He tugged his hat off and rubbed the back of his neck. "You know I have to account to the chief for every paper clip."

"I understand that, sir." The sergeant's lips flattened into a stubborn line. "I'll take care of it."

Crossin shook his head, "Setter. What's to be done with you? No wonder you never have any money to go on a holiday or take some nice young lady out dancing."

"Oh, I get along all right, sir." He made a business out of brushing flash powder off his sleeves. "But I suppose I'll have to continue being a non-dancing stay-at-home until the chief either increases the investigation budget or raises my wages."

"Well, you and I had better continue working in the vineyard to hasten that happy day." Crossin pulled out his watch. "Which means me reporting to the chief now ... and you getting things finished up here by 6:00 a.m. And don't speak to the press. The chief wants us to get more information out of the killer before the news gets out."

The door closed behind Crossin and Setter stood for a moment looking after him, absently pulling at the fingers of his gloves.

"Well, Mrs. Cliffe. Let's get on with it, shall we?"

2.

The chief was less than pleased at having been roused in the middle of the night, but he stood stoically in the early morning light with Inspector Crossin, straightening the folds of his tunic while Crossin, grasping the knocker, rapped loudly on the door at the Martland house. They were a little surprised when the door opened after about fifteen seconds to reveal a pale young man who was hoisting his suspenders as he drew the door inward. He was joined almost immediately by a young woman in a house coat, her hair in braids.

"Yes? What is it?"

"Inspector Crossin, sir. This is Chief Constable McMeekin. Is Mr. Martland at home?"

"I'm Mr. Martland —"

"— Mr. Frank Martland?"

"Oh, no, of course. You mean my father. Please come in. I'll just run up and —"

"What's all this, Trevor?"

The young man turned around to face an older man descending the stairs and pulling a silk dressing gown around his night shirt.

"It's the police, Father."

"McMeekin? What's happened?"

"Sorry to drag you out of your bed so early, Frank. I'm afraid there's been a terrible tragedy. I've just come from your offices. Joseph Asseltine was found in your office a few hours ago — dead — and there's evidence, I'm sorry to say, of foul play."

"Lord! Angus? What is all this?" Martland brushed his hair back from his face. "What the — are you telling me he was murdered?"

"I'm afraid it looks that way."

"Who would do that to him?"

"We have a man in custody, Frank. He was found at the scene in a drunken condition. He appears to have been one of Joe's — er — card-playing friends; something about a gambling debt."

"You say this happened in my office? Not Joe's?"

"It appears Joe was getting money from the safe —"

"The safe, good Christ! Don't tell me the fellow got into my safe. I'll have to go there immediately." Martland started for the stairs.

"You will certainly want to see to your office, Frank. But our people will have to finish in there first." He turned to the inspector. "How long before Setter and that photographer woman are finished?"

Crossin consulted his watch. "Should be done by now, sir."

"I'll just get dressed and go. Ethel, some coffee for these gentlemen. Trevor, you finish dressing and come with me." Martland started up the stairs, followed by the young man.

"Wait, Frank —"

Martland stopped and turned.

"The thing is, Frank, one of my men will have to be with you at all times while you're on the premises today."

"What? But these are my own offices. Are you saying I can't

set foot in my own office without a constable following me around like a dog?" Martland advanced on the chief.

"That's exactly what I'm saying, Frank. For the rest of today, while we are conducting our inquiries, no one will be admitted without our authorization. I've posted a constable at the door to turn your employees away this morning."

Martland paced up and down the foyer. "But all our most important legal documents are in that safe. And a certain amount of cash and bank information. I've got to make sure it's all still there."

"And we need you to do that as well. It's just that you'll have Constable Smithers for company. Just a formality, you understand. Why don't you have a bit of breakfast and we'll take you to your office in my carriage."

Martland scowled but, finally, heaving a resigned sigh, he motioned for the men to follow Ethel into the kitchen.

3.

"I'm going to cast you forth into outer darkness."

Charles picked up the blue croquet ball and cradled it against his own red ball, which he steadied with his foot. The mallet struck the braced ball with a mighty *thwack* and the blue ball ricocheted away, scudded across the lawn and came to rest in the far Caragana hedge.

"I thought you were a nobler man than that," Maggie said.

"I was, until you did the same thing to me in the last round. Revenge!" Charles capered nimbly around the girl, then tapped his ball through two hoops in a row, hit it again toward the next set of hoops and was just taking aim when the front gate creaked open and then sprang shut. A policeman was walking across the shade-dappled lawn toward them. He looked uncomfortably warm in his dark navy serge and did not hurry but walked deliberately, tugging with one hand at the white- and blue-striped arm band to make sure that the silver service number pinned to it was at the proper angle to be seen. He touched the hard peak of his helmet and briefly inclined his head to each of them in turn.

"Good evening, sir, miss. I'm Constable Gillies. Are you Mr. Lauchlan? The Reverend Mr. Lauchlan?"

Charles looked around for his suit coat as he rolled down the sleeves of his shirt and straightened his clerical dickey.

"I'm Lauchlan, Constable, and this is Miss Skene. How did you find me?"

"Your landlady told me I could find you here, sir. You're wanted at the station house on an urgent matter."

"What kind of urgent matter?" Charles was trying to find the sleeve of his coat as he spoke, slowly rotating backwards while Maggie danced around him, holding the sleeve taut in her outstretched hand.

"One of our prisoners wants to speak with you; I can't say anything more than that until you attend at the station, sir."

Charles did not hide his puzzlement. "Urgent? Look, I've got to lead the prayer meeting tonight. It's the last before the fall. Can I come along after that?"

"Well, sir, my orders were to collect you and bring you back direct if at all possible."

"Aha. Yes, well in that case I'll come right away. Maggie, tell your father I'm obliged to leave and thank your Aunt Jessie for a most excellent meal. Where's my hat? And could you send a note over to the church that I'll be late to the prayer meeting? Grand. Shall we go, Constable?"

"I'm coming with you." Finally she managed to stuff his arm into the sleeve.

"No, you're not. A police station is no place for a young girl. Isn't that right, Constable?"

"Oh, we get plenty of young women, sir, and our new station house has some of the most modern facilities in Canada to keep them while they wait their turn with the magistrate."

"You see, Charles. Mrs. Doolittle says that women need to see what's really happening in the world; not be shielded from the least unpleasantness."

"Well, my respects to Mrs. Doolittle, but she's a mature woman with children whereas —"

"Exactly. And how do you suppose she got all that maturity if not from a certain amount of experience. Aren't you always telling us in Bible study that we should take our faith out into the world? And anyway, stop acting as if you're called to the police station everyday because to my certain knowledge this is the first time and you don't know what to expect any more than I do."

Before he could be firm with her, she had disappeared into the house to tell her father that he should be prepared to lead the prayer meeting and that she must be spared to take advantage of a Maturing Experience. To Maggie's delight, they did not have to take a streetcar to the station. Constable Gillies handed her up into the police department's newest horse-drawn van, its sombre navy blue paint still fresh and smelling of polish with WINNIPEG POLICE stencilled in white on the side. She insisted on sharing the driver's seat with Gillies while Charles was wedged into a kind of pull-down seat behind them. Gillies shook the reins and they drew away from the curb at a stately trot.

"Look, Charles. There's Mrs. Dowdall." Maggie pointed in the direction of a plump lady pressing a Psalm book to her bosom and striding purposefully toward the tram stop at the head of the street. "Good evening, Mrs. Dowdall."

Charles smiled wanly and tipped his hat to the wife of his clerk of session.

This will hardly mend my fences with Dowdall, Charles thought. He pictured the woman describing the scene to her anxious, methodical husband. "Making a display of himself by riding in a paddy wagon — with Principal Skene's daughter, of all things. And the prayer meeting to start in less than forty-five minutes!"

From his perch in the police van, Charles watched the sights of Broadway roll past. Streetcar rails bisected the wide avenue and the elms alongside the tracks — just saplings, really — did little to impede his view. After the mansard roof of the legislature on Kennedy and the red sandstone turrets of the new law courts building to the north came the ample houses of the city's first magnates. He named them off to himself as the van passed by: *Ashdown, Brydges, Robinson, Schultz. Funny how these homes, so impressive only a few years ago, now looked a little behind the times.* There was talk that the lots that were still open closer to Main Street would be taken up with blocks of apartments for the newly married young lawyers and real estate executives.

Charles tilted his face upward into a breeze that was scented with honeysuckle. *Could there be anything finer than an evening in June?* He thought. *Especially if you could spend it in Winnipeg, where we're busy giving the cities of old Canada a good shaking up.*

But then he was not out for an inconsequential evening drive. Maggie was right; he was not in the habit of "attending" at the police station. Who was the prisoner that wanted to speak with him? His church was in what the professional men and business owners of his congregation called "a bad section of town": on Dufferin Avenue, near the grease and soot of the Canadian Pacific Railway line. He thought about the young railway and factory workers, with their rough hands and slicked-down hair, who sat in pews on the other side of the aisle from the businessmen. He would have been surprised if it were one of them. As long as they were employed they had little time to get in trouble with the law.

What about the Ruthenian families who increasingly populated the neighbourhood around the church? Many of his parishioners expected the worst from them and — to his shame — he had shared their sentiments. When raising money to build the church, he had written articles for the newspapers and given lectures at the YMCA, thundering against the stealing, bootlegging, drunkenness, and prostitution that went on near the rail yards. That was before he had been inside the shanties and tin sheds some Ruthenians had built for themselves. Using cast-off packing materials and anything else they could scrounge, their ramshackle homes occupied fetid alleyways and barren road allowances. If he had been forced to live like that, he might well be selling illegal liquor, too, or fencing stolen goods, or worse. And then the families who attended the English classes given in the parish hall had surprised him with their eagerness to learn, pushing their children into the front seats so that they could hear better. Had the summons to the police station come from one of these poor souls?

Once they had passed through the stone portico of the police station, Gillies led him up the stairs to the main floor, down a hallway, and into a cramped office in which an officer in plain clothes sat huddled over a desk covered with papers and files. He was about forty and as he murmured a distracted greeting and rustled among the papers, Charles was struck by the singularity of his features. The high bridged nose, flatter and wider at the nostrils, and the burnished expanse of cheek bone suggested native Indian blood, yet his eyes were blue, and his hair was wavy as it fell heavily in a chestnut-coloured swatch over his forehead.

Charles introduced himself and Maggie.

The officer belatedly sprang to his feet to acknowledge Maggie, his face betraying some surprise. He shook Charles's hand and bobbed his head to Maggie. "Miss Skene, how do you do? Setter. Andrew Setter. I'm sergeant of detectives for the Central Division. I'm sorry for all the secrecy Mr. Lauchlan. We haven't released the news to the papers yet. Reporters have been sniffing around here all day hoping someone would let something slip."

"Let what slip? Sergeant Setter, what is this all about? Why have I been sent for?"

"At approximately 11:30 p.m. last evening, Mr. Joseph Asseltine was found dead in his place of business, apparently the victim of foul play."

"Asseltine!"

"You know him then?"

"Yes — no. I know *of* him. His partner, Mr. Martland, is a member of my congregation."

"As it happens Mr. Asseltine's body was discovered in Mr. Martland's office. The suspect was apprehended there as well."

"The suspect?"

"Yes, soon to be the accused. That's why we called you in. He wants to speak to you. Come this way please. Miss Skene, please make yourself comfortable here until we come back." This last was an order rather than an invitation.

4.

Charles was full of questions, but Setter had walked briskly out of his office and then disappeared down a set of stairs. Charles gave Maggie a severe look to make sure she didn't follow and hurried after Setter. The stairway led to the basement where the cells were located. He caught up to the sergeant as Setter was asking the on-duty constable to show them to cell number 11. They walked down a narrow central hallway with cells on either side. Charles sensed rather than saw that most of the cells were occupied. It took a moment or two for his eyes to adjust to the dim light. The constable stopped at number 11, inserted a key in the lock, and swung the door open, gesturing for Charles to enter. Setter remained in the hallway.

Charles felt an inexplicable pang of fear. The figure lying on the bottom bunk had been startled from sleep by the sudden opening of the door. He was shambling to a seated position. The voice, when it came, was a like a dry reed.

"I'm afraid there isn't any place to sit, Charlie. Would it be possible to bring Mr. Lauchlan a chair?" This was addressed to Setter, who turned and spoke quietly to the on-duty constable.

Something was tickling at the back of Charles's brain. "I'm

afraid I don't …" The accused man rose from the bunk and his face broke through into the glare of the sputtering gaslight from the hall outside the cell.

"Peter? … Pete!"

"Hello, Charlie." The words came out quietly, the eyes bright and huge in the thin face, the spare frame pulling itself erect as if preparing to fend off a blow.

Pete and Charlie. Peter had been Charles's roommate at the University of Toronto. "Madman McEvoy" they had called him behind his back, a nickname earned after he had spent three full days and nights constructing a model of a building that was so unlike anything that then existed on the streets of Toronto that fellow students who wandered into their room had just gaped and shook their heads. Flushed with pride, Peter had tried to explain the structure and how it worked and what had inspired it, but his listeners just looked at him blankly. Two days later he had returned drunk and sullen after curfew and, before Charles could stop him, had demolished the model with two not very deft kicks.

As his closest friend, it had fallen to Charles to mediate between Peter and a world that did not understand him. *Charlie and Pete.* In spite of his best efforts, Charles couldn't achieve for Peter the accepting comradeship that he himself had gained so easily. How often had a group of roaring lads run by their room, calling for Charles to join them? Charles would say, "Right, grand! Hang on till I get Pete." No one would say anything but Charles could read the looks.

That kind of thing just made Peter more determined to steer into the wind. Famously, he stood up in one of Dr. Skene's Sunday afternoon Bible study classes and declared that the Westminster Confession may have suited the believers of 1646, but, since he had read Darwin and Huxley he could not, in good conscience, subscribe to it. With this he quietly left the room, packed up his effects, and had left the university before Charles had even realized he was gone. And that was the last Charles had seen or heard of Peter McEvoy until this moment.

Charles gripped Peter by one elbow, grabbed his hand, and gave it a thorough shaking. "Pete, for goodness' sake! After all this time — it must be fifteen years. Why didn't you write? I tried and tried to find you but nobody had a blessed idea where you were." Behind this bonhomie, Charles was fighting an urgent desire to get out — down the hall, up the stairs, out the door, and into the sweet evening air.

"It's good to see you, Charlie," Peter said, his head bobbing as he tried to withstand the handshake. "Yes, I know, I should have written, I suppose. It's just that I was doing a lot of travelling. Seeing a lot of things, never settled enough to have an address for long. You understand."

Charles didn't understand anything but he said, "Well, yes, I suppose, but ... well, it's good to see you; how have you been keeping?" The absurdity of that question was instantly apparent to both of them. He tried again. "When did you get to Winnipeg?"

"Oh, well, not that long ago, really. Ah ... about a year, I suppose."

"A year! And you never called on me? And I've never run into you on the street?"

"Well, Charlie ... we probably don't move in the same circles." Peter made a sweeping gesture with his arm to refer to his current residence.

"Ah, right. Yes, I see." He forced himself to look around the cell. "Mind you, it does remind me — uncannily — of our old room."

Peter gave an obedient laugh. "Minus the view, however."

The on-duty constable returned with a chair, which Charles took and carefully placed as far back in the cell as he could manage without actually having the chair back touch the far wall opposite the bunks. Charles looked in Setter's direction, waiting for him to leave, but Setter remained leaning against the frame of the open cell door. Peter resumed his sitting position on the bunk and Charles sat on the chair.

There was a silence that both tried to end by speaking at the same time. Then Peter said, "I suppose you're hoping this is some kind of mistake." He let the air out of his lungs, sighing deeply. "I'm hoping that too. They're trying to say that I killed him, Charlie."

"Asseltine?"

"Yes. I was there, I know. I can remember that. And I saw him there on the floor. But I didn't kill him. At least I don't think so." He cleared his throat and looked Charles directly in the eye. "I'd had a few drinks, you see."

Charles took in the shabby suit, bagged at the knees and elbows, the smudged shirt, the hair that hadn't seen a barber for about three months, the four-day beard. A sour smell wafted off of Peter.

"Forgive my appearance. They don't let you have razors in here — for obvious reasons." Peter's hands were shaking. He reached down and gripped the straw mattress. "Just hear me out. I need to tell you what I remember. I've played cards with Asseltine a number of times; he wasn't a very good player, but he was keen. Always looking for a game at the Metropole or the Express — any backroom setup he could find. He'd bet on anything, too. Horses, dogs, lacrosse matches, boxing. He had enough cash, I guess, to cover all his losses. Anyway, he owed me some money and I had pressed him for it a few days ago. He had said to come to his office late because he kept cash in the office safe, so that his wife wouldn't know about it. I was playing cards at the Metropole to put in the time before my appointment with him. Then everything gets confused. I've got little snatches of things, like lantern slides — only faster. I was there, in Martland's office. Asseltine was on the floor and I couldn't make out why he was there. Some man in overalls was kneeling over Asseltine and shouting at me. Someone was slapping my face. There were policemen ... that's about all I remember, until I woke up here."

"You mean you can you make a living playing cards?" Charles couldn't quite take in what Peter was saying.

"No ... yes. Look Charlie, you've got to listen to me. The last thing I wanted was to drag you into all this. But I'll be frank; my back is to the wall. Can you help me get out of here? Is there a chance of bail? Do you know a lawyer who could help me? I don't have any money at all and I've lost touch, you could say, with any family I have, but if I could get a loan —"

"Pete, I'm not ... — there's —"

"I know you don't have much, but you know people, well-off people who —"

"Well ... Pete ... I don't know about that. It's not that easy." Charles turned to Setter. "Is there a possibility of bail?"

"It's a bit unusual in murder cases but bail is sometimes granted. There would be conditions."

"What kind of conditions?" asked Charles.

"The court would likely require a sum of money to be put up — perhaps several thousand dollars and someone — probably you — would have to stand surety for him," said Setter.

"'Surety'? What does that mean?"

Setter looked uncomfortable. "Because of Mr. McEvoy's ... tendencies, the judge may fear that he wouldn't appear for his trial, or that he would turn up in an unfit mental state. Someone who stands surety would have to guarantee his appearance in court and be liable for the fee if he didn't appear."

"Several thousand! I couldn't put up even a fraction of that. I don't have any assets. My God, this place — Charlie, you can't imagine. They won't even give you a lamp when it gets dark …" Peter put his head in his hands.

Charles was in turmoil. Where was the long-ago comrade of the rugby field, that worthy adversary in late-night arguments on ridiculous subjects, that fellow contestant in the bewildering rites of manhood? Charles couldn't find him in this dishevelled stranger. He was appalled that he had been calculating the extent of his obligation to Peter — and even more appalled that he had been asking himself what Maggie and her father would think of his friendship with a person like Peter. Even if they could deliver the bail money, could Peter be relied on to turn up for his trial sober? Why not step back and let the law do what it would; if Peter was really innocent, surely evidence would be found to prove it. Charles made an effort not to remember various texts he had quoted from the pulpit as he looked at Peter, who now sat miserably with his head bowed. His hands, as they hung over his knees, trembled.

"Pete?" Charles said.

"Yes." He did not look up.

"I — I can't promise you anything, but I'll try. I'll see what can be done."

Peter raised his head. "I'm telling the truth, Charlie. If I killed him, I think I would feel it."

Charles said, in a rather flat voice, "Then I think, Sergeant, that I should start — right away — looking for someone capable of putting up the bail money. And I'll have to find a lawyer."

Setter immediately moved to clear the doorway. "We can go over the technical details of the bail application upstairs."

"Thank you," Charles said as both he and Peter stood. Charles was afraid that Peter would weep and he held his hands suspended on either side of Peter's arms, bracketing rather than touching — as if to hold him together. "Pete, I'll do my best. Try not to worry. I'll come back and see you as soon as I can."

Peter, his jaw and throat working hard, simply nodded.

5.

Maggie had been pacing slowly in Setter's cubbyhole of an office. *Two steps, turn, two steps, turn.* She was wondering if Charles ever took her seriously. In spite of the fact that she was now a student at the university and had just celebrated her nineteenth birthday, he treated her in a familiar, off-hand way, the way one would act toward a younger sister. It was annoying. She had known Charles since he had been a student himself and she had been prepared to make allowances for him. But his picture of her seemed to be stuck in the time when they had all lived in Toronto — when she had been a little girl and when Mother and Ralph were still alive. She had made a concerted effort not to be stuck in that time herself. And because there was just the two of them now, herself and Father — and, of course, Aunt Jessie — Maggie had needed to grow up quickly. Surely, Charles should be able to see that. He was still her favourite partner for japes and fun, but that didn't mean she was a floss-headed little ninny, incapable of holding up her end of a serious conversation.

Setter's sudden entrance with Charles startled her. They seemed full of purpose; Setter almost bowled her over as he reached for a file on his desk. The two men ignored Maggie while they discussed the technicalities of the bail application.

Then Charles said, "Maggie, will your father be at home when we get back to your house?"

"I'm not sure." She looked at the watch that she wore pinned to her dress. "The prayer meeting should just be over. He'll probably have reached home by the time we get there."

"The prayer meeting! I'd forgotten all about that." Charles smacked his forehead with his open palm.

"Don't worry. Father was there and he's perfectly capable of leading a prayer meeting. Who wanted to speak to you down there? What is this all about?"

"Oh ... an old friend ... well, not — yes, an old friend. One I haven't seen in a long while." He explained, as delicately as he could, about Peter and his predicament. Maggie was an extremely bright girl but she was, after all, still a girl and he felt compelled to shield her from the details exposing the kind of life Peter had obviously been leading. Charles sometimes wondered if he had been wise to let her to read some of the books and pamphlets he had ordered from the United States.

"Father will know someone who can put up the bail money," said Maggie.

"Yes, er ... that was what I was thinking, too."

"Charles, we have to do everything we can to help Mr. McEvoy. Did you get him to tell you exactly what he remembers? Did you take notes?"

"Well, no, come to think of it." Charles, a little late, caught up to Maggie. "Now listen, there is to be no 'we' about this. 'We' are not going to help Mr. McEvoy. *I* am going to work on this and *you* are going to work on your German and see to whatever vile potions you have brewing in the chemistry laboratory."

"Taking notes is my department, Miss Skene." Charles

and Maggie had almost forgotten Setter was in the room with them. "And as it happens, now that he's more himself I will be interviewing him at length about what he remembers; how he got to the crime scene and so on. Members of the public do not conduct murder investigations and I would ask you to remember that."

"Well, no, of course not, Setter. We'll leave that to you. But isn't it a little premature to charge Peter if your investigation isn't more advanced than that?"

"Well, now, that's a fair question, Mr. Lauchlan." Setter sat down on the edge of his desk and looked down at his boots for a second. "I asked the inspector that same thing. The chief seems to be of a mind that it's an open-and-shut case. Mr. Asseltine's taste for gambling was well known to us. The one coherent thing Mr. McEvoy said last night was that he had gone to Asseltine's place of business to collect on a gambling debt. Maybe Mr. McEvoy saw his opportunity to get more money out of Mr. Asseltine than what was owed to him. In his inebriated condition a struggle took place during which Mr. McEvoy inflicted the blows that led to Mr. Asseltine's death."

"Who found Peter there? Did they actually see him inflicting harm on Mr. Asseltine?"

"It was the janitor. He lives in the building and was making his last round for the night. And no, he did not see Mr. McEvoy attack Mr. Asseltine. McEvoy was sitting with Mr. Martland's whisky decanter cradled in his arms, 'like the dearest infant,' as the janitor described it. He locked McEvoy in the office and got his boy to run for the police. By the time he returned to the scene, McEvoy had lost consciousness altogether."

"Well, if no one saw the struggle, doesn't that mean there is no conclusive evidence that Peter was the one who killed Asseltine?" Charles said.

"That's correct — for the moment. The whole matter requires further investigation," Setter replied.

"And how do we know that Mr. Asseltine didn't attack Mr. McEvoy?" said Maggie. "Mr. McEvoy might simply have been defending himself and the whole thing was a terrible accident."

"It might have happened that way, right enough. We just don't know at this point until I conduct more inquiries. My inspector has decided that McEvoy's presence at the scene is grounds enough to charge him and he so recommended to the Crown." Setter looked down at his boots again.

Charles gave Setter a long, appraising look. "Sergeant, you don't think it's an open-and-shut case, do you? Otherwise you wouldn't be telling us as much as you have."

"Mr. Lauchlan, all I can say is, do all you can to get your friend bail and a lawyer."

"But, Setter —"

"No, Mr. Lauchlan. I've said more than I should already. Now if you don't mind, I have notes to prepare for Inspector Crossin."

"Very well, thank you, Sergeant Setter. Thank you very much." Charles extended his hand and Setter shook it firmly and saw them to foyer of the station.

Setter watched as Charles shouldered open the front door and conducted Maggie through it. *Well, that's done,* Setter thought. *Seems a good enough fellow. If he can save McEvoy from whatever lazy incompetent the Law Society Charitable Committee sends over it will be worth a dressing down from Crossin.*

He took out his watch as he walked back down the hall to his office. Smithers was fifteen minutes late, which surprised Setter, since the boy was, if anything, too hurried and inclined to rush to conclusions without sufficient thought. Setter wondered if he should have interviewed the cleaning staff at Martland and Asseltine himself. As if on cue, he heard quick, brogue-clad steps in the hall, and Smithers almost fell through the doorway.

"There you are. Have you finished with the cleaning ladies? What did they say?"

"Sorry, Sergeant — ran the last six blocks — knew you'd be waiting." Smithers flipped open his notebook and tried to catch his breath before beginning. "Right. The cleaning staff consists of the janitor's wife — a Mrs. Orelia Fuchs — and another woman — Mrs. Alice Gillespie, a neighbour." He stopped to breathe again. "I spoke to them both. They clean the whole office every second night, after supper when the offices are closed, including sweeping the carpets. They cleaned the office last night before the — um — alleged murder. I replaced the button right where you found it, near the leg of the desk. Neither of them recognized the button and Mrs. Janitor said — and she was definite — that she had used the carpet sweeper around and under Mr. Martland's desk last night and if the button had been there, she would have seen it and picked it up."

"So they cleaned the office a few hours before Asseltine died?"

"That's right."

"And Mrs. Janitor swears the button was not there when they cleaned?"

"Right again."

"Did Mrs. Janitor seem a credible witness?"

"Well, sir, she reminds me of my Aunt Florrie. She is a woman who knows her own mind and yours, too, if you know what I mean."

"Good, that's grand." He looked at his desk calendar and made a note on it. "Bring them along in the morning and I'll take a formal statement from Mrs. Fuchs. You can do the one for Mrs., Mrs? —"

"Gillespie, sir. That's all fine. What's next?"

"Well, we keep trying to find the person who belongs to the button, I suppose. It didn't come off of either McEvoy or Asseltine, at least not from what they were wearing last night. And the janitor was wearing overalls and a flannel shirt, so he's out, too."

"What about Mr. Martland?"

"Oh, well, after you had escorted him off the scene the inspector and I went back with him to his house to ask him a few more questions and I searched his closets."

"Well, sir, I hope he was a little more pleasant to you than he was when I supervised his search of the safe and the office."

"Not really. Hated the fact that I wouldn't tell him what I was looking for, of course, and didn't bother to hide how he felt about me searching through his closets and drawers. Probably sent the works out to be cleaned after I had left."

"Oh, well, uh, hmm. Was there anything there?"

"Nothing like the button we found. I expect we're going to be royally sick of buttons by the time this investigation is through."

6.

Maggie was full of questions on the way home on the street-car, but Charles was only half listening to her and after a few moments she gave up in disgust, spending the rest of the journey with her head resting against the frame of the open tram window, letting the breeze stir through her hair and play on her face.

Charles was busy working out how to frame Peter's situation when he talked with Maggie's father. He found himself at the Skene house often, dining with the family at least once a week and dropping by at other times with the easy assurance of a warm welcome. He felt completely at home in the large, bright house, which, though modestly furnished, provided more creature comforts than his cramped suite of rented rooms on Edmonton Street. He was a particular favourite of Miss Jessie Skene, who stuffed him with food and pricked up her ears at the mere mention of any unmarried ladies he had met; news which he dangled in front of her and then playfully withheld.

The confidence to be on teasing terms with the family had only come with long association. With one or two other theology students, Charles had become a fixture at Sunday lunch, or tea, when Dr. Skene had been minister at St. Andrew's in

Toronto. Over the crumbs of buttered scones, Charles had nervously voiced his idea about setting up an itinerant mission for the miners and lumbermen along the railway between Prince Arthur's Landing and Rat Portage. It was an idea that for many of his elders smacked suspiciously of Methodism. If Dr. Skene had not seen the value of taking the church to where the miners and lumberjacks actually lived, and had he not pushed for the scheme in synod and general assembly meetings, Charles would never have been able to carry out his plan. It was the same when Dr. Skene had become principal of the new college in Winnipeg, where Charles was struggling to persuade skeptical church authorities to found a mission for railway and factory workers. That was the beginning of what was now Dufferin Avenue Presbyterian Church. He owed the older man a great deal and was a bit ashamed of being more intent on pleasing James Skene than he was at pleasing his own father.

That was why it was terribly important to demonstrate that Dufferin Avenue was worthy of the dearly won resources the church had devoted to it. And so, from morning till late at night, he busied himself setting up and running the soup kitchen, the clothing depot, the English classes, securing a doctor and nurse for a weekly free clinic, and finding books for the free library. That was in addition to the regular duties of sermon writing and leading the Sunday services morning and evening, Sabbath school, weekly prayer meetings, confirmation classes and Bible study, Young People's Society meetings, session meetings, and taking part with his clerical brethren in presbytery and synod. In six years he had established a full-fledged congregation, which included a growing number of influential but reform-minded parishioners like the Skenes and a small number of wealthy businessmen whose patronage was essential to the continued operation of the church and all its programs.

The Skene residence on Balmoral Street was a large and rambling house of yellow brick with an octagonal turret, a bow window, and a broad, ivy-covered verandah that embraced both the front and the side of the house. The college owned the house and provided it for Principal Skene and his family; it was understood that prospective board members would be courted there and, in its comfortable parlour, Presbyterian businessmen would be gently turned upside down and all the money shaken out of their pockets. This was as important as anything the Reverend Dr. James Carmichael Skene might do at his office on the second floor of the barely completed St. Giles College building on Colony Street, a building for which the principal was still anxiously soliciting donations. With the help of Jessie and Maggie and the services of a part-time cook and full-time hired girl, Dr. Skene kept a good table. A dinner invitation to the Skene house was as valued as any in Winnipeg although, of course, there would be no sherry before dinner and no claret with the Sunday joint. For that, one needed an invitation to the Archbishop of Rupert's Land's drafty residence at the foot of Machray Avenue, overlooking the lazy brown current of the Red River.

When Charles and Maggie arrived at the house, Aunt Jessie was on the verandah having just settled with her mending. A young man had been sitting on the porch steps toying absent-mindedly with a croquet mallet and engaging her in conversation. He stood when he saw Charles and Maggie coming through the front gate.

"Here she is, Mr. Martland," said Aunt Jessie. "Maggie, Mr. Martland was kind enough to bring us home from the prayer meeting in his carriage. He wanted to return those books you lent him."

"Hello, Trev. You won't believe where we've been! What happened to Mr. Asseltine is simply awful but wait till I tell —" These words were no sooner out of her mouth than Maggie remembered with horror whose partner the dead man had been. "Oh, Trev, I'm sorry! But maybe you haven't heard?"

"It's all right, Maggie. The police informed my father early this morning. There was some cleaning up to do and the office staff had to be told not to come in to work until tomorrow. Good evening, Mr. Lauchlan." Trevor extended his hand to Charles.

"Please convey my condolences to your father, Trevor," Charles said as he shook hands. "The circumstances must be particularly shocking for him."

Maggie sat down on the steps with Trevor and launched into an account of their experience at the police station while Charles looked on, content to let Maggie relate the news about Peter, which now seemed all the more awkward considering the relationship of the Martlands and Asseltines.

In fact, Charles was vaguely annoyed at seeing Trevor Martland. This was the second time in as many weeks that he had found Trevor at the Skene house. Not that he disliked the boy; Trevor had the makings of a fine young man if he settled down and resisted the distractions all too common in the lives of wealthy families. Trevor's clothes were always in the latest style — or so Charles supposed, since he himself knew little of such things. Trevor had not one but two horses: one to pull his carriage and another stabled outside the city to ride alongside other fashionable young people on picnics and in impromptu races. There was even talk of organizing fox hunting, of all things, out among the prairie chickens and wheat fields. Trevor was also good-looking, a fact Charles had to acknowledge; whenever Trevor was at Bible study there was a palpable vibration among the females and Charles had to use all his best tricks to lure them back to the mysteries of text explication.

Trevor was listening intently to Maggie's story, sitting as close to her as propriety allowed while Aunt Jessie wielded her darning needle and strained to hear the grim details. "And he honestly doesn't remember coming into the office?" Trevor said.

"No," Charles said. "The only thing he remembers is being there and looking down at Mr. Asseltine. Everything else is jumbled in his mind." The whole topic was uncomfortable; Trevor seemed to be feeling the same. Charles attempted to change the subject. "Say, Trevor, how is your mother? We hardly see her at church these days. I hope her lumbago is improving?"

A bit disconcerted at that turn, Trevor popped up from the steps in order to be on the same level as Charles. "Oh, well, the lumbago is better but now she's having some difficulties with her knees."

"That's bad luck. I'll be sure to drop by and pay her a visit this week."

"Well, I'm sure she would appreciate that, Mr. Lauchlan. Just one thing though; she might not be receiving callers when you arrive. She's having a lot of dresses made for the winter season and, well, she seems to spend an awful lot of time with fittings. You know how these things go." Trevor smiled charmingly and some colour came into his face. "And, of course, there are endless details to do with the new house."

"Well now, the ways of ladies and their dressmakers are a mystery to me but I take your point about the house. I'll be sure to drop off a card before I call." Charles turned to Maggie. "I'll just go in and see your father."

"He'll be in his study," said Maggie. "Be sure to tell me everything you discuss."

Charles started to say something to her, stopped, and simply wished Trevor goodnight.

7.

The house was cool and still as he made his way down the hall to Dr. Skene's study, which overlooked the small garden in back. James Skene was writing a letter when Charles knocked on the door frame and entered. The study was filled with bookshelves and tidier than Charles could ever hope to keep his own cramped office. Skene greeted him warmly, despite his unexplained absence from the prayer meeting.

"Assuming that you led the meeting in my absence, sir, thank you, — most sincerely — and I'll try to explain why I left you in the lurch."

"Not at all, Charles. As a matter of fact, I rather enjoyed leading the responses tonight. Don't get into the pulpit much these days." Skene moved to a reading chair beside the small brick fireplace and motioned Charles into the chair opposite. "Now, tell me where you've been."

Charles related the details of the murder and of Peter's predicament.

"McEvoy. Yes, I remember him. A good, keen mind — but troubled. I wish that he had come to me with his difficulties. There was no need to remove himself from all his friends and from the university just because of some views he had come to hold."

"I'm not sure it would have helped. I think Pete needed an excuse to leave the college. He was never comfortable there. Never comfortable in his skin either, I suppose."

"Well, if what you tell me is true, he and his skin are still warring." Skene paused to fill his pipe and light it. He leaned back in his chair, drawing in carefully on the old briar. "It seems far from clear what really happened between Mr. Asseltine and McEvoy. But drunkards in my experience are all drunk in their own way; there's no two alike."

Charles looked puzzled. Skene gave a slight, snorting laugh. "I see that I confuse you. What I mean is a man who is drunk is still himself. He may exhibit coarser, more hidden parts of his nature; he may do something in drink that he would restrain when his mind is clear. But he will not do something, drunk, that is completely outside his nature. You and Peter were close once. Do you think him capable of deliberately harming another person?"

Charles thought before he spoke. "I want to say 'no'. But I don't know what has happened to him in these last few years. I'm not sure that he really is the same person I knew. If he was desperate — like a cornered animal — he might be capable of violence. Perhaps nothing is outside our nature at those times."

"Well then, we've nothing much to go on, I'm afraid, except the benefit of the doubt." He took another contemplative puff. "At the least, Peter deserves our help in securing a full defence. I suggest we decide who to approach about the bail money and payment for a lawyer. Blakeley Campbell owes me a favour. Perhaps he has a fine young lawyer in his firm who wouldn't mind taking a lesser fee if the case were interesting."

Their plan was quickly formulated. They named three men

who were likely to help, divided the list between themselves, and agreed upon the tenor of the approach to each one. Dr. Skene would address the need for legal defense by asking Blakeley Campbell to lunch with him the next day. Skene walked Charles to the door and they greeted the others, who were still relaxing on the verandah.

Maggie said, "I'm glad you've finally come out. All our problems are solved. Trevor has agreed to post the bail money and pay for a lawyer." She made a triumphant gesture toward Trevor, who was now standing, hat in hand.

"Good gracious, Mr. Martland," Dr. Skene said. "We couldn't ask this of you. If Mr. McEvoy is less of a man than we think he is, you might be out of pocket. And anyway, won't your father look rather askance at your paying for the defence of someone who is accused of murdering his business partner?"

"The money in my trust fund is my own to do with as I please, sir," said Trevor, his face now flushed. "I've studied the presumption of innocence and the right to a full defence. They shouldn't just be abstract concepts, should they?"

"No, though too often they are. But are you sure, Trevor? Your father won't object too strenuously?" Charles said. The boy had a funny look on his face for a second that was quickly replaced by a roguish smile.

"Well, sir, my father is always pressing me to take my legal studies more seriously. This may not be exactly what he had in mind, but I'll certainly have some stake in Mr. McEvoy's appearance at the bar of justice. And anyway, Maggie says there's no evidence that Mr. McEvoy intended to kill Mr. Asseltine. It may all have been a terrible accident."

"That is certainly our hope," Charles said as he exchanged a glance with Dr. Skene. "Well then, Trevor, if you're absolutely sure, we accept your offer. It's extremely generous, really. I can't thank you enough. I suppose the first order of business is to find a lawyer. Dr. Skene will be seeing Blakeley Campbell about that tomorrow and perhaps we should both join him."

"I'm at your disposal, Dr. Skene. Just let me know when and where," said Trevor.

They arranged a time for lunch the following day, to be confirmed with Blakeley Campbell. Charles felt that Peter's condition was sufficiently fragile that they should proceed with the bail application as soon as a lawyer could be assigned, tomorrow afternoon if possible. When the discussion had concluded, Trevor bid them all goodnight in turn, leaving Maggie for last and whispering something to her that the others could not hear.

As they watched Trevor step up into his trim, four-seater phaeton and glide away from the curb, geeing softly to his horse, Aunt Jessie asked Maggie to come inside and help her settle on the menus for the next three days. The girl complied, after a reluctant glance at Charles and Dr. Skene. The two men were alone on the verandah as dark blue clouds enveloped the last traces of pink in the western sky.

"Well, that was rather a surprise. Imagine young Martland riding to our rescue," said Dr. Skene.

"Yes. You don't suppose ..."

"Suppose what?"

"Well, you don't think he did it to please Maggie, do you? He's been buzzing around her a lot these last few weeks; why, I don't know. He should be spending time with his law books and not lollygagging on verandahs with girls who are too young for that sort of thing."

"Charles, you've suddenly aged about forty years," Dr. Skene said, laughing. "They're just friends. They discuss everything from suffrage reform to the finer points of lacrosse. I'm sure Maggie enjoys the attention and all the trappings that a wealthy young man brings, but it doesn't amount to much more than that."

"Well, that's just the point, sir. He'll turn her head with his carriages and clothes and oyster suppers and then he'll be on to the next flower and she'll be left alone and disappointed."

"I'm sure Maggie would be delighted with the bee analogy, but to extend it further, she may well be disappointed — but only until the next bee happens along." Dr. Skene clapped him amicably on the back. "No, Charles, if Maggie has tender feelings for Trevor Martland, I'm sure I would know about it."

Thinking back to what his own parents had known of his doings as a young man, Charles was not reassured. He bid Dr. Skene goodnight and began the walk back to his rooms, pulling his hat low over his eyes and stuffing his hands in his pockets. A thin crescent moon had risen in the southeast over the Assiniboine River. As he passed by the rows of tall, narrow houses, some with their curtains still open, he saw a quick series of little dramas: shadowy figures in conversation on a verandah, a hand languidly sweeping a fan, the sudden brightening red dot of a lit cigar; in a foyer through a screen door he glimpsed a child who couldn't sleep being cajoled back to bed by her mother; at a dining room table, a tired man stripped to his shirt and suspenders reading the newspaper by lamplight. There was the distant sound of dishes being stacked for the next day, the fizzy hiss from the filaments of the electric lamps at street corners, the satisfying musical ring of his heels on the wooden planks of the sidewalk.

The sound of a door opening high above his head made him look up. Someone, a woman in a light-coloured dress, had come out onto the balcony above the verandah three houses ahead. He slowed his pace. She was leaning on the railing, with her head thrown slightly back, taking in the scent of lilac. Pretty; maybe very pretty. As Charles came closer, a dark shape materialized behind her, which resolved itself into a man. *Now he's spoiled it,* Charles thought. *Now she'll go in* — and sure enough, she did. *Watch out, there, Lauchlan, my lad. Or you'll have to recite Psalm 100 backwards again.* Last time it had been the hired girl bent over the laundry tubs, the intoxicating movement beneath her skirts as she scrubbed. Better stop it right there. If it was marrying or burning, he would have to choose the latter for a while yet, no matter if he was thirty-two. Because with marrying you got a wife, infants, in-laws, mortgages, and other encumbrances that he didn't have time for right now.

As a distraction he began to review the evening's strange events in his mind, sifting through the information he knew while crossing the bridge over Colony Creek. He took the shortcut across the driving park, opposite the ornate wooden facade of the Fort Osborne Barracks drill hall where he heard the occasional snuffling of the army horses in their stalls.

Charles rented part of the second floor of Mrs. Gough's two-and-a-half-storey cedar shake and clapboard house at 315 Edmonton Street, just north of the dusty, track-rutted breadth of Portage Avenue. He had a bedroom and a small sitting room that he also used as a study. He shared a bathroom with Mr. Krause, the third-floor tenant, and took his meals, when he was there to share them, with Mrs. Gough and her children, Bertie, Hilda, and Dottie. If, as was more often the case, he arrived home late in the evening, his landlady kindly warmed something for him and hovered, telling him the news of the neighbourhood as he ate. He got a slight discount on his rent by cutting kindling for the stove and, in the winter, giving the furnace its final filling with coal before he went to bed.

He swung open the wrought-iron gate at the end of Mrs. Gough's walk, having progressed in his thoughts to the finer points of his sermon for the coming Sunday — and found himself pushed roughly sideways into the enveloping boughs of Mrs. Gough's prized Mock Orange bush. As he was struggling to right himself, he heard the sound of hastily retreating footfalls but, when he got back to the street and looked down the sidewalk, he saw no one. He thought better of his first response, which was to run after the individual. Instead, he dashed up the steps of the house and through the unlatched door. He almost tripped over a package on the hall rug, grabbed it quickly, and went in search of Mrs. Gough, who was found folding laundry in the dining room.

"Are you all right Mrs. Gough? Has anything happened?"

"Why, bless you, Mr. Lauchlan, what do you mean?" Mrs. Gough seemed startled by the intensity of his expression.

"Well, someone just bowled me over trying to get through the gate. I thought he might be a burglar or worse. I've had such a night."

"I did hear someone on the verandah. It sounded as if he pushed something through the mail slot. I was just going to check after I finished the laundry."

Charles remembered the package in his hand. He looked at the large envelope, somewhat scuffed by being folded and crammed through the slot. "Oh, it's addressed to me." Something about the whole business made Charles cautious about opening the envelope in front of Mrs. Gough. "Well, whoever it was may just have been in a great hurry."

"Isn't that the way of it these days, Mr. Lauchlan. People are just going and going and where it will end I don't know." Casting a glance at the package, she said, "Sit down now and I'll fix you something to eat."

"Oh — thank you — but I've already eaten, Mrs. Gough. I ate at the Skenes' earlier. I think I'll just collect the rest of my mail and go upstairs."

Picking up the small stack of mail on the hall table, he sorted through it half-heartedly on his way up the stairs, knowing that he would open the mysterious envelope first. He had one arm-chair, a little threadbare, but comfortable for reading, which he sank into after lighting the coal oil lamp on the nearby table. When he opened the envelope, he discovered that it enclosed yet another envelope — but there was a loose sheet of paper on which he found a note.

> I trust you to keep this for me. For the sake of
> your own safety don't open it and don't show it
> to anyone else. And don't tell anyone that you
> have it. Just keep it for me until I ask for it back.
> You are the only one that I can trust and I need
> your trust in return.

The note was unsigned. Charles stared intently at the unfa-miliar handwriting, but the hastily scrawled sentences refused to reveal anything more. He rolled the sealed envelope between his fingers. Papers, that was all he could feel, no other objects. Who could the owner of this package possibly be, and why had he entrusted it to Charles?

The package rested like a dead weight in his hands. Should he take it to the police — in spite of what the note said? The sender might be some unfortunate madman suffering from delusions. If he opened the package would he find blank sheets or scribbled nonsense? Or, was it all a joke? Would Sanders or Whitman reveal themselves as the perpetrators sometime next week, after he had suitably made a fool of himself? He had only the vaguest recollection of the figure running past him on the sidewalk. Just the impression of a long coat, inappropriate for the warmth of the night, and a hat pulled down low. Whoever he was, he plainly did not want to be recognized. And then there was the note. The person who wrote it seemed painfully in earnest. *You are the only one that I can trust.*

Members of his congregation sometimes confided things to him that they told no other living soul and, consequently, keeping that trust was a sacred duty. Mind you, he couldn't be sure that the man who had knocked him into the orange bush was someone from the church. It was all too quick. But if he wasn't a parishioner, did that really make any difference? Just because he didn't know the identity of the writer of the note, did that make it any less necessary to keep his confidence? He tapped the package against his knees.

I really should get back to my sermon, he thought. But all he did was stare blankly at a coffee stain on the carpet. He wanted very much to start this evening over again, omit all this business with Peter and the bail and the note and the package, and get back to the more familiar complications of his life. Strange how every step since dinner seemed to be taking him into unknown territory.

> Midway upon the journey of our life
> I found myself within a forest dark,
> For the straightforward pathway had been lost.

He grunted. *Dante. Don't be so pompous.* He heaved himself out of the armchair, moved to his desk and put the envelope in the centre drawer. Unearthing his partially completed sermon manuscript from the general chaos of the desktop, he cleaned his pen nib on a scrap of cloth ripped from an old night shirt, opened his inkwell, and reviewed the last sentence. After scratching three new words, he put his pen down, fumbled for the keys in his pocket, and carefully locked the centre drawer.

8.

Trevor walked the three blocks from the commercial stables, where he kept his carriage and horse, to the Martland house on Carlton Street. His father said that when the new house was finished, across the river in Fort Rouge, they would have stables and a groom. Trevor smiled to himself. He had heard that Augustus Nanton was going to buy a motor carriage, in which case Trevor's father would have to have two and a mechanic to keep them both running.

"Never forget, Trevor," his father would say. "Keep your eye on the kind of life I'm building for you — you and your sisters." That last was added as an afterthought. Although his father cared for the girls, he reserved for Trevor a fiercer kind of love. As a boy, Trevor had tried desperately hard to be worthy of this unlooked for singularity. He hadn't done too badly. School in Toronto at Upper Canada College; mixing with the right sort of people; rugby, lacrosse, and rowing to seal those bonds with boyish sweat. Then Queen's, Gaelic yells, and more sweat, accompanied by modest success in the classroom. Top marks in the venues that really count for a young man: the rugby field, the ballroom, and the card room. It was enough that when he returned from university Trevor carried with him a tantalizing air of manly refinement that made him, not just acceptable to the small top crust of Winnipeg society, but in demand. The impression of old money was heady, no matter how different from the prosaic reality, in a city where the oldest fortune had been acquired a scant quarter of a century before.

Trevor and the girls would laugh about their father's frequent references to his shanty Irish roots and his days rolling beer barrels across the floor at Dawes Brewery in Montreal's East End. "That was my university," he would say, that and the rough handling he got when, as a green young businessman, he came out to Manitoba and banged head-first into the awful bust of 1882. His father had been forced to beg his suppliers for extensions of his credit and that, Trevor knew, was not a subject for teasing. He was careful about teasing his father at the best of times; you could never tell where the line was with him.

Trevor found that he was sweating a little as he quietly entered the house. He leaned against the newel post in the darkened hallway, took out his handkerchief, and blotted his brow. *Need to think.* If he was lucky his father would have gone to bed early and he could put off the conversation until tomorrow when he would have more time to plan how to steer it. He took off his shoes and padded carefully up the stairs. Damn.

"Trev?" The voice came from behind the closed library door. The creaking stairway had given him away.

"Yes?" He hesitated slightly before opening the door to the library then put his shoes down outside the door and went in. Frank Martland sat at his desk hunched over his papers in the glow of an electric lamp. Although middle-aged, he had not lost the thick chest and powerful arms first developed by lifting barrels at the brewery.

"I was just going to say goodnight to mother."

"She'll be asleep already. Don't disturb her."

"Is she —"

"She's fine, Trevor. A little upset over this damned business with Asseltine, that's all. Come and sit down. Come —" He waved Trevor into the room. "— I was just reading over my partnership agreement. The lawyers will be in clover trying to sort out Asseltine's interests from mine for the settlement of the estate. Why we didn't incorporate years ago, I don't know. You'll have to handle some of it for me."

"Of course, Father." He walked over to the desk and sat on the edge of it. Better to get it over with. "I went to the prayer meeting tonight."

"Did you?" Martland said as he paged through the agreement. "That's good. Who else was there? The Davidsons?"

"Yes. And Dr. Skene had to lead because Mr. Lauchlan was ... detained."

Martland looked up, having heard the slight hesitation. "Detained? Where was he?"

"Well, it's the oddest coincidence. You won't believe it. He and Maggie — Miss Skene — were at the police station talking to the man they arrested for killing Mr. Asseltine."

Martland lurched back in his chair. "Why would Lauchlan do that?"

"Well, that's the amazing part. It seems the man — his name is McEvoy — was Lauchlan's roommate at university. They're old friends."

"But, how's that? From what the chief said, the man's a vagrant, a hopeless drunkard."

"Yes, he seems to have had it pretty rough. Mr. Lauchlan had completely lost touch with him."

"Well, he has rougher times to come. I warned Joe about mixing with scum but the cards had a grip on him and no mistake. I can't abide that kind of weakness in a man."

"Mr. Lauchlan has taken on the responsibility of finding bail for McEvoy and seeing that he has a lawyer. He was worried about raising the money." Trevor looked carefully at his father before continuing. "So I said that I would pay."

"You what!?"

Trevor jumped to his feet, placing the desk between himself and his father. "I said that I would put up the bail money and pay for a lawyer. You have to admit, father, every man deserves a fair trial and a full defence, even this one."

"But how is this going to look, Trevor? Think, boy." Martland stood up as he spoke, propelling the chair backwards on its wheels. "We need to show our support for the Asseltines. How am I going to face Millie Asseltine and say, 'By the way, my son is paying the legal fees of your husband's murderer.' She'll go straight to her lawyers and tell them to snoop in every corner of the accounts, squeeze every last dime they can out of the company."

"Mrs. Asseltine isn't like that; she doesn't know the first thing about the business," Trevor said.

"Ha!" said Martland and cast his eyes heavenward.

Trevor pressed on. "It just needs to be handled in the right way. If we explain it in a way that she'll understand I'm sure there won't be a problem." He was balanced lightly on the balls of his feet as his father leaned on the desk, his head jutting toward Trevor.

Martland narrowed his eyes. "Suppose you explain it to me in a way that I understand. What's this about, Trev?"

Trevor could feel the sweat forming on his brow again. "I — I just felt that I needed to help them, Miss Skene and Mr. Lauchlan."

"And what about your loyalty to me and to this family?"

"I'd match my loyalty to this family with yours any day." The anger in Trevor's voice surprised both of them. He took a deep breath. "Look, a man's being charged with murder and he may be innocent. That's what Maggie thinks and she may just be right."

"Miss Skene is a young lady with too much education and Lauchlan is …." He searched for the right word. "An idealist."

"He just wants to help an old friend. That seems very reasonable to me." Trevor stopped himself. Better to keep this as short as possible. "I've made up my mind, Father. That's the end of it. I'm going to meet Mr. Lauchlan and Dr. Skene tomorrow to settle on the lawyer and arrange for the bail application. If you like, I'll talk to Mrs. Asseltine. Goodnight, Father." He turned and walked toward the door.

"Trevor?"

"Yes." He did not turn back.

"We used to agree on most things. Not everything, of course, that's natural. But I always thought you would back me up on the important things."

"I'll see you in the morning, Father." Trevor closed the door of the library behind him. Martland stared at the closed door for a very long time.

9.

Enclosed within the dancing sphere of light cast by the coal oil lamp he carried, Setter negotiated the length of the dark cell block following behind the on-duty constable. When they reached number 11, the constable turned his key in the lock and stood back. Peter was sitting on the edge of his bunk. He had flinched when Setter threw open the bolt on the cell door but he seemed to have regained his composure since the meeting with Lauchlan earlier in the evening. Setter motioned for the on-duty constable to wait.

"Is there anything you want, Mr. McEvoy?"

"Apart from getting out of here?"

"Some water? Some tea?"

"Oh, Yes. Water. I've been drinking the wash water and now it's gone. So thirsty." He ran his hand through his hair.

The constable went off, his keys jingling. Setter walked in, put the lamp on the small washstand and sat in the chair that Charles had vacated.

"A few more questions, if I may." He took out his notebook.

"I hope you don't want to search my clothes again. And anyway, I've already told you I don't remember much."

"How do you live, Mr. McEvoy? I mean, how do you put food on the table, pay your rent?"

"I manage. Not easily, but I manage. I don't see what this has to do —"

"Yes, but how, specifically?"

"I'm a trained draftsman." He straightened his shoulders. "I get the odd bit of drafting. Nothing steady. But there's always building going on."

"Did you ever get any work from Mr. Asseltine?"

Peter shifted on the bunk. "Well, not directly, exactly. But he was well-connected. Sometimes he would give me a name."

"A name? Someone to contact for work?"

"Yes. I don't see the relevance —"

The on-duty constable came back with a pitcher of water and a tin cup. He put it on the washstand and took his leave. Peter poured a cup unsteadily and drained it, his Adam's apple pumping in his thin neck.

"And apart from that, it was money won at cards?"

"Just when I needed something to tide me over. It wasn't —"

"And Mr. Asseltine was always a willing player? And one you could usually beat quite handily?"

"Usually —" Peter jerked his head up. "— Look, I know my rights. Gambling under the Criminal Code doesn't apply to games of poker between friends."

Setter looked up from his notes. "You and Asseltine were friends, then?"

"We were friendly. Is that so hard to believe?" Peter was now quite flushed.

"McEvoy, a gaming charge is the least of your worries. I want to know how things stood between you and Asseltine."

"He owed me money and I needed it. It's really quite simple."

"Yet when we searched you, you had no money on you,

though there was money in Asseltine's wallet and money in the safe. Can you explain that?"

Peter drank from his cup and looked down into it. "Maybe he misunderstood about the amount. Fifty dollars. I can't ..."

"You had an argument?"

"No. That is, I don't think so. I don't remember arguing with him."

"Mr. Asseltine had more than enough money to cover the debt between what was in his wallet and the money in the safe. Was he —"

"A bilker? A piker?" Peter was looking out at the hall, almost talking to himself. "No. Not before at any rate. He was a straight enough fellow, even after a few drinks."

"And he opened the safe?"

"I suppose so. The safe was open. I remember that. And papers on the desk."

"Papers from the safe? Did you see any of them or read them?"

"No. They had nothing to do with me. They were just there."

"And there were some on the floor?"

"There may have been. But I didn't touch them. I was there for the money that was owed to me. I can't remember what ..." He put his hands up to his face. "It's a blur, that's all. If I could explain it, don't you think I would have by now?"

Setter flipped the cover of his notebook over. "Thank you, Mr. McEvoy. That'll be all for now." As he stood up, he pulled something out of his pocket and laid it on the bunk. "In case you need something to read in the morning. I wouldn't let the on-duty constable see it, if I were you. Sorry I can't leave the lamp." Peter took the newspaper and shoved it under the mattress.

10.

Rosetta closed the door of the darkroom and fastened the thick, rubberized canvas apron so that it was snug about her waist and its bib was taut against the front of her shirtwaist. "If a customer rings down below, Sergeant, they'll just have to wait or come back later. Mrs. Harbottle has one of her sick headaches."

Setter brightened noticeably at this news. He was always acutely aware of people who did not approve of him and after one brief meeting; Mrs. Harbottle had fit the bill. "That's unfortunate," he said. "I hate to think of you losing customers because of me, Mrs. Cliffe. Perhaps you'd better charge me more."

Rosetta shook her head. "Or perhaps I should hire you in place of Mrs. Harbottle. You've shown more interest in darkroom technique in three months than she has in three years. And your questions have been more than thorough." She removed a pair of wooden tweezers with rubber tips from a hook on the wall and placed them on the counter. "But now you'll have to be quiet and let me get on with it."

"Sorry. Too much thinking out loud to myself, I suppose. It's a habit of people who live alone."

"I know what you mean. The house gets very quiet when

Ellie goes back to school. Sometimes I'm not sure whether I've actually said something out loud or just thought it."

"If you shared an office with Constable Smithers, that question would be answered for you. I often catch him looking at me with a vague, alarmed expression."

Rosetta laughed and he smiled broadly. She had firmly refused when he first asked if he could observe how contact prints were made but after his sixth or seventh request she relented — only on condition that he keep quiet, stay out of her way, and tell no one.

That last got his back up a little. Was she ashamed to be seen with him? But then when he told her that he was not an Indian, but rather a half-breed, and that his people had been farming here in St. Andrew's Parish since the 1840s, she had actually laughed and said that back then her own family were still mucking out byres for the toffs in Ireland. There was a warmth in that joke that made him think she wasn't bothered much about his brown skin. That only left the fact that he was a man. Well, if that was it, she needn't worry. No matter how much he wanted to, and he often wanted to quite a lot, he had never known what to say to a lady to turn the conversation to softer things. How the devil did other fellows manage it while he stayed tongue-tied? Not that he would say such things to Mrs. Cliffe, of course. There was an invisible boundary between them that he must not cross if he wanted their professional association to continue.

Setter stood as far back as he could since the darkroom had not been built for two. This was his second time observing but he still had to curb his habit of trying to see everything close up, as it was happening. He liked being there with the red safety sleeve over the gaslight creating velvety shadows, watching the images slowly forming on the paper, the lines cutting in until they reached a burning clarity. Maybe he would even invest in a camera of his own and try his hand at darkroom work. Give him that interest outside of his work that Crossin was always at him about.

Rosetta took down a series of brown glass bottles from the shelves above the counter and filled three large enamel pans with chemicals. She replaced the glass stoppers with a brisk, *thrip*.

Grasping the photographic paper by its edges, she carefully removed it from the wooden developing box and immersed it in the first enamel pan. As she bathed the paper gently by manipulating it with the tweezers, the image began to appear. Once she had moved the print along its liquid way into the fixer and then into the washing bath, he would be able to ask questions. She fished the sheet out of the bath, holding it by its top edge and hung it to dry on the clothes line, then turned to place another negative in the box and repeated the whole process until fifteen prints hung on the line. They recreated the scene in Martand's office, its masculine opulence marred by the sprawled body and displaced furniture and papers cast along the desktop and across the rich Turkish carpet.

"Yes, wonderful. Already I had forgotten some of the details but now I have them back again," he said. "The depth of field you achieved is splendid. I wondered — could you take a close-up of a very small object?"

"How small?" she said.

Setter reached into his inside jacket pocket and drew out a white envelope. He removed something from it and set it on her work table. She was hanging a wet print on the line and returned to pick up the object.

"A button? Is it the one you found on the floor?" she said.

"Yes. Can I see the one that shows the desk?" He went over to the dripping prints on the line. "Yes. This one. Here's the button lying by the leg of the desk." He pointed with his pencil.

She peered at the photograph. "Yes, I see it."

"I wondered if you could photograph the button again, both sides, very close up."

"Yes, I expect I can. I'll use my new camera — the one I use for botanical illustrations for the university. Why do you want me to photograph it again?"

"I want to avoid showing the button itself as much as possible. And Smithers can double my efforts by using photographs in his inquiries."

She slipped the safety sleeve off the gaslight and held the button up to the lamp. It was made of mother-of-pearl and tinted a greenish-blue. "Pity we can't show it in colour. It's quite an unusual colour for a man's button."

"You think it could belong to a lady?" Setter crowded under the lamp with her and squinted at it. "It matches the size of my jacket and vest buttons so I just assumed — I'm afraid fashion — for either sex — is an unknown land to me."

"I could say the same. But some of the new ladies walking suits are quite mannish. I'm just not sure. You think this button is important, then?"

"Yes. Of course we may yet find that it was innocently dropped by one of Martland's clients and missed by the cleaners, or —"

"Or there was someone else there, someone besides McEvoy and Mr. Asseltine?"

Setter was unaccountably pleased. It had taken Smithers a while to reach that conclusion. Then he remembered himself. "Er — yes, possibly so; but it could still be just a wild goose chase."

11.

As a result of the luncheon meeting that day at the offices of Campbell and Bentinck, Barristers and Solicitors, Charles and Trevor found themselves walking briskly, almost trotting, to keep up with Chester Jessup as he led the way to the police station, bail application in hand. Jessup, small, bespectacled and intense, had been the junior lawyer chosen by Blakeley Campbell to take on the McEvoy case. To add to the credibility of the application, Dr. Skene had attached a letter stating that Peter had once been a young man of good behaviour and outstanding promise and that he, Skene, would stand with Charles in providing surety for Peter. It would be an uphill battle, but Jessup said that the support of people respected in the city might well move the judge to approve. Before filing the documents at the court house, Jessup wanted to meet Peter and talk over the specifics of the bail application. They met Setter in his office.

"Come this way and I'll take you down to see McEvoy," said Setter.

"I'd rather wait here. You go ahead," Trevor said.

"Come on now, Trevor, I'm sure Peter will want to thank you personally for your generosity." Charles smiled but looked puzzled.

"Yes, that's the trouble. I'd rather be in the background, frankly. The fact is my father isn't very happy about my being the banker for Mr. McEvoy. I'll be as good as my word — but the less of a personal role I take in all this, the better."

"Of course, it's up to you. Whatever you prefer," said Charles. He left Trevor in the office and headed toward the stairs to the cells with Setter and Jessup.

Setter sent the other two down ahead of him and grabbed Constable Smithers by the arm for a quick word. Smithers nodded and walked over to the closed door of Inspector Crossin's office. He straightened his tunic and badge and knocked. After a muffled reply he entered and stood in front of Crossin's desk, his nose wrinkling slightly from the cigar fug that permeated the small space.

"Excuse me, sir?"

"Yes. What is it?"

"Sergeant Setter said to let you know that you'll be needed to sign Mr. McEvoy's bail application when they're through downstairs."

"Fine. Tell him I'll be here until six. Then Mrs. Crossin requires my presence at supper."

Smithers remained in front of the desk.

"Yes? Something else?"

"Well, sir. I was just wondering if you'd had time to go over my request for a transfer."

"Hang it, Smithers. Don't I have enough to worry about?" He sighed and stubbed out his cigar. "You'd better close the door and sit down."

Smithers did as he was told.

"Now, what's all this about? You've only been assigned to Setter for three months and even then we pull you away for other assignments."

"Well sir, I'd like to write the sergeant's exam after I've put in enough time in the division. And, well," He lifted his jaw and focused on a point just above Crossin's head. "I want to get a range of experience before —"

"Lad, you can't get any better experience than where you are right now. You can learn things about investigation from Setter that none of my other sergeants have thought about. He's like a terrier with a bone. He won't quit till he's worked out every angle and he won't let you quit either."

"I know that sir, it's just that, well ..." He fretted at the cuffs of his tunic. "I've heard that Sergeant Setter had to write the exam four times before he finally made sergeant."

"And you think you'll be held back because you're working for him, is that it? And the boys are ragging you and making jokes behind Setter's back."

"Oh, give me some credit, sir." Smithers jumped his chair back a few inches. "I like the sergeant fine, though he does have his funny little ways, and I don't pay any attention to what they say. It's just that, see —" He dropped his voice a little and bent forward. "I have to get on. I got engaged last month. And her father says we can't get married until I make sergeant."

"Oh, it's like that, is it?" Crossin opened his desk drawer and pulled out a sheet of paper that Smithers could see was his transfer request. Crossin ripped it in two, then in four, then in eight, and dropped the whole business into the waste paper basket beside his desk.

"Sir! —"

"All right, now you listen to me, Constable." Crossin leaned forward on his elbows, glaring at Smithers. "I'm going to tell you something and if you repeat one word of it to anyone else, and I mean anyone, I will personally break both your legs."

Smithers sat up very straight.

"Setter scored top marks in each of those four exams and in the interviews," Crossin said. "After a few years it got to be embarrassing. If the premier — who happened to be Setter's uncle — hadn't weighed in, he'd still be wearing blue serge."

"Crikey," Smithers said and then narrowed his eyes. "But, if he scored so high, why was he held back?"

"There was some nonsense about Setter not making an effort to fit in and work with the other men." Crossin brought his fist down hard on the desk. "It was all a load of steaming ... manure! They were afraid if Setter made sergeant, the constables under him wouldn't take orders from him and there'd be trouble in the locker room."

"Oh, I see," Smithers said, looking as if a smell worse than cigar smoke had just wafted in. "Well, that seems pretty hard to me, sir. 'Specially since he proved four times over that he was qualified."

"Exactly my point; so, Constable Smithers, it behoves you to get just as qualified and the way to do that is to stay where you are and do every blessed thing that Setter asks of you. And when Setter thinks you're ready, he'll recommend you for the exam. Not before. You tell your young lady that you'll be working your blasted arse off for the next two years. And then when there's a position open at that rank, She'll be right proud of you when you get those stripes. Anything else?"

Smithers looked crestfallen. "Two years, sir? I'd been hop-ing —"

"Two years is average, Constable. Less if you're a bloody genius. Are you a bloody genius?"

Smithers cleared his throat and stuck out his chin. "I, uh, don't know about that, sir. But I intend to do my best."

After the meeting with Peter, Crossin signed the application and Jessup set off for the court house, looking determined. Charles and Trevor left the police station together and headed down Rupert Street as a light rain began to fall.

"That's a God-forsaken place isn't it?" Trevor said.

"Yes, well, no, not literally —"

"I'm sorry. But you know what I mean."

"I know," Charles said. "Actually the cells are not as bad as I thought they might be. They're bad, I grant you. But you hear of so much worse in older cities."

Trevor was quiet for awhile. They risked their lives by crossing Main Street, dodging wagons, carts, bicycles, and streetcars, and feeling lucky that in the rain the roadway hadn't yet been churned into thick mud. When they reached the other side, Charles was faintly surprised that Trevor continued walking north with him instead of turning south toward the offices of Stobbart and Long, where he was a clerk in articles and studying for the bar examination.

"I hope you will visit my mother, Mr. Lauchlan," Trevor said.

"Yes, I intend to — and call me Charles — but you said she was very busy these days?"

"Yes. You'll need to be persistent. Once she sees you I know that she'll feel better for it." Their progress was halted by a large cart loaded with vegetables and they had to wait for it to pass.

Charles stepped closer to Trevor to make sure he could hear properly. "You know, it's strange, but I don't think your mother has ever been very comfortable with me."

"Well ..." Trevor looked a little ill at ease, himself. "... Because of her upbringing, she's had difficulty adjusting to things here in the West."

It was an awkward subject and this was as close to candid as Trevor had ever been about it. Trevor's parents and, indeed, he himself had been baptized and raised as Catholics in Montreal. When they made the move to the West they decided, or rather his father decided, that they would make a completely fresh start — including changing their religion. Of all the family, this had been hardest on Trevor's mother. Even after eighteen years, Agnes Martland still seemed uncertain when to stand and when to sit in church, and visibly restrained herself from genuflecting before entering the pew. The Martlands baffled Charles and he had always attributed this to their Catholicism, which was as strange to him as if they had come from a foreign country. Now he felt that he should have made more of an effort to get to know them.

"I have things to attend to today. But I'll see her tomorrow if she's at home — and I won't take 'no' for an answer."

"Thank you, Charles." Trevor nodded a goodbye and turned back toward Stobbart and Long, leaning briskly into the rain.

12.

Charles walked on, turning his conversation with Trevor over in his mind. Sounds of activity greeted him when he arrived, a little rain soaked, at the church. Miss Perrin, the nurse who visited three days a week, was in the parish hall teaching some young mothers-to-be about the care and diseases of newborn infants. In the basement a group of neighbourhood women were sorting household goods and clothing for distribution. This was a highly coveted job; the sorters got to take some of the best goods home with them.

The rich contralto cadence of mostly Slavic back-and-forth chatter was suddenly punctuated by, "teeeeee paaawtt?" And a choral reply of, "teeeeee paaht!" One bright, slightly raucous peel of laughter above the rest told Charles that Maggie was with them, taking her turn at helping the women with their English. He was tempted to join them but there were some repairs to the gallery in the sanctuary that needed his urgent attention and so he made his way back to his office.

The paint-stained corduroy trousers and thick blue cotton shirt he changed into felt like old friends as he carefully hung up his damp suit jacket and pulled his trousers into tight creases before laying them over the back of his office chair. With his shirt, clerical collar, and black dickey laid over the other chair, the small office resembled a laundry. He looked quickly at the messages on his desk. There was one from Erling Eklund, saying that he would be slightly later than he had anticipated with the equipment to repair the gallery. Charles took advantage of the delay to go down and have a word with Maggie.

The gaslights were on full in the centre of the large basement room, revealing the new wood of the bare rafters and making a pool of light for the women to work in. There was a definite increase in the level of chatter as he joined them and some of the women giggled, their aprons raised in front of their faces. He nodded a greeting to Maggie.

He knew one or two of the women by name. "Mrs. Morosnick, how do you do? Mrs. Sloboda? Very nice to see you." The women eyed him with sidelong glances.

"And this is Mrs. Kodalek," said Maggie, indicating a small woman hanging back a little from the main group. "This is her first time here."

"Mrs. Kodalek, hello. I hope you will come back again," Charles said, enunciating clearly. Mrs. Kodalek bobbed several times from the waist and gave Charles a wide smile, smoothing her apron with reddened hands.

"*Vin krasniski yak ya doomala! Trocha kygey ale maye mochni nohi*," said Mrs. Morosnick to her neighbour, pointing to Charles and slapping her thigh, and both whooped with laughter, which set the whole group off.

Charles, a little self-conscious, shot a questioning look at Maggie.

"Apparently they're not used to seeing you looking like a farm hand. I'm not sure, but I think they just said that you're a bit thin — but you have good strong legs," she said.

65

"Oh, hahah!" Charles blushed but then struck a circus strong-man pose, crooking his arm to show off his biceps, and off they went again. Once the women had dried their eyes with the ends of their kerchiefs, Maggie seized the opportunity to go through the names of various body parts, pointing to Charles who obligingly flexed or waggled the part in question and gestured to the women to repeat the name. At the end of this game he helped Maggie and the women put the clothes and housewares into boxes. The group dispersed, each one carrying a few prized articles homeward, while Maggie stayed behind to put the boxes away.

"Why are you dressed like that, anyway?" she said.

"A beam supporting the gallery is cracked. People up there were getting a sinking feeling — completely unrelated to my sermon. Mr. Martland is sending one of his work crews over to help me repair it."

"What would we do without the Martlands?" she said, closing some cardboard cartons. "And what about the bail application?"

"It's being filed at the court house by one Chester Jessup of Campbell and Bentinck."

"Wasn't it fine of Trevor to offer the money?" she said. Charles, putting a padlock on a storage locker, did not immediately reply. "Well, I think it was fine of him," said Maggie.

"Yes, yes, it was generous of him."

"Extremely generous, I'd say. And you would too, only you seem to think Trev is shallow and stuck-up."

"I don't," Charles protested. "But he's had the best of everything and I think that can be very — I don't know — distracting, I suppose. I'll tell you one thing though; I didn't think his father would take very well to Trevor footing the bill and apparently he hasn't. Maybe we shouldn't have accepted his offer."

"Nonsense; it won't do Trevor any harm to stand up to his father. It makes his gesture all the nobler."

"Do they get along, Trevor and his father?"

"I'm not sure. We talk about all kinds of things. People we know; what he wants to do after the bar examination; sports; politics; religion, of course —" she nodded in his direction. "And I go on about my family, which he actually seems to find interesting. But then if I ask him a question about his family, nine times out of ten he'll make a joke and we'll go off in another direction entirely. And ten minutes after he's gone, I'll realize he changed the subject."

"Perhaps he's doing that deliberately. Trying to make himself ever more fascinating," Charles said, only half joking.

She laughed. "I hadn't thought of that. He's that way with everyone though. Charming and good at drawing people out. But there are certain topics he doesn't care to discuss." She looked suddenly thoughtful. "But, I suppose men are like that."

There was a door open. All he needed to do was walk through it.

And then it was closed. "Oh, look. Some children's shoes came in this morning," she said, picking up two impossibly small black boots from a carton. "Since we already have some on hand we should send the new ones over to the children's home. Mrs. Forman says they're desperate for them. And by the way, Trevor is running in the All Charities Foot Race next week — did you know? And his law firm is sponsoring him at twenty dollars a mile. That's one hundred and twenty dollars for the children's home if he finishes the race."

"Well, that's good work. As a matter of fact, I'm thinking of entering the race too."

"You're not! Charles! You'll fall over after two miles."

"Why do you say that? I do a little road work with the boy's

67

boxing club," he said, "And I'll have you know I was very highly thought of on the University College track and field team."

Maggie just snorted. "Your road work consists of watching the boys run around the park and your glorious sporting career is, shall we say, receding into the distance. I suppose I'll just have to make sure there's a wagon at mile three to bring you home in." She looked at her watch. "Oh, my goodness! My German lesson's in ten minutes!" She grabbed her hat, handbag and umbrella, and ran up the stairs, hiking her skirts clear of the steps.

Annoying girl, Charles thought. *Just assumes I can't do it.* In truth he hadn't had any intention of entering the race. He had been as surprised as she was when those words popped out of his mouth. But now a granitic determination formed in his mind. Of course he would enter the race. The church was a member of the All Charities campaign and he had been thinking of taking more exercise. This would be the start of a new health regime.

He took the stairs two at a time up into the cool, white-washed brightness of the sanctuary. The rain was drumming lightly on the roof and he stopped, cocking his head. So pleasant just to be still and listen to it. *Come on*, he reminded himself, *there's work to be done.* While climbing the narrow stairway to the gallery, he mentally reviewed the steps he needed to take to get some working room around the sagging beam that supported the front portion of the gallery floor. First the front railing and the parapet on which it was fastened would be removed; then the floorboards over the beam; then the decorative boards and mouldings hiding the beam. He set to work with a crowbar, taking down the railing which only two years before he himself had made.

As he carefully loosened the groaning boards of the parapet from their nails, trying not to split the boards, he began to hum softly. Some of the men on the session thought it less than respectable for their minister to undertake this kind of work. But Charles had convinced them that most of the money they raised for the church should go to the programs and services they offered in the building and not to adorn its place of worship. They were lucky that he was able to do a few things around the place; it meant that the church could make do with only a weekend caretaker. They would expand and decorate as money could be spared. And anyway, he enjoyed the work. A well-mitred joint in the wainscoting was a gift to God, a prayer made with his hands.

There was a great deal left to do, though. The interior of the sanctuary furnished the basics for worship but little else. The chancel was a bare platform with a borrowed lectern in place of a pulpit; the choir loft behind was comprised of second-hand chairs on unfinished risers and a small harmonium served in place of a piano. For a baptismal font he used an old Spode ware basin set into a converted fern stand that, to Maggie's delight, Charles consecrated to its new use with elaborate solemnity.

The long, pointed windows, six on each side of the sanctuary, bore the only touch of richness. They were filled with ordinary glass except for the pointed sections at the top. Mrs. Lydia McCorrister had insisted on paying for stained glass panels — from McAusland in Toronto, no less — in memory of her haberdasher husband. The geometric pattern of yellow, opalescent white, and clear bevelled glass was understated but when the sun shone small rainbows appeared on the opposite wall, which captivated children and not a few adults whose attention had wandered from the sermon.

A thumping of boots sounded beneath him and a baritone voice reverberated in the empty sanctuary. "Hello? Mr. Lauchlan? Reverend?"

"Eklund? Just wait, I'm coming down." Charles set a board down at the back of the gallery and clomped down the stairs to greet Erling Eklund, Martland's foreman, and Kauffman, another worker from the Asseltine and Martland yard. Eklund was tall and solidly built, and though still a young man, his sheer physical presence and booming voice gave him an aura of command. He wore his weathered cap pulled down low on his forehead but it did not quite hide the wine-coloured birth mark above his left eyebrow that extended, jagged like a bird claw, across the bridge of his nose.

The three men finished unmasking the sagging beam, and then wandered around beneath it, eyeing it from various angles. The damage was worse than Charles had expected. Eklund clambered up a ladder, ran his fingers along the widening crack and furrowed his brow while sighting along the beam to where it disappeared into the plaster wall on each side.

"I'm afraid we're going to have to replace it, Mr. Lauchlan. I guess we should have used fir after all," Eklund said from atop the ladder. "I thought this grade of spruce would be up to the job but it looks like there was a fault in the grain."

Charles felt a sting of annoyance with himself. "That's my fault, Eklund. I shouldn't have talked you into the spruce. I was trying to shave a few dollars off the budget."

"Oh, it's just the luck of the draw at the lumber yard sometimes." Eklund smiled ruefully as he climbed down the ladder. "I can get a wholesale price for you on the fir beam and Mr. Martland will give you half-price on the labour. I'm afraid that's the best we can do."

Charles sighed. "That's more than generous, of course. All right, I guess we'd better go ahead. If you can get me an estimate for the new beam and the work then my board can approve it fairly quickly."

"If you can spare a few hours to help, the three of us can get the old beam out today. Then in with the new one whenever you get the go-ahead and we'll leave the mouldings, plastering, and painting to you."

They hauled in some hydraulic jacks and lumber for temporary supports from the wagon parked outside. Then Eklund sent Kauffman to return the wagon to another work site. Charles and Eklund removed some pews underneath the gallery to provide working space. Then they measured the lumber and prepared to cut it into the right lengths for temporary posts and a plate to support the gallery floor.

"I feel guilty monopolizing your time like this, Eklund," Charles said. "I know you're of more value to Mr. Martland supervising the hotel site."

"That's all right, sir. Mr. Martland wanted me to make sure the job here was done right." They manoeuvred a twelve-foot length of eight-by-eight timber onto a series of saw horses.

"Well be sure to thank him again for donating his top man to the cause here," Charles said as they clamped the timber firmly to the saw horses.

"I'll do that." Eklund said, "Oh, Mr. Martland said you know the man who was arrested for killing Mr. Asseltine? That's a hell of a thing. Can you take the other end of this?" He picked up a two-man crosscut saw and slid the other handle toward Charles.

"Yes, true enough." Charles wrapped his hands around the saw handle. "We're old friends from university — hadn't seen him in fifteen years." They lined up the saw on the pencil line, bracing the timber with a leg on each side. The first passes of the saw bit tentatively into the wood but then they established a rhythm, extending their arms more confidently with each stroke until the saw broke through at the bottom.

"I hear he was so drunk he can't remember what happened," said Eklund, loosening the clamps. "But maybe if I did something like that, I'd say the same thing."

"Well he was certainly drunk enough. By the time the police came he was more or less insensible." Charles positioned the timber for the next cut. "Just there?"

"Yes, tighten away — I suppose he might not have been alone?" Eklund picked up some sawdust from the floor to dry the sweat from his hands.

"Yes, I wondered myself whether Peter had brought someone else with him."

"So, he said he was alone then?"

"Yes. He said he'd come to collect a gambling debt from Asseltine. No mention of anyone else." Charles was taking a grip on the saw handle again, waiting for the other man.

"Still, an open safe would be an awful temptation. Probably tried to take more than he was owed," Eklund said, taking up his position.

"Well, I don't think that's what happened, though. All the police found on him were some drafting pens, a train schedule, and an empty old wallet. It's pretty awful, really. He as much as told me all he had in the world was what he stood up in."

"And you believe him?" Eklund said.

Charles suddenly felt a little offended on Peter's behalf. "Pete's clearly made some bad choices but yes, I do believe him."

"Sorry, Mr. Lauchlan, it's none of my business, really." They lined the saw up on the pencil line. "Everybody around the work yard has been talking. You know how it is."

"That's human nature, I suppose. Ready?" The saw teeth ripped through the pencil line and deep into the wood, sawdust dropping lightly to the floor as the two men pushed and pulled back, pushed and pulled back.

Kauffmann returned and the three men were wrestling the new supports into position when a boy of about fourteen, in knee breeches and a cloth cap, appeared at the back of the church.

"Excuse me. Do you know where I can find Mr. Lauchlan?" The boy dragged his cap off his head.

"I'm Lauchlan."

"Mr. Jessup says come to the police station right away. There's a prisoner to be released." He held out a folded piece of paper to Charles.

"Just a moment," Charles said and handed Eklund the sledge hammer he had been using to tap the new support posts into place. He took the note from the boy and read it quickly. Jessup's small, neat script told him that the court had released Peter on bail, with Dr. Skene and he listed as sureties. Peter was to be released into their care upon Charles presenting himself at the police station. The judge had instructed Charles to keep Peter "under close supervision." With a guilty, fluttering sensation just under his rib cage, Charles realized he had made no firm plans about what to do with Peter, should he be released. Indeed, he hadn't really believed that Peter *would* be released.

13.

"Have this filled at Bannerman's. He'll put it on my account. It's a tonic. Mr. McEvoy is undernourished, as I expected. It will also help with the headaches and the insomnia. I'm afraid I can't do much about the shakes, McEvoy. Mind you drink plenty of water." Dr. Herzinger turned again to Charles. "Let me know if the withdrawal symptoms are severe. I can prescribe a mild sedative, but I'm loathe to do it — unless he really needs it. It only encourages the dependency."

"I'll get that filled right away, Doctor. Thank you for fitting him in on such short notice."

"Yes, thank you, Doctor."

Charles and Dr. Herzinger were a bit surprised when Peter piped up. Until then he had been quiet and hang dog as Charles steered him from the clothing depot — where he picked out several shirts and sets of underwear — to the clinic, where Herzinger had given him a brisk once-over. Peter jumped at every sound and seemed to be two beats behind everyone around him.

They left the church with the new clothing wrapped in a bundle and began walking to Mrs. Gough's. The fresh air and light did little to revive Peter's spirits.

"Just like old times, isn't it Charlie? You bailing me out of a scrape."

Charles sidestepped the remark. "Cheer up, Pete. We're going to get to the bottom of this. I can't imagine that these charges will hold up."

"You haven't had much to do with the police, have you? If you lived around the tracks, you'd learn that the policeman is somebody's friend — but he certainly isn't yours."

"Oh, I don't know. That Setter fellow seems all right."

"Yes, he's not bad. At least he listens to what I have to say — such as it is. I don't think he believes that I just don't remember."

"He's got to ask you questions about it, doesn't he? You shouldn't blame him for doing his job."

"Well, it's not helping. I've been trying and trying to pull something back. It's still just a jumble of pictures and sounds."

Charles thought it best to drop the subject, for now. Something Eklund had said earlier came into his mind and he tried to push it away. If Peter didn't remember something more about that night, it might be because it was convenient not to. They walked the rest of the way in silence. Charles was still running over the details of the bail and surety in his mind. Either he or Dr. Skene was to see Peter a minimum of once a day and Peter was to report to the police station once per week. Peter was to abstain from drinking alcohol of any kind. He was not to enter any commercial establishment where liquor was being served or sold and would be required to obey a curfew of 11:00 p.m. He was not to take part in any card games or gambling of any kind. The judge made it clear that if he was in default of any of these conditions, his bail was forfeit and he would return to jail and Charles and Dr. Skene were obliged by law to report any breach of the conditions that they personally observed.

They had gone straight from the police station to the church and he had not had time to ask Mrs. Gough whether Peter could stay with him in his rooms. He would not have thought twice about it, had he been bringing any of his other friends home. She was fond of him, he knew, and gave him latitude that even extended to letting his friends from out of town stay at the house for a few nights as paying guests. But this was different and he regretted not being able to talk with her about it beforehand. He rather hoped she was out so that he could spirit Peter upstairs and directly into a bath. But as they came in the front door, she was carrying a load of laundry down the stairs from the second floor.

"Oh — ah — good, good — Mrs. Gough, I would like you to meet a friend of mine from university days. This is Peter McEvoy. Pete, my landlady, Mrs. Emmeline Gough."

He could see Mrs. Gough's smile slacken, just for a moment, as she took in Peter's unshaven face, matted hair, and shapeless, dank-looking clothing. Then she smiled harder than ever.

"Well, now. How d'you do, Mr. McEvoy? Always a pleasure to meet friends of Mr. Lauchlan."

"How do you do, Mrs. Gough." Peter took little furtive glances at her through the hair falling across his eyes and extended a tremulous hand which she shook warily. "Um ... it's a nice place you have here."

"Yes, yes. We're quite cozy here, aren't we, Mr. Lauchlan."

"Yes. Yes indeed. If you don't mind, Mrs. Gough, I thought Peter could take a bath and change and then I'll take him for something to eat at the café on the corner."

"Yes. Yes, certainly. Make yourself at home, Mr. ... Mr.?"

"McEvoy." Charles and Peter spoke at once.

"Mr. McEvoy, yes. I'll just get you a fresh towel." She looked Peter over. "Or maybe two."

"Thank you, Mrs. Gough. That's very kind." Charles hustled Peter up the stairs. It was a bad sign that she hadn't insisted on feeding them supper, but perhaps it was just that she was busy with the laundry. Had she had time to read the paper? She usually read at least the headlines with her afternoon tea. While Peter was getting cleaned up, he would take her aside and tell her the particulars of his situation. Of course, he would have to pay for Peter's board until — until what? It occurred to him that if Peter was convicted, he would not long be a burden on his pocketbook — or on the state's for that matter.

Peter emerged from his ablutions less skittish and smelling considerably better. He put on an old suit of Charles's that was slightly too long in the pant legs and a bit big at the shoulders. Nevertheless, noting Peter's washed and combed hair, Charles found him quite presentable though his now clean-shaven face was lined and pale, a fresh dew of sweat already forming on his brow. While Peter had been in the tub, Charles had gathered up his things and, trying not to inhale or look too closely, had taken them to the back yard and hung them on the line. He had wanted to burn them, frankly, but Peter had been unexpectedly shocked at the whole idea and said, whether true or not, that Sergeant Setter had expressly forbade him to dispose of any of his clothes.

"Sorry, Pete. But they are in pretty awful condition, you have to admit."

"Maybe so. It's just that they're mine, that's all. We've been through a lot together."

On his way back from hanging the clothes on the line, Charles had found Mrs. Gough alone in the kitchen and, taking a deep breath, he had laid out Peter's story factually, dispassionately. But she was, as he feared, more than slightly taken aback at having an accused murderer so near at hand.

"Dear Lord, Mr. Lauchlan! Och — my heavens! Oh —" She clutched the cameo at her throat. "I thought the name was familiar. Dear, dear. But the paper said the murderer was in jail?"

"He was granted bail this afternoon. On the condition that Dr. Skene and I supervise him closely. I know this is very short notice and I'm asking a lot, but if Peter could stay with me here, I can keep an eye on him. He's quiet and shy by nature. I'm sure he wouldn't be a bother to you."

"Well, according to the paper, he was more than a bother to Mr. Asseltine!" Then she looked ashamed to have raised her voice to him in that way. She beckoned him to come closer and spoke more softly. "I've the children to think of, Mr. Lauchlan. And there's Mr. Krause."

"I know that, and I understand how you feel. But you've seen Pete. He's as frightened of you as you are of him. I know what kind of person he is and I think when the police do their work, the charges against him will be dropped."

"Well, I don't know, Mr. Lauchlan. I'm all at sea —"

"Mrs. Gough, you've known me a long time haven't you?"

She hesitated for a moment, and then nodded.

"If you could just see your way clear to try out this arrangement for one day," Charles said, "I would be extremely grateful."

He could see that she was far from easy in her mind but, finally, she agreed. It made him uncomfortable to have made it an issue of loyalty to him. He could only hope that Peter would catch on to the rhythm of the house and move with it, a rhythm he himself knew so well that he could take it for granted.

14.

Setter peeked around the half-closed door of Crossin's office. "Progress report on the Asseltine case, sir? Is this a good time?"

"Come in." Crossin put the cap on his new-fangled fountain pen and dropped it into a tarnished silver lacrosse trophy on his desk. "I'll try to tear myself away from my monthly statistical report."

Setter took a seat in the chair in front of Crossin's desk and laid out his notes on the only space available that was not occupied by Crossin's files. He placed a manila envelope beside the notes and laid his hand on it briefly, and inwardly told it to wait for the proper moment.

"Right," he said, and launched into a review of what had been found at the crime scene, of the subsequent interviews with Peter, the janitor, Martland, the office staff, the two cleaning ladies, and ending with the various wardrobe searches. Crossin leaned forward on his elbows, concentrating hard during the sergeant's account of the button searches.

"So we're throwing our net wider on the wardrobe searches to include young Martland and other family members," Setter said.

He looked up from his notes. "And that's the way things stand at the moment, sir. Frankly, the more I look at it, the more questions I have about what actually went on in that room. For instance: why didn't McEvoy just run off after the struggle with Asseltine?"

"Too bloody drunk to do it, maybe?" Crossin cocked his head to one side, the better to cogitate. "There's Asseltine dead on the floor. McEvoy sees the whiskey decanter. At first he thinks, 'just one for my nerves.' In short order, he can't form the intention to take the money and leave."

"Mnmm." Setter shook his head. He got up and began pacing. "Well sir, you've been drunk and I've been drunk. But — supposedly — McEvoy's just killed a man, for God's sake. It's not likely something he does every day." He looked pointedly at Crossin.

"All right. Agreed. He doesn't seem the type."

"So why didn't the shock of that burn right through the alcohol? By rights he should have grabbed the money and staggered out as fast as his legs could carry him."

Crossin leaned forward, picked up the stub end of a cigar and stared at it. "And instead he stayed put." He picked up a box of matches. "Didn't even try to get out after the janitor locked the door on him."

Setter leaned on the desk. "Exactly. All he had to do was break the glass in the door."

Crossin fished in the box of matches and took one out, not striking it but flipping the match over, rolling it backwards and forwards across his undulating fingers. He seemed mesmerized but Setter, who had seen the trick before, waited impatiently.

Crossin snapped back to reality. "What have you got in the envelope?"

"Ah, well. Some photos of the button. They're —"

"No. Don't tell me. Hell's bells, Setter —"

"Sir, before you get up a head of steam, I can explain. They'll actually save us time, if not money in the end, guaranteed."

"How, pray tell?"

"Smithers and I can divide up the list of tailors and gents clothiers between us, thus completing the searches faster and making more efficient use of staff time." He nodded toward the monthly report on Crossin's desk. "Besides, if I hadn't asked Mrs. Cliffe to make the photographs, I would have missed — er — the woman's point of view."

Crossin's drew his eyebrows together. "Which is?"

Setter sat down again and pulled the photographs out of the envelope. "Up till now I've assumed that this button came off a man's clothing. But Mrs. Cliffe said there's a chance it belongs to a woman. That means we'll have to widen our search to include the female staff members, any female clients who visited the office that day, and Mrs. Martland and Mrs. Asseltine — to be absolutely thorough."

"Well." Crossin leaned back slowly in his chair and smiled coyly at his sergeant. "By all means be thorough."

"Yes, certainly. I intend to, sir." Setter tried to ignore the heat that had crept up his face.

"Give me the receipt for the photographs." The older man was back to business. "I'll pass it through somehow. We can only pray that this is not just a trip down the garden path —"

"I wouldn't suggest this expenditure of department time if it wasn't absolutely essential, sir. We need to confirm whose button this is and when it was dropped in Martland's office."

Crossin pursed his lips and nodded. "Agreed. Oh, by the way, I persuaded Smithers to drop his transfer application."

"His transfer? — I didn't — is that right? —"

"Blast. He didn't tell you, did he?"

"Well, sir," Setter began quickly gathering up his notes,

"There's no requirement for him to tell me. Things like that are entirely his own business." He tucked the sheaf of notes under his arm and headed for the door.

"Steady on, Setter. The point is the lad wants to stay with you. There was just —"

"No. Really, sir. No explanation necessary. Shall I have these notes transcribed for the file?"

"Look — yes. Go ahead —" Setter was out the door before he could finish. Crossin sighed and looked at a framed portrait on his desk. "Mrs. Crossin, your husband needs to think before he speaks."

The brethren milled around folding their aprons and helping themselves to strong tea from three large, squat teapots. The worshipful master had more than once wondered if such an early meeting caused the members to yearn more for their dinners than for the perfection of the Masonic craft. Still, the men of Northern Light Lodge no. 63 often had business to attend to later in the evening and an early meeting time was their decided preference. The master had been rewarded tonight with a most commendable turnout. He saw Frank Martland's greeting from across the room and responded with a dignified and condoling inclination of the head.

Martland reciprocated and tucked his regalia case under his arm. He caught a glimpse, through the crowd, of the dark, military-style frogged tunic and peaked cap of the chief constable and steered in his direction, shaking a hand here and receiving a solicitous pat on the shoulder there. The news about the murder had been leaking out to an ever-widening circle and had finally furnished the headline for the late afternoon edition of the *Free Press*. The chief, too, was working his way through the crowd. He paused for a few moments of earnest conversation with one group then detached himself and moved on to the next. Martland kept him in view and slowly gained on him.

"Good evening, Chief," Martland said as he grabbed the chief's hand.

"Martland — Frank — grand to see you." The chief lowered his voice slightly. "I hope you've got the wind back in your sails after that terrible shock."

"Thank you, Angus. My employees are quite shaken, but I've got the office functioning at least. And thank you again for personally giving me the news. I know how busy you are."

"Not at all. A crime like this — a prominent man — needs delicate handling and reassurance. Decent people need to know that they're safe in their beds at night."

"But are they, Angus?" Martland drew him a little apart from the rest. "When I got home from the office Monday I had to put up with a visit from one of your sergeants. Setter, I think he said his name was. Indian fellow."

The chief rumbled in his throat and nodded. "Ah, yes?"

"Asked me a lot of questions," Martland said, "and then insisted on pawing through my closets, for heaven's sake. And now I've just heard that the killer has been granted bail! I was shocked, I can tell you."

The chief took an involuntary step backward. "News travels quickly." He closed the gap again. "But then perhaps you heard from your son?"

Martland sighed and nodded his head. "I know. Trevor put up the bail money. Cut me to the quick that did. But a father's wishes don't seem to count for much when there's a pretty face involved."

"Oh, was that it?" The chief smiled. "An angel of mercy, I suppose. Well, Frank, children go their own way these days. But if it had been up to me the fellow would have stayed in my jail until the call from the hangman."

"Quite right, too. There's more of these kinds of people coming into the city every day. And Jews — and now these people from Galicia." Martland looked around to see if others were listening. "Shite from the manure pile of Europe, Angus. We have to make a stand for British justice or they'll swamp us. People want this McEvoy fellow to pay for what he did and believe me, we appreciate your leadership in these matters."

"Thank you, Frank, I'm just trying to do —"

"No, no, you're too modest." Martland took the chief by the elbow and drew him into the empty cloak room. In a hushed voice he continued. "You'd make a fine mayor, Angus, and I'm not the only man here that thinks so. There are seven or eight of us who would back you to the hilt."

"Well, Frank, I don't know what to say." The chief's chest expanded, and the ribbons trailing from the frogs on his tunic stirred. "I really haven't given the matter much thought. But I suppose if you and the others feel I could make a contribution —"

"The election is six months away — plenty of time — and I'm sure we can run a strong campaign for you."

The chief looked pained. "The thing is, Frank, I would feel duty-bound to resign my present position in order to run. And then if I lose —"

"If you lose, which you're not going to do, every man here would jump at the chance to use your talents. I'd like to speak to one or two of our friends about this, if you'd allow me. Get a committee rolling, that sort of thing."

The chief leaned in closer to Martland and his voice dropped almost to a whisper. "I have had conversations with one or two people, just in a hypothetical way, you understand —"

"Good work, Angus," Martland said. "Now, the next step is

for you to get this McEvoy business settled. Let the city see you at your best."

The chief drew himself up to his full height. "Well, I've always been four square for the law, Frank. We won't have quiet streets unless we can demonstrate to the criminal classes that we are prepared to deal firmly with them."

"That's what we've been waiting to hear. Keep talking like that, Angus, and the mayor's gavel is as good as yours." Martland grabbed the chief by the shoulders and looked him in the eyes. The chief found himself caught in the intense blue gaze of the other man.

"I know you won't let us down," Martland said.

After taking his leave the chief walked down the steps of the Masonic hall slowly, feeling for the next step with his outstretched foot. At the bottom of the steps he smiled and lifted his face up to catch the early evening sun. He set out for home, walked several paces, stopped, and then turned back toward the Central Police Station.

15.

Supper at the Colony Café had not been a success. The little corner place had smelled inviting but the plates set before them contained gluey mashed potatoes and overcooked chops afloat in grease. Peter had barely touched his and, in fact, had left the table abruptly. The meal now sat like a par-boiled hockey puck in his stomach as Charles ushered Peter back through the front door at Mrs. Gough's. An evening in the parlour. A long evening. He had never had much time to sit around at home but he couldn't very well drag Peter along to his hospital visits or evening meetings. This was beginning to remind Charles uncomfortably of taking care of his younger sister and brothers.

When they walked into the parlour, Charles's fellow lodger, Mr. Krause, was seated in a tufted leather rocking chair with the newspaper spread across his lap. Mr. Krause sold plumbing supplies, as he liked to say in his scrupulously correct though heavily-accented English, "throughout the whole of the Northwest." It was an exaggeration but not by much; his territory ran from the Lake of the Woods as far west as Swift Current in the Assiniboia country. As a result, Mr. Krause didn't spend much time sitting in the parlour either. And when he was home, he certainly didn't fit the type of the garrulous commercial traveller. Even after five years of sharing a breakfast table with him, Charles had never felt comfortable addressing him by his Christian name.

"Mr. Krause, I'd like you to meet my friend, Peter McEvoy. Pete, this is Mr. Krause, my upstairs neighbour."

Mr. Krause rose quickly from his chair, catching his pince-nez spectacles as they fell from his nose and crushing the paper to his chest in the process. Charles could see part of a large headline: VAGRANT CHARGED IN ASSELTINE —"

"Ah, yes, yes, I see, yes." The older man shuffled paper and pince-nez into one hand and couldn't seem to decide what to do next. "Mrs. Gough told me that you had a ... a guest, yes." Finally he put out a hand to Peter, and after shaking, made a determined effort not to wipe his hand on his trouser leg. "Well, Mr. McEvoy, you will be staying with us for a while?"

"Yes. Yes, just for a while until I can get things settled."

"This is a very quiet house. I'm sure you will find it so. We all attend to our own affairs." There was something vaguely challenging about the set of Krause's chin when he said it.

Peter reddened slightly. "Well, you can be sure I'm not going to bother anybody, if that's what you're concerned about. I actually prefer to keep to myself." Now his chin was out.

"Now — Mr. McEvoy — don't ... that is, I meant no offence ... really ... I was only —"

Charles groaned inwardly while Krause stammered. *Pete! Can't you see that Krause is frightened, not angry? Do you think you could help yourself a little?* He tried to lead the conversation to safer waters. "No offence meant, I'm sure. Say now, Mr. Krause, I hear you went through quite a storm west of Brandon last week."

"What? Oh, yes, yes, quite a storm." It was a lifeline and he grabbed it. "Lightning, wind — I had to tether my horse to a tree and hide under the buckboard. I never heard such thunder."

"That — that must have been uncomfortable for you," Peter

said. "I've taken shelter in some pretty hard places myself during storms."

"Yes, yes." Krause's eyes darted toward the archway to the hall. "I expect you have." He stuffed his pince-nez into his pocket and placed his folded paper on a side table. "Well, gentlemen. If you will excuse me — em — I have some figures to enter into my sales book." He bobbed his head to them as he retreated from the room.

Mrs. Gough came in just as Charles and Peter were settling uneasily onto the rocking chair and the settee. "Where has Mr. Krause got to? He was going to hold my wool for me." She hugged a well-stuffed knitting basket to her bosom.

"He said he had some sales figures to go over."

Mrs. Gough glanced over in Peter's direction, then quickly looked down, fussing among her wool skeins. "Oh. Oh, I see. Well —"

"I'll do that for you, if you like."

"Oh — Thank you, Mr. Lauchlan. That's a help. I've got to make a start on Bertie's winter stockings."

She moved a petit-point covered chair to a position in front of him, sat down, and unwound the first skein into a long, continuous loop of wool. She found the end of the thread and dropped the loop over his outstretched hands. As she wound each skein into a tight ball, he tried to keep the thread moving into her quick fingers without tangling. He needed to keep his wits about him but all the while he was acutely conscious of Peter, who had the paper in his lap and was reading the article that belonged to that partially glimpsed headline.

As Mrs. Gough was tucking the neat, wound balls into her bag, Charles said, "Mrs. Gough, Peter here is pretty handy with a hammer and saw; how would it be if we made that new screen for the kitchen window I've been promising you?"

"What? Now, do you mean?"

"Yes, this evening. I've got the wood and the screening in the garden shed. With the two of us it shouldn't take much more than a couple of hours. We should have just enough daylight to finish." As Charles said this, he looked over at Peter, whose mind was still coming to grips with this new plan for his evening.

"Och, well. The mosquitoes are starting and I would love to be able to open the window while I work. Yes, Mr. Lauchlan — if it's not too much trouble."

"No trouble at all. Come on, Pete. I've got an old shirt you can wear."

The work was quickly in hand. As they put together a make-shift workbench on top of the clothesline stoop, Charles could tell that Peter was distracted, likely still focused on the article in the *Free Press*.

"I gather there was something in the paper?"

"Yes. Something." Peter compressed his lips and made an effort to steady his hand as he drew a diagram of the window frame on the back of a handbill. "Damn. I can't lay out much of a straight line."

"Never mind that. We don't need Rembrandt. What did the article say?"

Peter clutched at his right hand, massaging it. "That reporter talks about it so matter-of-factly. As if there's no other explanation possible except that I did it."

"Then he's not very good at his job. Anyway, you never used to set much store by what was in the newspaper. Come on, now." He gave Pete a playful box on the shoulder. "Don't give up before we've even started."

Peter cast a look of exasperation skyward, then pulled himself to mock attention. "Right; note to self: always look on the bright side and make sure you have a clean hanky."

Charles was not to be turned aside so easily. "Look, we've

got a fine lawyer in Jessup. According to Blakely Campbell, he's headed for great things." Peter had begun sorting aimlessly through the hammers, chisels, and clamps in the late Mr. Gough's toolbox, so that Charles had to twist around in order to look him in the eye. "Courts deal in facts, not opinions. And the facts are on your side."

Peter gave a grunt of acknowledgement and reached around Charles for his drawing. Leaning back on his heels, Charles sighed. The effort required to paint a bright picture was starting to wear on him. If Peter was going to make a good impression in court, he would have to dig in and find his own confidence. If he turned up looking like a defeated man, the jury would likely read that as guilt.

"So!" he said, biting back those thoughts. "Let's do lap joints. They're easier to make with the tools we've got."

"No. Not laps." Peter held up the finished drawing, pointing. "Mortise and tenon. Laps aren't strong enough."

"But —"

"You know it's the right thing to do. And I'm not interested in doing the other."

"Man of decision. Mortise and tenon it is." They tacked the drawing to the stoop and then began to measure out the boards and saw the lengths for the rails and stiles. Peter knew exactly how long and how wide the tenons would need to be for a strong join. Just as they were carefully chiselling wood away from the ends of the rails to make the tenons the screen door of the house sprang open and a small boy came hurtling out, jumped off the steps, and started running toward the stoop.

The boy bought himself up short about four paces from them. He grabbed at one stocking that had come adrift from his knee breeches and pulled it up, considering his next move. With a sly look back at the house, he said, "Don't tell Mummy I'm here."

Charles looked up, brushing some wood shavings off the rail he was working on. "All right, but you have to behave. Bertie, this is my friend Peter McEvoy. Pete, meet the man of the house."

Peter wiped the sweat off his hand and offered it to Bertie. "Pleased to meet you, Bertie."

The boy hung back, looked wide-eyed at Peter, then at Charles, who nodded encouragement. With a solemn look, Bertie walked slowly up to Peter, took the hand that was offered, shook it firmly twice then jumped back a step, as if he had been too close to a fire.

A look of triumph spread over his face. "Jeff Connolly's going to be mad when he hears that I shook hands with you."

"Why's that?"

"Because he bet that I would be too scared. But I wasn't."

"That's just what I would expect from you, Bertie," Charles said. "But there's nothing to be frightened about. Right, Pete?"

"Right." Peter went back to his work.

Bertie looked a little disappointed. He watched them working with their bright chisels for a while, the metal catching reflections from the setting sun. "Can I do that?"

Charles and Peter exchanged a look. Then Peter retrieved the sawn-off end of one of the boards. "Come here, then. I'll show you."

The boy hesitated, but he could not resist. He moved close to the stoop and watched, with one foot absently toeing the grass, while Peter drew a square on the face of the board with a pencil, then fastened the board to the edge of the stoop with two clamps and, using the hammer and chisel, began to cut into the lines, incising the shape of the square. Then he changed the angle of the chisel and began to cut wood away from within the square.

Bertie's eyes followed every move as the wood curled up and

away from the chisel, forming a neat pile of shavings that Peter periodically swept away from the hole.

"Now me!"

"All right, all right. Come over here." Bertie moved to a position in front of Peter, who stationed him at the proper angle to the board and handed him the hammer and chisel. Then, standing behind the boy, he put his own hands above Bertie's, gently guiding the tools. They were two intent and parallel forms: Bertie squinting at his work, concentrating hard, and Peter hovering over the boy, watching the bite of the chisel and steering it ever so slightly as the shavings magically curled away.

"Bertie!"

The voice was shrill, piercing. Peter jumped back from the boy; the hammer dropped from Bertie's hand as the chisel gouged the side out of the neat square.

"Now look what you made me do! You spoiled it."

"Come away from there. Now! This instant!"

"But I was just —"

"Never mind that. Into the house. Right now!"

"Look — Wait a minute. I wasn't hurting the boy. I was just —"

Charles grabbed Peter's arm. "Let me handle this." As Charles rushed toward the house, he missed seeing the look on Peter's face.

Later, even when she had calmed down, Charles had known that there was no point in trying to change her mind.

"I understand, Mrs. Gough. You've been very kind. We'll find somewhere else."

"Oh, no, no, Mr. Lauchlan, I'm not wanting to put *you* out of your rooms at all. No. You're a good tenant and good around the house. But could you not find another place for Mr. McEvoy?" she said.

Charles suspected that finding another place for Peter to

stay was easier said than done. He knew that Dr. Skene would feel obliged to offer but he simply could not foist the problem onto the Skenes. The only place he could think of was the church. There was a large room suitable for a live-in caretaker, if the congregation should ever be able to afford one. Peter and he would just have to bunk in there for the time being. He tried to soften the edges of their exile as they cleaned up the scraps and returned the tools to the shed.

"Might be best, anyway. It's really too crowded for both of us here. We'll be able to spread out more at the church."

Peter said only, "I suppose so," and then went rather quiet. He waited silently while Charles packed his shaving kit and a few clothes into an old leather grip. He nodded to Peter, who picked up his own bundle, and headed out the door and down the stairs. With one last look around at his nest, Charles pulled the door closed and locked it.

16.

The next morning, Setter was rooting through drawers in the file room when Inspector Crossin appeared in the doorway. "Ah — there you are. Come into my office, will you?"

Setter followed Crossin down the hall and into the office and was somewhat bemused when the inspector closed the door carefully. Crossin walked behind his desk and sank down into his chair with a tired explosion of air.

"The Asseltine post-mortem report's on the chief's desk. He asked for it to come directly to him."

"When can I see it?"

"He seems to want it all to himself just at the moment." Crossin pulled a cigar out of his humidor, bit the end off and spit it into a waste basket beside his chair. "Here's the gist." He paused to light the cigar and blow out several acrid puffs. "Severe compression fracture of the second cervical vertebra, almost certainly resulting from the fall onto the fender. Severe injury to the spinal cord paralyzed his diaphragm and that was the end of him."

"And the scalp wound?"

"Hard to say." He removed a piece of tobacco from his tongue. "The doctor thinks it was caused by the fall, but the chief thinks he was hit on the head by something. Judging by the amount of blood, he died pretty quickly."

"Well, if it's clear that the fall killed him we'll have a hard time proving intent won't we? Even if there was a fight between them, McEvoy might have been trying to get to the safe and just pushed Asseltine out of the way. He might even have been defending himself."

"Chief thinks the blow to the head is what caused him to fall. If McEvoy inflicted that blow, there's an argument to be made that he used force sufficient to be deadly and that speaks to intent."

"You saw McEvoy that night, sir. The chances of him being able to land even one blow, much less one with deadly force were, I would say, pretty slim. And besides, we didn't find anything except the fender that would cut the scalp like that. No, no." He shook his head. "It just doesn't add up to me, sir."

Crossin just nodded at him with a wry look, cast his eyes toward the door, and then beckoned Setter to come closer. "Look. The old man's got some kind of bee in his bonnet, so he's not seeing things right. He's bound and determined that we'll complete the investigations as quick as possible. That means we have to find something solid — something he can't explain away — sooner rather than later. I can string him along for about a week, I think."

"Give me Smithers for a week and we'll find something. I'll stake my badge on it."

"Done. But keep it quiet, and avoid the chief whenever possible."

Charles and Peter had spent the better part of the afternoon making their new living space at the church habitable. The room, large and with a high ceiling but no window, had been used for storage. All of that had to be relocated except for an old chest of drawers. To this they had added two ancient iron beds, which they had carried, crablike, from the second-hand store up the street. Charles had not asked the storekeeper where the lumpy, dispirited mattresses had come from; sometimes it was best not to know. Everything that didn't fit in the dresser was piled in an orange crate — one for each of them — or tossed on the beds. A basin and ewer stood on a wooden china barrel in the corner.

Charles had to admit to himself that fitting out the room had gotten slightly out of hand. The cart was squarely in front of the horse. If the board refused them permission to live here, all this would have to be disassembled and they might have to doss down in the cart. So be it. Although he wouldn't get a chance to ask about Peter staying at the church until the meeting the next day, Charles couldn't reconcile himself to sleeping on the floor another night. He'd just have to make the board understand.

They had been invited to the Skenes' for dinner and so they began dressing, trying not to elbow each other in the eye in front of a mirror, which they had "borrowed" from the dressing room used by the choir. *Here we are again,* Charles thought. They seemed to be acting out a weird parody of their student days, sharing a room as if the last fifteen years hadn't happened. So familiar, yet so strange. Charles handed Peter a can of bootblack which Peter took to his bed and, with an old rag, began polishing the scuffed leather of his shoes.

"I've found that if you polish and then buff and then put on a second layer of polish and then buff that very lightly, the scuffs almost disappear," Peter said, mostly to himself. "Unfortunately, it's just temporary." He gave a final pass with the cloth and put his shoes back on. Charles was pulling at the stiff celluloid of his clerical collar. He tried not to look at Peter too obviously.

Without the practical task of arranging a room to preoccupy him, the shaking and sweating was reasserting itself.

"Do I look all right?" Peter said, standing up.

"Yes, of course. You'll do fine."

"Wouldn't it be better if I just stayed here?" Peter said. "Dr. Skene is kind — and I'm indebted to him. But he just invited me out of a sense of duty. And because I might sneak off, I suppose. The whole business is pretty awkward."

"Don't be so worried. Dr. Skene spent five years at a church in the Gorbals. He saw worse than you every day. And as for Maggie, she'll be questioning the life out of you the minute you step over the door sill. You'll feel like a specimen in a glass jar."

"I'm more used to people trying not to look at me," Peter said as Charles herded him out the door.

When they arrived at the Skene house the whole family had assembled in the front hallway to greet them, everyone speaking a little louder than strictly necessary. Charles introduced Aunt Jessie and Maggie to Peter, who alternated looking at them and glancing off to the side, as if their faces were too bright for his eyes.

"How do you do, Miss Skene?" Peter said to Aunt Jessie, who murmured a shy reply, and, turning to Maggie, he said, "Very pleased to meet you, Miss Skene."

Maggie stepped forward and took Peter's hand in both of hers. "Mr. McEvoy, Charles has told me so much about you. I — we — all of us just want you to know that you're not the one — that is, we believe what you say, even if you don't remember — er, we've never met you before, but we're sure — oh, dear — I'm talking nonsense —" she flushed and laughed with embarrassment.

"What Maggie means to say, Mr. McEvoy," said Dr. Skene, "is that you are welcome in this house and we want to do all we can to help you through the ordeal you're facing."

Smiling at Peter, Maggie said softly, "Yes, that's it. Thank you, Father."

Peter shook Dr. Skene's outstretched hand. "Sir, you've already done so much for me. I'll never be able to repay your kindness."

"I hope you like lamb, Mr. McEvoy," said Aunt Jessie, "and there's plum cobbler for dessert." Since it was later than their usual dining hour, she ushered them directly into the large, bright dining room.

Once they had settled themselves and the soup had been brought in from the kitchen, dishes were passed and there was a lull in the conversation as they began to eat. Peter's spoon made a somewhat unsteady trip from the bowl to his mouth. Charles wondered if he would have any appetite since he had hardly eaten anything since leaving his cell. But, to his surprise, Peter seemed hungry and the soup was extremely good. With a furtive glance around the table, Peter moved his head as close to the bowl as good manners would allow and spooned in the soup with evident relish.

"Charles tells me you've travelled a great deal, Mr. McEvoy," said Maggie. "I would so like to hear about some of the places you've been. Germany and Austria, for instance."

"Maggie is in love with all things German at the moment," said Charles. "She says all the most forward-looking scientific discoveries are made there."

"I agree with you there, Miss Skene," Peter said. "When I was in Tübingen, I snuck into a lecture hall to hear Meyer give a talk on the Periodic Table."

"Oh please, tell me all about it!" Maggie said. "I have his textbook. Did he look as fierce as in his photographs?"

"He was very impressive," Peter said, his eyes lighting up. "He had an immense white beard and he pounded the desk to make a point. I had a hard time understanding what he was talking about, my German is so poor, but the fellow next to me knew English and translated a bit for me."

"Someday I would love to study there," Maggie said, sighing. "Maybe by the time I get there, ladies will be able to take degrees instead of just attending lectures. I can take a science degree of sorts at the university here but things are so much more advanced in Germany."

"I looked into studying there myself," Peter said. "But, well, there were so many other interesting things to see, I didn't want to limit myself."

Peter seemed to become self-conscious all at once and dropped his eyes to his plate. Charles realized that he had been staring at Peter. Had some of his anxiety about how Peter would fit in been written on his face? Happily, the lull in the conversation was camouflaged by the arrival of the lamb and vegetable dishes.

Best to direct the conversation elsewhere. "You don't know anyone in Germany, do you?" Charles said to Maggie. "Couldn't you study somewhere in Canada? Toronto or McGill, for instance?"

"You don't think I could manage by myself in a foreign country, do you?" she said.

"I didn't say that. I've been to Germany and those university towns are sometimes pretty rough. There's a lot of carousing and the streets are full of, you know, full of —"

"Full of men, you mean. Drunk and disorderly men," Maggie said.

"Well, yes. Respectable young women need protection from that."

"I don't need that kind of protection. While they're in the tavern singing drinking songs and inflicting duelling wounds on each other, I'll be snugly holed up in a laboratory or a library. There's more to German universities than swilling beer. Don't you think so, Mr. McEvoy?"

Peter, his mouth full of potato, nodded in the affirmative but then Maggie felt like kicking herself.

"Yes, of course, that's true," Charles said. "There are some wonderful professors and you can study almost anything you want. I'm sure you'd thrive in that atmosphere, Maggie. I just worry that you'll get caught up by accident in some of the tomfoolery that goes on there."

Maggie smiled, disarmed. "Charles. You think I'm worth educating?"

"Of course." He was surprised. "Why do you suppose I've been feeding you books all these years?"

"More potatoes, Mr. McEvoy?" said Aunt Jessie. "Pass the potatoes to Mr. McEvoy and the gravy."

As Peter took the potato dish it wobbled unevenly in his hand.

"Here, I can hold that for you." Charles said, taking the dish. Peter tried to steady his hand as he spooned the potatoes onto his plate.

"You'll never guess what Jenkins did today," said Dr. Skene and launched into a story, the latest in a long line, about the eccentric caretaker at the college. He was just getting to the best part, warming to his theme, when there was a crashing sound.

"Christ!" Peter had knocked over his water glass, splashing its contents over the table. In trying to save it, he had knocked the gravy boat onto the floor. With all eyes on him, his own eyes were screwed shut and his mouth was twisted. Then he let all the air out of his lungs in one long, dispirited sigh.

"Why doesn't somebody just say what you've all been

thinking? 'He's shaking like a leaf. Maybe we should hide the port we keep for the bronchitis.'"

The others all spoke at once. "No, Pete, it's not like — we're all trying to help — no harm done — just an old bowl —"

"— Do you really think you could stop me if I wanted a drink? As it happens, I've been trying to think of an excuse to go to the kitchen. Find that port or maybe some vanilla extract."

"Pete, we're not thinking those things. We're just trying to have a pleasant meal here and make you feel welcome. Here let me —"

"And if we're all comfy cozy, I won't think about sneaking a drink?" Peter rose from his seat. "You really don't know anything about it, do you? Well, the truth is there's no trick I wouldn't stoop to, believe me. I've been thinking about that drink every minute of every hour. Most of the time I can't think of much else."

"But why, Pete? Anyone can see that it's killing you. Why can't you?"

"You think it's just a question of — what? — pinpointing the problem?" Peter said. "Just reason it out and then don't do it anymore? — Christ! It's not the thinking, Charlie. It's the God-damned doing." He cupped his forehead in his hand and looked down at the ruins of the gravy bowl on the floor.

"I should have stopped you — back when we were students."

"Isn't that just like you!" The cords were standing out on Peter's neck and there were two patches of colour below each cheekbone. "You think you can manage almost anything. Manage me so that I don't embarrass you in front of your friends, more like. Well I'm not so easily managed. You may not like it, but my life is in my own hands."

Now Charles was angry. He lurched to his feet. "Then do a better job of running it! Because, I'm telling you, you'll have to do more than just feel sorry for yourself now. You're in a right mess, boy. So if ever there was a time to take hold, this is it."

Peter looked as if he had been slapped. Charles's angry voice echoed around the room and the others seemed frozen in place.

"Excuse me, Mr. Lauchlan." It was Lizzie, the hired girl.

"Yes? What is it?" Charles felt a bit stunned. He wondered how long she'd been standing there.

"There's a gentleman at the door wants to speak to you," she said.

Charles removed the napkin from his belt and walked to the front hall. He could feel the sick regret welling up in his chest. When he got to the door, he saw Erling Eklund standing just inside, cap in hand and still in his work clothes.

"Eklund, hello. What brings you here?" Charles said. Dr. Skene had followed him and he was vaguely aware of the women clattering dishes in the kitchen.

"Evening, Reverend, Doctor." Eklund nodded his head in Dr. Skene's direction. "I wanted to get this estimate for the beam replacement to you right away. Mr. Martland has seen it." If Eklund had overheard the argument, he gave no sign. He handed Charles a sheet of paper.

"That's really very good of you. Thank you for tracking me down." Charles tried to cover his embarrassment. "Sorry I had to leave you to carry on by yourself yesterday."

"That's all right, sir. I know you have other claims on your time. Do you have any idea when we might get on with the new beam? We don't want to leave those temporary supports too long," Eklund said.

"Well, I'm trying to get a meeting of my board together tomorrow afternoon. Let's see what we have here." Charles read the estimate while the other men looked over his shoulder. He looked immediately for the total at the bottom of the page and was relieved at both the amount and the presence of Frank Martland's scrawled signature beside it. He asked Eklund a few questions and Dr. Skene made some suggestions about the way in which the information should be presented to the board, of which he was a member.

"Charles, something's happened!" Maggie's voice was urgent. Her face appeared over Dr. Skene's shoulder.

"What is it?"

"We can't find Mr. McEvoy! He was here but now he's vanished," she said.

He asked, but Maggie had been through the whole house. Peter was gone.

Charles raked his hand through his hair. "Idiot! Why did I lose my temper?" He looked frantically out at the street. "Which way do you think he went? I'll have to find him somehow." He grabbed his hat out of the hall closet and rushed past Eklund, shouting at Maggie not to follow him. She made for the door anyway but her father caught and held her fast.

"No, dear. No. Let Charles go after him," he said.

Charles loped down the street, looking in every direction when he reached the corner of Balmoral and Broadway. There wasn't a sign of Peter. He asked a man watering plants on his verandah whether he had seen Peter. He had. He described seeing a man in a somewhat ill-fitting dark suit walking quickly in the direction of downtown.

17.

Maggie sat on the verandah steps with her German grammar book balanced on her knees. She had been going aimlessly over the same vocabulary list for the past twenty minutes.

"Wake up, dreamer."

"Trev? Where did you come from?"

"The usual place. I thought you might like to go for a ride and see how the new Martland estate is progressing." Trevor was sitting on his own bicycle and holding onto the handlebars of another bicycle, a shiny ladies' model.

"Oh, I'd like that." Then she thought of the events earlier in the evening. "Only, Mr. McEvoy's run away and Charles has gone to look for him." She hesitated. "I hope to goodness he finds him before ... "

"Before?"

"Before you actually end up paying the bail money."

"Now Maggie, don't go putting a fright into Mr. Martland before we know the outcome." Dr. Skene had been writing letters in the screened-in portion of the verandah, and had emerged at the sound of Trevor's voice.

"Oh, good evening, sir. And please call me 'Trevor'. McEvoy's gone, then?"

"I'm afraid so. Slipped away when we weren't looking. I suppose we should have known how difficult sobriety would be for him." He lit a match and drew the flame into his briar.

"I didn't help much by talking about drunken students in Germany."

"He didn't need reminding, dear. You heard McEvoy. Liquor is ever-present in his mind." He gripped the stem of the pipe with his teeth and a small, mushroom shaped puff drifted upward. "What a living hell that must be."

"I suppose I could help Charles search for him, sir, although …" He shook his head. "If he is in a barroom somewhere, the damage will already have been done, I'm afraid."

"I fear it's as you say, Trevor. Charles will have to handle it as he sees fit. Let's leave it to him." He saw Maggie's face. "But why don't you see if you can cheer Maggie up?"

The frown lines left Trevor's forehead. "I'm sure I could do that, sir. I was just going to suggest she take a bicycle ride with me to see the new house."

"Well …" Dr. Skene looked in the direction of the kitchen. "Jessie will worry about propriety. But, yes, go ahead. Real estate always has an uplifting effect on Maggie." He looked at her over the top of his spectacles. "Mind you're back by ten-thirty at the latest or we'll both have your Aunt Jessie to deal with."

In short order they were riding across the Osborne Street Bridge and onto the cool, less inhabited streets of Fort Rouge. They turned west on Roslyn Road, past the gates of Augustus Nanton's ample new house, still under construction and hidden from the masses by a serpentine drive through the dense forest of poplar and elm. Around the next bend in the road, Trevor turned his bicycle into a circular driveway, still composed of mud that had been temporarily gravelled to ease the way of the construction wagons. The house, which was set far back, was visible from the street with the drive passing underneath a porte-cochere that covered the main entrance. Trevor's father had considered building in Armstrong's Point on the other side of the river where several of the city's grandees had recently relocated. But when Nanton had chosen Fort Rouge, his father had changed his mind, muttering something about property values being more secure there.

They managed to ride over the bumps and ruts in the loose gravel and cruised in under the porte-cochere where the going was smoother. They leaned their bicycles against a huge packing crate with, MARTLAND — W.C. scrawled on the side. Maggie walked out from under and, screening her eyes, took in the full breadth and height of the front facade.

"I've never seen stonework like this, not even in Toronto. It's like a fantasy castle." She suddenly turned in his direction. "Your parents don't mind us poking around?"

"It's my house, too." He kicked at a clod of mud. "Sometimes I have to direct the workmen when father is out of town so I have my own key. Come on." He bowed deeply to her. "Would you care to be escorted to the drawing room?" He stretched all the vowels to the breaking point.

"I should be utterly charmed." She stuck her nose in the air, extended her hand and they ever-so-grandly ascended the front steps.

The huge cherry wood door swung silently inward to reveal a dark panelled foyer with built-in leather upholstered benches for removing boots. Then there were steps up to a central hallway, empty now, and almost the size of the street in front of Maggie's house. The door shut with a decisive engagement of fittings that echoed throughout the house. Halfway down the hallway the wide staircase, as yet uncarpeted, led upward to a generous landing and then up again to the second floor. They walked from room to empty room. There was a dining room that could sit thirty people quite easily although the table and chairs were not yet in place. Across the hall there was a large drawing room with fireplace and French doors that opened onto a conservatory. The plastering was not yet complete in some of the rooms and the floors not yet laid in others. They walked up the staircase and into the reception room where dances and parties would be held.

"Father had to bring in the plasterers from Boston. No one here could do these mouldings. He has to pay for their lodging and everything."

She looked up at the plasterwork on the ceiling, which looked like a ribbon complete with an ornate bow above the archway into the hall. There was a similar ribbon around the place where the chandelier would hang. She could see that the house was three times the size of the Martlands' current house. What must it all have cost? She couldn't imagine and it still had to be filled with flooring, carpets, drapery, furniture, lamps, and all the small touches and details that made a house a home. She had expected Trevor to be proud and excited, taking pleasure in showing everything to her and so she was trying to be properly enthusiastic. But his heart did not seem to be in this particular showing.

"Don't you like the house?"

"Oh, it's fine, I suppose."

"It's almost too big, isn't it? Still, it will seem more home-like when the furniture is in. If I lived here I might lose my way between the kitchen and the dining room."

He didn't laugh. *Oh no,* she thought. *What if he thinks I'm trying on chatelaine of the manor for size?* She hadn't intended that at all.

Then he seemed to remember himself and smiled suddenly. "Little ninny. If you lived here, you wouldn't be working in the kitchen; the servants would be carrying you around on a cushion."

Relief. She shoved him playfully. He stepped back and threw his arms wide. "In Xanadu did Kubla Khan a stately pleasure dome decree!" The shouted words hit the walls and bounced back as he turned around and around, wind milling with his arms.

The arms dropped so suddenly that there was a slapping sound as they hit his sides. "The truth is it is too big." He walked unsteadily toward a window that looked out over the soon-to-be park behind the house. "Too big for me, anyway; a house like this, somehow you have to earn it, though how a person would do that, I don't know. This —" He gestured at the fireplace, the ceiling mouldings. "It's more like a stage set. We walk through it and say our lines. And we hope the right people are watching us." He turned back to the window.

"Trev, is something —"

He turned suddenly. "Hey! I can't believe I forgot to show you the swimming bath off the conservatory. Come on. We've just got time before we have to go."

He grabbed her hand and hurried her out of the room and down the stairs. Later, on the ride home, she thought about what houses mean. After Trevor had begun to call on her, she had indulged in some daydreams of being with him in a house like that. But now that she had seen the house somehow she couldn't call back those pictures.

18.

Charles had begun the search by going through the hotel bars and beverage rooms, starting with the Metropole, the one Peter had mentioned. Each one had been more disreputable than the last. He tried to appear nonchalant while walking through the dark interiors of these high-ceilinged, narrow rooms with their scratched and stained tabletops, beer-soaked air, and sawdust-strewn floors. He hadn't thought about what he would do if he found Peter, only that he must find him. He did think, though, about what Peter had said to him at the Skenes'. He readily pleaded guilty to taking all the decisions out of Peter's hands, to barging ahead while thinking that he knew what was best. It was a fault that he had prayed over often. But it was the other thing that was still stinging, hours later. He had been ashamed of Peter; and he had been too busy worrying about what people were thinking about Charles blasted Lauchlan to really stand by his friend.

The manager at the Criterion said he hoped Charles wasn't there to lead a revival meeting; it was bad for business. He had personally escorted Charles off the premises. After that, he took off his clerical collar and dickey and stuffed them in his jacket pockets then undid the top button of his shirt. He was not proud of having done this but he needed to pass through these places without attracting a lot of attention. As it was, some of the regulars gave him looks that caused him to pat the inside pocket of his jacket. *Good. Wallet's still there.*

No one seemed to have seen Peter, though several people said they knew him. The Vendome was next. A burly man in a bowler hat, shirt sleeves, and a checked vest said that he had seen Peter that evening. Charles rushed through the passageway to the beverage room, blood drumming in his ears. No good. If Peter had been there earlier, he was gone now.

It was close to midnight. Mr. Checked Vest, who had stubbed out his cigar and returned to the lobby, was sympathetic. He said if Charles wanted to find Peter at this time of night he should look in the after-hours places — the illegal drinking and gambling establishments. He gave directions to two of these places. Charles thanked him and started for the door. A large arm with a bicep the size of a ham barred his way. Charles looked at him, recognized the situation, and reached for his wallet. He pulled out a one dollar bill and held it out. The arm stayed where it was. He pulled out a five and the arm reached out and took both bills.

Charles visited both establishments, one in what looked like a former livery stable, in which tables had simply been placed in the stalls; the other in a private house on Annabella Street in Point Douglas. At the latter, girls in cheap silk dressing gowns were serving drinks in the parlour. He was very tired. He sat down heavily on an overstuffed chesterfield while he explained to the older woman who seemed to run the place that he was looking for his friend. While he was doing this, one of the girls sat on his lap.

"No, Miss — um — pardon me. I think you misunderstand. I'm looking for my friend."

"We're all looking for a friend, dearie. I can be your friend, if you'll just let me." She tapped him playfully on the nose. "Whatever you're looking for, I've got it — in spades." With that she raised the hem of her wrap to reveal a garter around her abundant bare thigh. Stuck in the garter was a playing card, the ace of spades. She giggled and he felt the vibrations against his thighs, an unnervingly pleasant sensation.

"I'm sorry, but I really have to find my friend." He shifted her gently but firmly off his lap and onto the chesterfield.

"That's all right, dearie. You must have come to the wrong place. The nancy boys are at number 212 down the street." She sighed, got up and looked around the parlour for another friend-to-be.

Back on the street, he leaned against a tree. Things looked very bad. Peter had forfeited his bail and lost his opportunity to make a good impression on the judge and jury. Charles set off toward Main Street, crossed it, and trudged down Dufferin, wishing that his bed would magically appear in front of him. He could see the church ahead. When he came closer, he saw that there was a light on in the sanctuary. *Blast.* He went around to the side door. But when he got there, the dead bolt had been forced. The strike plate had completely broken away from the frame. He pushed the door inward but there was a heavy weight against the bottom on the other side. He pushed harder and the weight, whatever it was, slid along the floor with a scraping sound allowing him to enter.

Inside was silence; the hallway was dark. He bent down and felt for the weight that had held the door closed. A bag of what felt like sand. He took a deep breath and waited for his eyes to adjust to the light. Sweat pricked his upper lip. Then he remembered that the boys' gymnastic class kept their Indian clubs in a closet just off this hallway. Slowly and quietly he moved to the closet, eased open the door and felt along the floor. He gripped a club and, with some difficulty, shifted it noiselessly away from its mates. He felt its reassuring heft in his hand. *Now.* He walked down the hallway and turned the corner, heading toward the closed sanctuary door. He raised the club to his shoulder and rested it there, ready to defend himself. Then he opened the door — and stepped into a tableau from a medieval manuscript. On the pulpit platform an old door and two saw horses had been pressed into service as a desk and on its four corners, coal oil lamps were burning. In the soft light Peter sat drawing on what appeared to be an unrolled window blind.

Charles was rooted to the spot by the quiet concentration in that island of light. Utter relief and extreme annoyance careened wildly around his brain.

"Where have *you* been?" Peter said, but his eyes did not leave his drawing.

Charles was jolted back to reality. "Where have I been! Where have *I* been?" Then he began to splutter, still holding the Indian club at the ready. "I've been at my wit's — hey! — are you responsible for that broken dead bolt?"

"Sorry," Peter said. "But you never gave me a key so I had to break through the frame. I'll fix it in the morning. You really should have a better lock set. I'll see to that in the morning too."

"But — do you realize I've been in every — you know, I could have been robbed or worse in some of those — do you know it's one o'clock in the morning, for heaven's sakes —"

"Oh, never mind all that now," Peter said. "Come and look at what I'm doing."

Charles let the Indian club fall heavily to his side and exhaled through clenched teeth. Then he remembered the reason for his frantic tour of the worst watering holes. He eyed Peter's work area and looked for suspicious bulges in his jacket pockets. In a low voice he said, "That large fellow at the Vendome. He said he saw you."

"The bouncer? Yes, I was there." Peter looked up at Charles for the first time. "I got to the door but I didn't go in."

"You didn't go in?"

"No. I just kept walking and walking after that and then I came here." Peter saw that Charles couldn't quite ask the next question. "I got here at eleven. I know that because the clock at Dingwall's store said 10:50 p.m., and it's only a ten-minute walk from there to here — maybe twelve, but you're not going to quibble over two minutes are you?"

"No, I suppose not."

"You didn't see anyone else out there did you?" Peter furrowed his brow.

"Where? Outside the church?"

"Yes. When I turned off Main Street I thought someone was following me," Peter said. "I headed down a lane and through some yards and then doubled back. Seemed to work. Couldn't see anybody when I got here so I wondered if he was ever there at all." He shivered. "Never mind. Probably just the jim-jams. Look what I've got here."

Charles climbed the steps to the makeshift desk and saw that Peter had placed a crowbar close at hand and that there was more than the usual dew of sweat on his face.

"How did you know it was me coming in and not him, whoever he was?"

"You already knew the way so you didn't stumble around in the dark looking for the right door to the sanctuary."

Clever, Charles thought. Then he saw the drawing Peter had been working on. It was a design for a chancel and choir loft, drawn roughly in freehand, but in enough detail to give a strong impression. Charles had never seen anything quite like it — plain, but with proportions that seemed just right. The pulpit had none of the fancy decoration he was accustomed to. Yet he could almost feel his hands gripping its smooth surface and his voice resonating outward from the handsome reading desk.

"Gives you some idea of what it would be like," Peter said. "I can do better when I don't have the shakes."

"No, it's good. Wonderful, really," Charles said.

"It's simple, so it won't take long for me to build. And not too expensive if we can get most of the wood wholesale. But I will need some things — the best quality saws, planes and sanders. Really, it'll pay off in the long —"

"Pete, hold on now, I'll have to talk to my board —"

"But, Charlie. See how beautiful it's going to be. I won't ask for any pay. Just some food. I'll work on the detailed drawings tomorrow while you get this on the road. What do you say?" Peter's face was glowing, pale and intense.

In that moment Charles knew that he must use every trick of persuasion, stake his job on it if necessary, to get his board of management to approve Peter's renovations.

"I'll get you what you need. I don't know quite how, but I will," Charles said.

Peter looked relieved, then rattled off a list of tools he would require and started immediately to weigh the virtues of maple versus cherry. Charles had to smile and shake his head.

It won't be difficult, he thought to himself. *I just need to convince my board to house a dipsomaniac accused of murder in the church and hire him to build a chancel and choir loft. Other churches will be jealous and want to hire him, too.* He thought of his snug little suite at Mrs. Gough's, of his comfortable old armchair. Then he looked again at the ferocious concentration with which Peter was calculating board foot measurements.

"I'll get some quilts from the storage locker in the basement. We'll get some real bedding tomorrow," Charles said.

Peter looked up from his calculations and sat back slowly in his chair, looking at the ceiling. He stretched and rubbed his neck. "Yes. Yes. I think I could sleep now."

19.

On Friday mornings Rosetta went to the university to photograph botanical specimens. She had told Setter, with a certain glow of satisfaction, of how she had filched the contract out from under the nose of Crooks and Feyer. It did mean that Mrs. Harbottle had to cover for her in the studio Friday mornings, a prospect that took some of the edge off the triumph. That was why Mrs. Harbottle came to be at the desk that morning, reading a novel instead of taking inventory of the frame stock. She was jolted into awareness by an airy tinkling of the bell that announced the arrival of a customer.

Erling Eklund, dressed in a rather garish window-pane check suit, was approaching the counter. Either the fashion in men's clothes had changed considerably or the suit was somewhat too short for him, both in the trousers and sleeves. He seemed all too aware of this and pulled at his cuffs as he walked.

"I've come to pick up some photographs."

"Oh yes, sir. And what is your name?"

"Brochmer. William Brochmer."

After asking him to spell it out for her, Mrs. Harbottle stepped over to the box of prints and framed photographs marked for pick-up that day. He was now standing close enough to her that the red wine birth mark across his nose was hard to overlook. If she noticed it, she was making an effort not to stare at him as she flipped through the contents of the box once, and again more slowly. Then she went over to the oak filing cabinets and checked several files of contact prints and negatives.

"I'm sorry, Mr. Brochmer. I can't seem to find them. Are you sure Mrs. Cliffe said to pick up today? She's usually very efficient."

"Yes. It was today. I'm sure she said today. Is there somewhere else you can look?"

"Well, I can look at the order book in the back."

"I would be obliged." He moved around the counter and stood in front of the oak filing cabinets. "Would you mind if I had a look? She may have put them under my company name."

As he was standing right in front of the cabinets, it was difficult for Mrs. Harbottle to refuse. She nodded assent. As soon as she disappeared into the back room, Eklund, keeping a furtive eye on the back room door, located a drawer, pulled it open, flipped through, pulled another drawer open and stopped at a file containing a number of contact prints and a heavy packet of glass negatives. He paged through the prints.

"No, Mr. Brochmer," She called from the back room. "I don't see any order for you either."

He pulled a print out of the file, folded it in two quickly and stuffed it into his inside jacket pocket a quarter second before she reappeared.

"I can't think what's happened. Mrs. Cliffe is very organized. She scares the willies out of me, quite frankly."

"I'm sure there must have been some mistake. I'll have to have a word with Mrs. Cliffe myself. When will she be back?"

"This afternoon about two o'clock."

Eklund furrowed his brow and made quite a show of pulling a small appointment book out of his inside pocket and consulting it. "Too late, I'm afraid. I have to be on the 1:30 p.m. train for Calgary this afternoon." He sighed deeply. "I suppose I'll have to write to her."

"I'm very sorry for this, sir. I'm sure Mrs. Cliffe will want to make it up to you in some material way."

"Don't fuss yourself, dear lady. Probably an honest mistake. Thank you for your trouble." He tipped his hat and left the store, tugging at his jacket sleeves.

20.

Hat in hand, Charles banged the heavy brass knocker on the front door of the Martland house. It was an attractive house, certainly, but he had heard that the Martlands' new house across the river would be much grander, with an upper floor room big enough to hold dances. He imagined such events would be referred to as balls, not dances, given the resplendent surroundings.

A girl, plainly dressed, answered the door and Charles gave her his card, and asked if Mrs. Martland was receiving. The girl launched into what sounded like a rehearsed speech when Agnes Martland herself walked briskly into the hallway, stopped, looked for a quick exit, and realized one was not to be found.

"Oh — I thought it was the draper. Well — Mr. Lauchlan, how nice to see you. I wasn't — please — please come in. Unfortunately my husband is at the office. So many things to attend to with the — the death of his partner."

"How are you, Mrs. Martland? It was actually you I came to see. We haven't seen you at church lately and, what with Mr. Asseltine's unfortunate death, I wanted to see if there was anything I could do for you. Trevor mentioned that you've been a little unwell?"

"Oh, Trevor is exaggerating. I'm perfectly all right. Well — of course — I have had some trouble with my hip."

"Oh, your hip. And Trevor said your knees too?"

"My knees? Oh well, yes. My knees are not what they were. It's age, I suppose. Nothing is what it was."

Charles could well believe that; she said it so sadly. But he did not believe that he was hearing the real reasons for her absence from church. Agnes Martland was an extremely pretty woman, despite her claims of decrepitude. Delicate-looking, she was, with a slender, graceful frame, and an oval face with a lustrous head of auburn hair, only lightly touched with grey, piled up high but with curled tendrils close around her cheek bones and forehead. And Trevor's tale about the dressmaking must certainly be true, for she was dressed expertly and expensively in shades of lilac-coloured silk that both hugged and flowed around her and rustled as she moved. But her dress made no allowance for the unseasonable heat; she was covered from the ruffles about her chin to the long sleeves banded at her wrists.

"Won't you come and sit down? Ethel, some tea — and some biscuits, please."

She lead Charles through a set of pocket doors into the parlour, a large comfortable room with a bow window facing onto Carlton Street and a grand piano in its own alcove. Charles had never seen one outside a concert hall. She motioned him toward an over-stuffed settee and sat down herself in a low brocade-covered chair with no arms that allowed her to spread her skirts elegantly. This accomplished, she sat very erect, hands folded tightly in her lap.

"There must be many things for you to attend to what with your new house and all."

"Yes, yes. So many things."

He waited in vain for her to enlarge on those many things.

"I gather your daughters are away at school?" he said.

"Yes — well, no. School is out just now. We send them to the Trafalgar School in Montreal. At the moment they're visiting friends in New York."

"It must be a comfort that they are so near your family in Montreal."

But she looked anything but comforted and her left hand crumpled the fine stuff of her skirt. He was about to try yet another subject when she almost spit out. "They — they do not see them."

"Not see them? Are they —"

"My relations — my parents and my sister and her family —" She looked down and then toward the window, anywhere but in his direction. "They are Catholic, you see. I haven't seen them myself since we moved to Winnipeg." She forced herself to turn back to him. "I had hoped, with the girls so near ..."

"I see. That must be very difficult for you." As a response it was pathetic and inadequate but for now he sensed that she needed something else to concentrate on or it would be a very short visit.

"Say, that's a beautiful instrument. I understand that you've studied music a great deal, Mrs. Martland."

"Oh, yes. I played reasonably well when I was young. And I gave piano and singing lessons when we first came to Winnipeg. We needed every penny then, of course."

"I'd very much like to hear you play."

"Oh, no, Mr. Lauchlan. I never play for people now. Just for my own pleasure."

"It's such a fine piano. Could I try it?"

"Yes, of course. Here, I'll open it for you." She walked over to the piano and lifted the wooden cover from the keys, pushing it back into the recess above the keyboard.

Charles sat down and played a few random notes and arpeggios. The sound echoed, bright and resonant, off the high ceiling. He started into a simple arrangement of "Danny Boy," softly at first but playing out more, gaining confidence even though he hit several wrong notes. He was not a good player yet he could see that she was following the tune, singing it in her mind. She walked over to him, almost in spite of herself, placing her hand on the piano at the point where it curved inward. She swayed slightly as he hit the soaring conclusion.

"I'm sure you know the words," he said, playing the introduction of the song again. When she began to sing softly, he smiled and nodded encouragement. At first her voice was a little thin but soon she was burnishing her phrases with a honeyed vibrato — in the mezzo range, surprisingly — at odds with the delicacy of her frame.

When the song was finished, she laughed with pleasure. "Oh, I enjoyed that. I expected you to play a hymn, though."

"Well, hymns are grand, of course. But my sister needed an accompanist for musicale performances and I was the only one of my brothers who could play at all. So if you like Robbie Burns songs and the like, I can accommodate you."

"Do you know, 'Annie Laurie'?"

"I do. I can even sing the harmony. But my talent doesn't run to playing and singing at the same time."

"Oh, I can play." He surrendered the piano bench to her and she began the introduction to the song. She nodded to indicate the entrance and began to sing. He had to go searching for the correct pitch for the harmony, but soon found it, matching his light baritone to the lilting curve of her phrases above him.

Halfway through, "My Heart's in the Highlands," the maid brought in the tea things. At the end of the song Mrs. Martland performed a dazzling arpeggio, running up the keyboard and ending with two decisive, ringing, chords. They both laughed.

"Do you sing on all your pastoral visits, Mr. Lauchlan?"

"I may from now on, Mrs. Martland. If there was more singing — and more tea and biscuits — the world would be a happier place."

The tea wagon had been set beside her chair. She sat down there and motioned for Charles to sit on the settee beside her. Just as she was starting to serve, a gust of wind blew open the French doors to the verandah.

"We really will have to fix these doors before we sell. They're always blowing open." The wind caught her hair, blowing the tendrils off her face just for a moment before she got the doors closed. Something jarred in the back of his mind, but that was all, for she came back and was so much more relaxed that he was sure it was nothing.

Once she was finished serving, he said, "You sing so beautifully. I wish you would sing for us at church."

She faltered and looked down at her cup. "No, no, I don't have the confidence, I'm afraid."

"Is it confidence? Or is it that you're a little uncomfortable, still."

She looked up at him. "A little of both, I suppose."

"You know that if there was anything I could do to help you or set your mind at ease, I would be glad —"

"That's kind of you. And for Frank's sake, I know I should try harder — to fit in and learn and do my part, I mean. I've been such a disappointment to him."

Charles wasn't sure that they were still discussing church matters. "I find that hard to believe. Look at this house and your family. You've raised a fine young man and two lovely girls."

"The children were no trouble, no trouble at all. They've been my mainstay, really. But I'm afraid Frank should have married someone more outgoing. Someone who could entertain more, find the right people and cultivate relationships with them. But I really don't enjoy that sort of thing. Sometimes I don't blame him for losing his temper but that makes it worse because then I get rattled and I can't think …"

She had been twisting a delicate napkin between her fingers. Her face said — something — he couldn't quite name it. He put down his cup and folded his napkin slowly. "Would you like to pray with me, Agnes?"

She looked almost shocked; but then she nodded slowly. He leaned slightly toward her, bowing his head, and began, softly. "Lord, hear our prayers and let us draw near to you. Father, you know our inmost thoughts even before we give voice to them and there is no place so lost or remote that you are not there with us. But sometimes the sound of our own troubles din so loudly in our ears that we can't hear you; we can't feel the comfort of your presence. Be with us in our trembling. Help us to find the peace that is in your promise to us for we ask it in Christ's name."

She murmured "Amen," with him and then they were perfectly still. Agnes remained with her head bowed. Then there was a sound from somewhere at the back of the house, a door closing. She sat up in her chair, alert like a doe scenting the wind. Then she folded her napkin quickly and placed it on the tea tray. "Well — it was so kind of you to call, Mr. Lauchlan." She rose from the couch and extended her hand. "But now I'm afraid I must get back to some details for the new house."

"Yes, of course. Thank you for the tea and the music, Mrs. Martland. I enjoyed it very much."

"I did, too. Very much. Oh — and can I ask?"

"Yes."

"Do you still need used clothing? At the church, I mean."

"Yes, we're always looking."

"I have a boxful. I'll send it over tomorrow."

Charles nodded his thanks and took his leave. The intimacy of the visit had vanished abruptly with this sudden dismissal, yet he knew that he had broken through some kind of barrier with her. It was a start.

21.

Millicent Asseltine received Setter in what the maid called the drawing room. The maid was, of course, dressed in black — as was Mrs. Asseltine. Something about the sculptured bodice of her dress — with dagger-shaped jet beads dangling at regular intervals from its black lace gathers — and the dramatic pose she struck in front of the fireplace made Setter think that there were aspects of widowhood that Mrs. Asseltine was rather enjoying.

"Good afternoon, Sergeant. I wasn't expecting to see you again."

"I have just a few more questions, Mrs. Asseltine, if you would be so kind."

She arranged herself on the settee, leaving Setter standing. "Well, let's get on with it, then. I've been unable to complete final arrangements until the coroner releases my husband's, er, remains. Do you have any idea when that will be?"

"I think very soon. The post-mortem report has been completed." He told her the results, which she received calmly, having visibly braced herself. She got up from the settee and walked to the window.

"My husband had his failings, Sergeant. But he didn't deserve to die that way." She made a handsome figure but she seemed less aware of being on display now.

"I am sorry for your loss, Mrs. Asseltine."

She turned to look at him as if he were a canker worm on her best roses. "What I can't understand, Sergeant, is why you people continue to bustle around with your questions. That awful man killed my husband. And —" She broke off as if she had just remembered something else. She crossed the room and pressed a button concealed by the flocked pattern of the wallpaper.

"I think some refreshment would be best. You'd better sit down."

Setter pricked up his ears and, after looking around at his options, lowered himself into a tufted leather wingback chair. The maid came to the door and was duly dispatched. Mrs. Asseltine sat down again opposite him and fixed him with a steady gaze.

"I wanted —"

"No, Sergeant. My questions first. What do you know about Trevor Martland paying that man's bail — and his legal costs, too?"

It caught him unawares. "Well, nothing really — that is, Mr. Lauchlan was looking for someone, I suppose. Someone capable of putting up the bail and young Mr. Martland volunteered."

The maid reappeared. Not with tea things, to Setter's surprise, but rather with brandy, a soda dispenser, and two glasses.

Mrs. Asseltine picked up the brandy bottle. "Sergeant?"

"Oh — that's kind, Mrs. Asseltine, but unfortunately, not while I'm on duty."

"Oh. Very well, then." She poured a generous glass with a short dash of soda for herself and then returned to the matter at hand.

"I call what Trevor did peculiar — decidedly peculiar — and I do not appreciate it." She rapped on the arm of the settee. "If that man doesn't hang, I will never forgive the Martlands. And now you're poking around here again. What the devil is going on?"

"I am as eager as you to find the answer to that question, Mrs. Asseltine. Sometimes things are not as they appear. Even a policeman knows that."

She sat back in her chair and, for the first time, smiled at him. "So — we're both intent on penetrating mysteries. Are you married, Sergeant?"

"Ah, well — hem. No. Not at present."

"Well, if you ever get married you will see that wives know all about appearances, too. For instance, I knew when Joe told me he was having dinner with a client, that the 'client' would have a deck of cards or a racing form in his pocket."

"Then you —"

"Oh, yes. I knew about Joe's diversions. Most of the time, they were harmless enough. I would have put a stop to them if they had been a serious drain on our finances."

"What about the finances of the firm? Did your husband ever mention any arguments between himself and Mr. Martland?" He was determined to gain the offensive again.

"I'm afraid my husband never discussed his business affairs with me. We were always on good terms with the Martlands socially — at least I thought so until this last development. Now, what were you going to ask me?"

Blast the woman, thought Setter. "I, er, well, the fact is, I need to look through your closets — if you don't mind." Oh Lord. A constable on his first day would have sugared the pill better than that.

"First Joe's closets and now mine!" She sat up bolt upright.

"Sergeant, if you have found a fan or a glove in Frank Martland's office, I can assure you that it does not belong to me. Frank was very careful about the people he let into that room. He wouldn't even let Joe have a key."

Setter ruffled the pages of his notebook so as to gain time to think. "Really? Well — of course — but wouldn't the cleaners need a key?"

"That's what I mean. The cleaners had a key but his own partner did not." She took a gulp from her glass and took a deep breath. "Mind you, I think it was the whiskey."

"The whiskey?"

"The whiskey was bought by the firm to entertain clients and investors but Frank insisted on having it in his office." She put on a prissy expression. "Frank doesn't drink, you see. But Joe does — did. The impertinence!"

"I expect that was why your husband chose that particular night to meet with McEvoy, then. The cleaners would have been cleaning Mr. Martland's office between eight and nine o'clock." And he thought to himself that there was a little added indignity for Asseltine, knowing that the company safe was in a room to which his partner controlled access.

"Yes. That's right. He left here at seven-thirty — some work to do on the Bates building project, he said. That would put him at the office by eight. Of course, he could have asked Mrs. Fuchs for the key at any time. She lives in the building, after all."

"Ah, no. Because, you see, he wouldn't have wanted to attract undue attention to himself. He thought — wrongly — that his gambling debts were a secret."

"Yes. So he simply told the cleaners that he would lock Frank's door after they left." Setter reflected that Mrs. Asseltine would've made a fine policeman, and this added to his discomfort. He flipped his notebook shut. "Well, um, this has been very pleasant, Mrs. Asseltine. But I'm afraid there is still the matter of your closets."

She leaned back against the cushions of the settee and tilted her head to the side, fixing him with a look so direct that he had to fuss with his pant leg to escape it.

"I must say, you have the most extraordinary duties. What is it you want with my clothes?"

"You know I can't tell you that, Mrs. Asseltine." He stood up with as much authority as he could muster. "Now, if you would be so kind."

She gave a little puffing sound with her lips and raised her eyes heavenward, then lifted herself from the settee, glass in hand. "Well, come along then. I'll have to show you the way. Gertie is busy in the kitchen."

Setter would wince at the memory of the next twenty minutes for a long time. He stood in her dressing room at the door of her closet, pulling hangers across, checking the buttons on a dizzying array of dresses and suits with her distinctive scent warm in his nostrils. She sat on a dainty satin-covered chair throughout this performance, sipping brandy. He was proud, nonetheless, when he looked back on it, that in spite of the sweat rolling down his neck and sinking into his collar, in spite of the blushing and the fumbling, he had checked every damned button in the closet.

22.

Charles had returned to the church from the Martland house and was feverishly preparing for the board meeting that was to begin in an hour. Peter had only just completed the formal drawing of the chancel and Charles was setting it out on a table across the room from the table in the parish hall where the board held its meetings. He heard steps in the hallway.

"Pete?"

Frank Martland walked into the room carrying a large cardboard box. "Lauchlan, hello. That young man in the sanctuary said I could find you here."

"Mr. Martland. This is a surprise. I was just visiting with your wife an hour or so ago. Can I take that from you?"

"Yes, thank you. It's a box of old clothes we had around the house. My wife wanted to give it to you."

"That's very generous of you. But we could have arranged to have it picked up."

"No need. No need; thought I would just bring it around myself since I was coming this way."

"I'll just put it on the table over here." There was an awkward moment as Charles went to put the box on the table, realized he had no hands left over to push the drawing aside, and Martland stepped in to slide the drawing farther along the table.

"I want to say, Mr. Martland, how saddened I was to hear of your partner's death. That was the reason for my visit to Mrs. Martland. I wanted to see if there was anything I could do to help." Not quite true but, somehow, he felt cautious about telling Martland that Trevor had urged him to make the visit.

"Very kind, I'm sure, Mr. Lauchlan. We're coping as well as can be expected under the circumstances."

"Well, I'm very glad to hear that. Please let me know if I can help you out in any way." Charles, anxious to get on with things, prepared to usher Martland to the door but Martland stood his ground, smiled, began a sentence, stopped, then began again. "You and my son are friends, I think?"

"Trevor? Yes, yes. He's in my Bible study class and in the Young People's Society, of course. And I hope to get to know him better. He'll make a fine man one day."

"Yes, indeed. That's what I intend for him. He could be a very important man, achieve ten times more than I have." Martland walked over to the window.

"Is anything wrong?"

"We used to be great friends, Trevor and I — but lately ..." Martland paused, "It's hard to pinpoint. Then there was that business with the bail money. I wondered if he'd done it just to spite me." He turned again to face Charles. "Or, maybe, he did it to please you?"

"Oh, I can assure you, Mr. Martland. I was as surprised by his offer as you were."

"You didn't press him for it, then?"

"Not in the least. Dr. Skene and I planned to approach two or three others for the money. Then Trevor volunteered it — completely on his own. To be honest with you, I thought you might well object. But I was so grateful to Trevor for making my life easier; I couldn't really see the thing from your point of view."

"Well it's damned awkward, I can tell you that, and I said as much to Trevor."

"Yes. I think he felt badly having to cause you distress. But he was standing up for the right of everyone to have a fair trial, even those too poor to pay. That speaks very well for him, I think."

Martland looked at Charles through narrowed eyes. "Is that what he said?"

"Well, words to that effect. He and Maggie had apparently discussed it while Dr. Skene and I were in his study making plans."

"Miss Skene? Yes. Young ladies can put strange notions into the heads of their beaus. I hear Miss Skene has advanced ideas; votes for women, temperance, and all that." Martland furrowed his brow. "Trevor knows what I think about these things, but perhaps she has a hold on him."

"Are you suggesting that Maggie has something to do with Trevor's attitude toward you?"

"I don't know, Lauchlan. I'm just trying to understand why he's changed; why he doesn't seem so interested in taking his place in the business."

"Mr. Martland, I've known Maggie Skene since she was a toddler. If Maggie is exercising a magnetic influence on Trevor, it will be the best thing that ever happened to him. She's intelligent and spirited and cares about other people. If there is a serious connection between them, you should be thanking your lucky stars that he's picked such a fine girl."

Martland's eyebrows shot up. "Has it gone that far, then? I didn't know. Has she confided something to you?"

Charles finally caught sight of the red flag that had been waving just outside the range of his vision. "If she had confided something to me, I would be a poor friend if I shared that confidence with someone else behind her back. I'm not sure that I should have told you even the things I have."

Martland gave him a dark look.

"Look, Mr. Martland, it's none of my business I know, but at a certain point, children will make their own way, mistakes and all. How will Trevor learn to be the man you hope he will be if he isn't allowed to learn from the decisions that he alone makes?"

"Have you got children, Lauchlan? If not, stay out of it."

"No. I don't have children. But I am a son and I know that you can lose your son by trying to keep your hands on the reins too long." Charles pushed his hair off his forehead. "Look here, before you go I should go through the box in case there's anything we can't use that could go to another agency."

Ordinarily he would take pretty much anything for the clothing depot, but he wanted an excuse to change the subject. They went over to the box and Charles started sifting through it. Most of the items were men's shirts, jackets, and trousers. All of good quality, with only slight signs of wear.

"Yes. These are very good. We're always short on clothing for men." He fingered a jacket. "Are you sure you want to give this away? It looks almost new."

Martland put a hand on the jacket. "That's Trevor's." He snorted and took it from Charles. "Only a few years old." He turned it over in his hands. Charles watched him as he continued to hold it — running his hand down the fabric of the front and turning the cuffs over. Martland's irritation turned into to a kind of blankness.

"Well," Charles said, "From my observation Trevor has no lack of clothing." He heard his own voice and didn't like the tone of it.

Martland handed the jacket back to Charles. "Yes, that's the problem," he said. "Throwing away perfectly good things; I know we have money enough for new, but I wish he didn't need to pay attention to every little change of fashion."

Martland patted the pockets of his vest, pulled out his watch and looked at it. "I have to get back to the office, Lauchlan." He stuck out his hand. "Kind of you to talk to me about this— and don't mind me." He favoured Charles with a smile that did not extend to his eyes. "I'm always a little direct in what I say." He nodded a farewell, turned on his heel, and was gone without waiting for Charles to say goodbye.

23.

Though the conversation with Martland had left a bitter taste in his mouth, Charles had no time to brood over it. The board meeting was starting in half an hour and he still had much to do. He had decided to put the beam replacement first on the agenda since he felt it would be smooth sailing. In the sanctuary, Charles could hear Peter busily cleaning up around the temporary supports under the gallery. The old beam was still in the narthex awaiting removal and its splintered crack would be more persuasive than any words he could say.

The meeting was underway before he had quite finished his preparations but, as he had supposed, the approval for the new beam was quickly given. After a few more routine matters, they broke for tea and brought their cups and biscuits back to the table. Charles swallowed hard as the men around the table rustled their agenda papers and the chairman nodded for him to begin the next item, enigmatically titled, "New Chancel."

"Right. I'm going to lead on this one. Let's turn to item number three." He cleared his throat. "Some of you have, perhaps, heard rumours about the man who has been arrested for Mr. Asseltine's murder and was recently granted bail. His name is Peter McEvoy. You just met him in the sanctuary." A sharp intake of breath was heard around the table. "It happens that he is an old friend of mine. I have agreed under court order to stand surety for him, to keep an eye on him, and make sure that he appears as scheduled for his trial. This undertaking affects us all here in the church."

The chairman's mouth dropped open and he pushed himself back in his chair.

Charles held up his hands for silence and as he pressed gently against the air the men settled once more.

"I would like to have prepared you more for what I am about to say. I would have liked to give you time to pray and reflect. But life does not always offer us time. The events of the last several days have been tumultuous and confusing. If you can, please let me get through this whole story before you ask questions. I will say that what I am going to ask you will test your faith — or, at the very least, your faith in me. I can only ask you to suspend your judgement and hear me out." He stood up and took another deep breath.

"I've preached sermons on *agape*, that patient, humble, and selfless love we ought to extend to our fellows, no matter how unworthy they might seem to be in the eyes of the world. I should have been listening myself, because like all the things that Jesus asks of us, this is so much harder to do than it is to prescribe from the pulpit. Peter McEvoy is about as needful of that kind of love from us as any man can be." Charles went on to describe his relationship with Peter, Peter's dilemma, his status as an accused murderer, and his self-confessed addiction to alcohol. His hearers received this story with growing alarm. More than once Charles had to hold up his hand and beg again for silence. He had deliberately said as little as possible to the chairman of the board, James Arbuthnot, so that all the members with the exception of Dr. Skene would hear what he had to say at the same time without having any opportunity to form an opinion beforehand. The risk of this strategy was at this moment very clear; the whole thing was teetering on the edge of a very deep precipice.

"Whatever else Peter McEvoy is, he is also a gifted designer and craftsman in wood. I want you to look at the drawing he has made for us on the trestle table over there. No — please — just come with me and look at it while I explain how it came about." With considerable wariness of expression and some murmuring, the men left the board table and walked over to the trestle table ten feet away. Charles had covered the drawing with his black silk Geneva gown, which he now removed carefully and set aside. At first, there was no discernible reaction from the men as they clustered around the drawing. The new drawing was really a thing of beauty. Charles marvelled again at the absolute rightness of all the proportions. He explained how the design would work; how well it suited their needs; how it expressed in its simple forcefulness what the mission of the church was about. Then he talked about how it would be built and what economies might be available in choosing the materials and how they might be able to borrow the necessary tools. Arbuthnot began asking questions about the technical aspects and a few others chimed in. Some clearly didn't know what to make of it but most of the men whose opinions tended to sway the others appeared at least intrigued at the design. For the first time, Charles began to hope.

"This is what I am asking of you today. Peter needs a safe place to stay until his trial; a place where I can keep an eye on him. He also needs, above everything, to have something to focus his energies on, to keep him busy. I'm asking you to allow him to live here in the church — in the janitor's room with me — and I'm asking you to approve our borrowing the money to build the new chancel and choir loft over the course of the next few months. He has asked for no pay for this work, which I can attest he is more than capable of performing. He asks only for his board here at the church." Charles paused and drew a sheet of paper out from underneath the drawing. "We have prepared a preliminary budget for the work, the details to be finalized as we negotiate prices with the lumber yards and the hardware suppliers. I think you can well appreciate the money we will be saving on labour and the fact that, at the end, we will have the most beautiful and distinctive sanctuary in the city." He laid the sheet of paper on top of the drawing and the men crowded around it.

"I suggest we take this back to the board table." It was Arbuthnot's voice, firm, but not censorious. He picked up the budget sheet and walked with it back to the table. The others followed him. They shuffled into their seats again and there was an awkward pause as the sheet was passed around from group to group. Charles's heart sank. *It's too much for them; they're thinking only of the things that can go wrong. It's too much of a risk.*

Arbuthnot finally broke the silence. "Mr. Lauchlan, I'm just a practical man of business and I'm trying to come to grips with what you've just told us. It's a lot to take in." He paused and smoothed the table top in front of him with his hands. "To me, it comes down to the man himself. Are you sure you're seeing him clearly? Or is friendship clouding your judgement? Because I will tell you frankly that, if that man did what he's accused of, I will not have him in such close proximity to my wife and children here." There were nods and low sounds of assent around the table.

Charles knew now was the moment. "I don't blame you for having doubts. And I'll tell you freely that I've had doubts myself during the course of the last few days. You're absolutely right. All this boils down to one ultimate concern. What kind of a man is Peter McEvoy? Will he prove to be the kind of man who fulfills our worst fears? Is he the kind of man who is capable of violent, senseless behaviour? The kind of man who will take advantage of us, take our money, and perhaps run away and leave undone the job we have entrusted to him?" He got up from his chair and leaned forward on the table, so that everyone at the table could both see him and hear him. He could feel Dr. Skene willing him onward, nodding slightly.

"Or will he turn out be the man I believe him to be. A fundamentally good person; albeit one who has lost his way. I believe that what happened to Joseph Asseltine was a tragic accident to which Peter was an unlucky accessory, and I believe that this will be proved in court. I won't absolve him of all blame for the situation in which he found himself. Peter would be the first to tell you that he is the author of his own misfortune to a large extent."

"See here Lauchlan, that's all very well." It was Harman Fraser, who was never very friendly to Charles's proposals. "Guilty or not, I can see that you need to do your duty by him as his friend. But why drag the church into it? Why put him up here, of all places? And because he needs to keep busy, we rush out and borrow money to install a new chancel in the sanctuary? When we just decided in the spring to delay for at least a year?"

Murdo McGillivray chimed in. "And don't you think the bank will want to know what kind of a risk we're taking in hiring him to do the work? And what about that drawing? It doesn't look like anything I've ever seen in any other church. We're risking being made laughing stocks."

This opened the floodgates. From all around the table questions came about Peter, about his drinking, about his bail conditions, about the strange, stark beauty of his drawing, about the money for construction, about Charles's judgement, about his highhandedness and lack of consultation. Charles fielded the questions calmly, keeping his temper, and Dr. Skene spoke eloquently in support of the plan, yet they both could feel the sickening drag of the undertow as the momentum shifted to the negative.

"We hear you say, 'I believe he is innocent; I believe he will complete the work.'" It was Fraser again. "What assurance do we have to back up your opinions? You're asking us to take an awful chance, aren't you?"

"Yes, it's an awful chance, as you say. I'm afraid there is nothing to fall back on if I'm wrong. I have no collateral to offer you except myself." Charles played the last desperate card. "If this ends badly, if Peter is found guilty, or if he proves unworthy of the trust we place in him — in any way — or if his actions prove harmful to what we have all built up here together, you will have my resignation on your table."

"Very noble of you, Lauchlan," said Fraser. "But in that case the damage will already have been done. I hardly think throwing yourself on the funeral pyre will help matters at that juncture."

"Um, excuse me. I — I think we should go ahead." The voice was a little tremulous. Every head turned to see who had spoken.

"What? What was that, Mr. McAlistair?" Arbuthnot said. He was addressing Hamish McAlistair, the Latin teacher at the Central High School, who hardly ever spoke at meetings.

"I said, 'I think we should go ahead.'" McAlistair blushed to the roots of his hair. "I've heard Mr. Lauchlan's assessment and I'm persuaded by it. Mr. McEvoy is asking us for a place to stay and for a chance to do some useful work. Mr. Lauchlan has vouched for him and will be here to supervise him. And, well, I for one don't see what we really have to lose by giving McEvoy this chance to make a turning in his life."

"And I suppose you think that is what Christ would have us do, McAlistair?"

"Well, um, I was thinking more about Marcus Aurelius, but I take your point Mr. Arbuthnot."

Charles held his breath. After McAlistair had spoken, several of the other quieter members rallied around him. In the end, the matter was decided by three prudently worded motions, with enough escape hatches provided to permit that matters be put to a vote. The first passed fairly handily; the last two squeaked into the affirmative column by a margin of one vote — that vote being cast by the chairman. It all amounted to an agreement to proceed to final drawings and specifications with the building to commence only on final approval. Charles felt like a wrung-out sponge but it was enough, enough to keep Peter at the church for a while, at least. Peter's own attentiveness and ability would have to carry it the rest of the way.

After the others had left, Charles shared a spartan supper with Peter in the church kitchen, talking about the details from the board meeting. Peter was unsurprised at the success of their plan. He seemed to have taken it for granted that once the design was explained to the board members in all its details, reasonable men would have no option but to approve it. Charles was beginning to appreciate the difficulty Peter had with social and business relations — he was a true innocent. *Yes, that's right.* When he had said in the board meeting that he believed Peter to be innocent of the murder, he had really meant it. And he had no idea why he was so convinced of this, nor of when this conviction had come upon him. They washed the dishes together in companionable silence and then Peter went back to his makeshift desk.

Charles had promised Maggie to help her with her German that evening, so he settled his hat on his head and set off toward the Skene house. He'd already decided to treat himself to a streetcar ride home. He took a shortcut through the rail yards — which was illegal, but all the men knew him by now and he tried not to overuse this privilege. He lifted his legs over one set of tracks after the other, and felt the steel giving back some of the heat of the day.

The board meeting had pushed all thoughts of the conversation with Frank Martland out of his mind but now they came creeping back. The better acquainted he became with the Martlands, the more questions he seemed to trip over. He wished that the sweetness of his visit with Agnes had not been wiped out by the grilling Martland put him through about Trevor — and Maggie. How incredible that Martland would think his son too good for Maggie. The thought of it set his teeth on edge again. He had reached the gates of the rail yard and continued on through the streets crowded with tiny houses, some only a few years old but already showing the effects of their hasty erection and shoddy materials.

He had defended Maggie eloquently, if he did say so himself. He stopped dead in the middle of Alexander Avenue. Maggie and Trevor. He could see them in his mind's eye. Maggie in an elegant travelling dress; Trevor, handsome, with a red rose in his lapel, looking at her with a shy smile. He puts his arm, in a proprietary way, around her waist. They wave from the back of the train. Maggie throws something at Charles and laughs happily. Rice. Rice caught in folds of her dress and in the brim of her hat, the hat made especially for her by Varennes of Montréal. The train whistle blows insistently.

The train, at least, was real. It was the 7:19, bound for Regina, Calgary, and points west, pulling out of the station a few blocks behind him.

"Hey, mister! Would you mind moving your arse out of my way?"

Charles looked up and into the cavernous nostrils of a dray horse whose breath, not entirely unpleasant, now lifted his hair slightly. "Sorry — excuse me!" He sprinted to the far curb. The wagon, laden with tight bundles of lathe, and its glowering driver, moved on past him and down the otherwise quiet length of the avenue.

The realization that Maggie would marry someday, perhaps soon, had come to him rather late. She was a young lady now, a fact that everyone except Charles had acknowledged. Yet, instead of the happiness he expected to feel for her future with Trevor or with some as yet unknown man, he felt only an ache — the exact location of which eluded him. He took a deep breath and turned again toward the Skene house, walking a little faster this time.

24.

"*Ich ginge, du gingest, er ginge* — oh, what's next? Oh, yes — *wir gingen, ihr ginget, sie gingen.*" She tapped the end of her pencil on the table in triumph and waited. And waited.

"Charles?"

"What?"

"The next verb, please."

"Oh, sorry." He had lost his place in the grammar text.

"Are you tired? If you're tired, we can do this another time."

"No, no, it's fine." He turned back to the text then put it down again. "I went to see Mrs. Martland today. Trevor particularly asked me to see her."

"That's funny. I had the impression that he was trying to discourage you the other night."

"Yes, I did too. But then yesterday he was anxious for me to see her."

"Is she ill?"

"No. She seemed fine, really. Well, except —"

He could see that she was waiting for him to finish the sentence but he was still groping toward a conclusion.

"Except?"

"Well — it's just a feeling I got — I couldn't quite put my finger on it while I was with her. But I've been thinking about it. When she talked about her husband, she built him up to the skies and chopped herself down. There was something —"

"What kind of something?"

"At first I thought she was just deferring to him. But — no — I know that wasn't quite it. She was afraid of him. I'm sure of it now. And ashamed of herself in some way."

"Afraid of him? What, exactly, did she say about him?"

"Nothing that specific. It was more the way she said it. He is overbearing — I've been on the receiving end of some of that myself. I mean, he seems pleasant and jovial but there's something he's angling for behind it all." Charles sighed. "I know we owe a lot to Frank Martland — and we'll continue to owe him a lot, I hope — but I just can't bring myself to like him."

Maggie made a *hmmn* sound and furrowed her brow even more. "Go on."

He was in the Martland parlour again. The joy Agnes took in the singing, the pleasure he took in singing with her. And then that briefest moment when the wind blew the hair off of her face. Had he really seen it? It had jarred so much at the time that he had half persuaded himself that he had imagined it. A bruise, faded now, but clearly it had been darker, angrier.

"Sometimes it's a lot easier to skim along the surface of things, like a water bug," he said.

She was puzzled. "You mean, with the Martlands?"

"Yes. And with everybody else. When you go under, down to the muck of the pond bottom, it's confusing and frightening. Water bug longs for the smooth, bright surface. But he knows that all the really important things that happen in the pond go on there in the murky half-light."

"Are you sure you're all right? It isn't like you to use zoological references."

He laughed. "I can never take myself too seriously when I'm with you. I think I could probably tell you just about anything and you'd hear me out and give me that little 'hmmn' sound. It always reminds me to spare the dramatics and just work at the knot, whatever it is."

"Yes. Except you haven't really told me anything, have you. I am up to it, you know. I won't faint or scream. Or talk about it to anybody else."

"I know that." He righted his coffee cup in its saucer and turned its handle just so. "But I came very close to betraying a confidence — inadvertently — today. So this water bug had best swim alone." He made a melodramatic waggle of his eyebrows. "Where were we? Right. *'Sagen.'*"

"Now I'm going to be wondering all night about whatever it could be."

"Sagen," Charles said, more insistently and with his best German accent.

She sighed and began. *"Ich sagte, du sagtest, er sagte, wir sagten, ihr sagtet —"*

There was a knock at the door and Maggie, eager for a distraction, called out to her aunt, "I'll get it."

When she opened the heavy door she found Sergeant Setter standing in the long shadows, fingering the brim of his hat. "Ah. Good evening, Miss Skene."

"Sergeant Setter — Come in. I'm sorry if you've come to see Father. He's still at the college."

Charles came into the hallway. "Setter, how are you?"

"Oh, Mr. Lauchlan, Good evening, sir." Setter continued to fidget with his hat. "Actually, it was you I came to see. Mr. McEvoy said you were here. Could I have a word with you, er, in private?"

147

"Yes, um, of course." Charles looked at Maggie. She arched her eyebrows slightly, nodded, and shifted her gaze to Setter.

"I'm sure Father wouldn't mind if you used his study. And when you're done, come out for some tea and cake." She held out her hand for Setter's hat.

Handing it over, Setter said, dutifully, that he couldn't put her to such trouble but Charles could tell that the siren call of cake had enchanted a fellow bachelor. Once they were in the study, Charles closed the door and motioned to Setter to sit in one of the chairs by the fireplace while he took the other.

"Well, Sergeant?"

"In a way, I can't believe that I'm asking you this. It's hardly standard procedure. But the fact is, we don't have much time, or I would find another way."

"Much time? I'm afraid you've lost me."

"Yes, sorry." He brushed the heavy thatch back from his forehead. "I've been living inside this case so long — McEvoy's case, I mean — that I expect people to read my mind." Charles continued to look confused. Setter leaned forward in his chair. "Here's the nub. Asseltine's dead and can't tell us how he died. I've got a few bits of evidence that could mean something but I'm running short of time. Unless McEvoy can remember something — something substantial that will help us interpret those bits and pieces — I'm afraid that appearances will carry the day and he'll be convicted."

Charles pulled back in his chair. He had almost convinced himself that Peter's exoneration was just a matter of fair play and right reasoning. Cold water. "What can I do? Is there something?"

"Here's the thing. McEvoy is not comfortable with me. I've tried to gain his trust, but, well, he shies like a skittish colt. He trusts you, though."

"But he doesn't remember —"

"I know, I know. But there's something. It's as if part of him wants to remember and part of him would rather not."

"Yes. Yes, I've felt that too."

"The drinking complicates things, of course. But I'm convinced — based on some articles by a French doctor — that those memories are still in his head somewhere. It may just be a matter of getting him in the proper frame of mind to find them again."

"I see." Charles picked up Dr. Skene's tobacco pouch from the small table by his chair and absently squeezed the leather between his fingers. "But how would I go about that?"

"That's where I can't help you. McEvoy trusts you and that's the first step. Put him at his ease, I suppose, and then get him to go over what he remembers in a methodical way."

Charles blew air slowly out of the sides of his mouth. "I don't know, Sergeant. I have tried to talk to him about that night. But he resists thinking about it."

"Yes, but you can try different approaches with him. I can't." Setter paused. "It's a chance — maybe a long chance."

"Yes." Charles met the other man's eyes. "Yes, all right. Leave it with me. I have some ideas." They were quiet for a moment. Then Charles slapped the tobacco pouch back on the table and stood up. "Cake?"

Setter brightened. "Well, only if you're having some."

"Never miss an opportunity to try some of Miss Skene's lemon pound cake, Sergeant. How the woman has remained unmarried all these years, I don't know." Charles opened the door and motioned Setter through.

"One last thing." Setter dropped his voice and moved closer to Charles.

"Yes?"

"If McEvoy remembers something, send me a note at the

station or at my boarding house — here, I'll give you the address."
He fished in his inside pocket and handed Charles a card. "I'll
meet you somewhere convenient."

"It isn't a problem for me to drop by the station, you know."

"I understand, but, well, it's better if we meet somewhere
other than the station for the time being."

Charles cocked his head and shrugged, "Whatever you say."

Setter preceded him out the door. "You know, Setter, I
wanted to be a policeman when I was a boy."

"Is that right? What changed your mind?" The aroma of
burnt sugar and vanilla met them in the hallway as they walked
toward the dining room, talking comfortably of boyish things.

25.

The next day, being Saturday, was a half-day for articling clerks at Stobbart and Long, and Trevor usually found it hard to concentrate on civil procedure or the dog work of case law research while anticipating the pleasures of the rest of the day. This morning, however, he was oblivious to the outside world, reading intently and making notes almost fiercely. At the stroke of noon the other students clapped their case books shut and vacated the office for cooler and more pleasant pastimes in the grotto bar at the Marriagi. Trevor listened as the sound of their larking and stamping down the stairs ended with a definitive slam of the front door.

He slowly put his work to bed and set out for the warehouse on Amy Street, near the docks where the Martlands stored the family boat for the winter. On the way he bought a ham roll and coffee at the Leland Café and dawdled over them until he was almost late. He had promised to help his father clean and set up the boat for its first launching of the season the following day. It was something they had done together every year since he was about sixteen, usually on the first Saturday after he arrived home from boarding school or university. The plain but well-made rowing skiff of his boyhood had been succeeded by a highly varnished low-riding motor launch, the latest thing in pleasure boats, with a sun canopy that looked like something from the Arabian Nights. What hadn't changed was his father's pleasure in the job of getting the boat river worthy. Martland could easily have paid someone to do the job for him but he loved to clean and prime the motor and wash the boat, reserving his most loving attention for a careful polishing of its varnished top deck and brass hardware.

When Trevor rounded the corner of James Avenue and Amy Street his father, dressed in overalls, had already pulled the boat on its trailer out of the warehouse and onto the concrete apron. He was stripping off the tarpaulin, in which the boat had been tightly wrapped. Trevor hurried to help free the boat from its canvas shroud.

"She's not looking too bad, Trev. Not much harm taken by sitting all winter."

"That's good, Father. How's the canopy?"

"I had it cleaned after last year. It's in the garage at home. We'll put it up tomorrow when we take her round to the club."

They folded the light canvas tarpaulin between them, feeling the pleasure of pulling it taut and then folding, pulling again, and folding again, until it was a compact rectangle. Trevor took off his suit jacket, his vest, and his necktie, laying each over the weathered fence next to the warehouse. Then he put on the overalls that Martland had brought with him from home. They washed the boat inside and out with rough brushes and soapy water smelling of pine resin. They stripped the engine down with the tools from Martland's box, putting each part down in order on a chamois cloth, then cleaned and oiled the parts and put them back in place. They removed and cleaned the propeller, reinstalled it on its drive shaft, and filled the tank with gasoline.

Martland motioned to Trevor to stand clear. He climbed into the boat and sat at the controls. There was a sluggish cough, then silence, then another, more throaty cough. And then a roar, at which father and son gave a whoop of delight. Then they turned the motor off and settled into the final and most pleasurable task, waxing and polishing the warm, dark mahogany of the bow, stern and gunwales.

Martland smoothed on the wax in broad swipes. "Now, Trev, I wanted to talk to you about this McEvoy fellow."

Trevor missed a fraction of a beat in his tight swirling of wax across the grain of the wood. "All right, Father."

Martland was jovial. "You might not credit it, but I was young once myself. An innocent bit of fun and suddenly you're out of your depth. If you needed money to settle a card debt and that fellow was pressuring you, why didn't you come to me?"

"It wasn't like that."

"If he has you under some kind of obligation, if he has something on you, this isn't the way to handle it, you know." Trevor said nothing but paid rapt attention to a fold in the grain of the wood. Martland pressed on. "I mean, why pay his lawyer and give him a chance to come after you again?"

Trevor pushed harder on his rag, his face almost touching the gleaming surface. He did not look at his father. "As a matter of fact, I don't even know Mr. McEvoy."

"You didn't meet with him the night of the murder?"

Both rags were still. They looked across the gunwales at one another.

"No, I've told you I don't know him." A bead of sweat rolled down from Trevor's temple to his jaw before dripping onto the collar of his overalls.

"Well, where were you on the night of the murder?"

"I think that's my business."

"Just tell me. I'm your father, damn it!"

Trevor bent down over his rag, "I was with Maggie — with Miss Skene."

"All evening?"

"Yes. All evening."

Martland didn't seem to know where to let his eyes rest. He finally chose the brass bowsprit ornament on the boat, which he began to buff gently. He smiled but the planes of his face seemed to resist and something shiny in his eyes caught the sun.

"That's good. That's fine, Trev. Just trying to understand why you're bankrolling that sod. No offence, boy. A commitment to justice. That's good. Especially if you go into politics. People like to vote for someone high minded. That's why I've spent my life making the money that allows you to be high minded."

Trevor looked miserable as he continued to polish away, raising a high gloss from the cloudy wax swirls.

"You're a bit soft, Trevor. I've always known it. Not much good in a back alley punch-up. I've watched you box. You could never deliver that final punch. The one to use when the other fellow is just getting up off his knees, the one to finish him off. But it's all right. It's all right because I've fixed it so you won't have to do the kinds of things I've had to do."

"I didn't ask you to do those things for me."

"No, but you've been happy enough to take the money, haven't you!" It was a shout and when it left his mouth, Martland looked around quickly, to see if anyone else had heard. He dropped his voice to an anguished whisper. "And now, I'm not good enough for you?" His hands were splayed over the deck as he leaned over them and thrust his face toward his son.

"Let's just leave it, Father," Trevor said. "Let's just leave it alone now." He walked around the boat giving it a thorough look-over and ran his hand slowly over the warm wood. "That's it. It's done." He turned back to face his father. "She looks fine, but you may have to re-paint her next year."

26.

Peter was in the sanctuary, removing his temporary desk and drafting equipment from the platform so that services could take place as usual the next day. He was not altogether happy at this task for, as he had said to Charles, "How can I get my work done if you keep interrupting me with needless distractions?" At which Charles had simply smiled.

The sudden scraping of a key in a lock at the back of the church made Peter look up; he jumped off the platform and had walked halfway up the aisle to investigate when one of the large doors to the narthex opened. A dark figure loomed in the sudden brightness of the open door.

"Steady those horses, Kauffman. Don't want to break it before we get it in. Just wait till I see if Mr. Lauchlan's around." The figure emerged from the sunlit door frame and squinted at Peter.

"Hello there." Noting Peter's cautious look, he held the key up so that Peter could see it. "Mr. Lauchlan gave me a key. Eklund. Erling Eklund from Martland and Asseltine? With the lumber for the new beam?"

"Oh, yes. Of course. McEvoy. Peter McEvoy." Peter shook

Eklund's outstretched hand. "I'm — well — helping out for a while here."

"Don't suppose you could give us a hand to get 'er in?"

"Yes. Of course." They went out and, after some head scratching, decided that the new beam should be stowed temporarily in the parish hall, where it would be out of the way. Then Peter, Eklund, and Kauffman wrestled the timber off the wagon and carried it around the side of the church and to the back where the door of the parish hall was located. With some considerable back and forth manoeuvring and raising and lowering of the long timber over obstacles and through door frames, the three men managed to carry the beam into the large hall where they lowered it to the floor on the long side of the room.

They rubbed their hands together to remove the sawdust and restore circulation and the air was filled with the comforting odour of newly sawn wood.

"There," said Eklund. "It'll be fine here until Monday morning. I've told Mr. Lauchlan that I'll send a crew over then."

"I'll work with them. Charles — Mr. Lauchlan — will be busy, so I volunteered."

"Oh, that's grand. You're staying here then, in the church?"

"Yes. Yes. Just for a while."

"And you've got some experience of building?"

They continued to talk, Eklund asking questions and Peter being pleasant but giving only as much information as necessary.

"Oh, yes. It's a great town, Winnipeg. Lots of opportunities for a man that's willing to work," Eklund said. He pulled a flask out of his breast pocket, uncorked it and took a drink from it. "Of course, you have to prove yourself, sometimes. Bosses here are tough. I am myself, anyway." He took another swig. "I won't stand for any laziness in a man. Want some?"

Peter said, perhaps too quickly, "No. No thanks."

"Sure? It's McQueen's Select. I probably paid too much for it, but there isn't a finer whiskey."

"No, thank you, no. Really."

Eklund shook his head in mock wonder and replaced the stopper.

"Say, I left something here the other day. I'd better go and find it." With that Eklund put the flask on the edge of the small stage platform near where they were standing and strode out of the hall.

A flush of blood rose in Peter's face and drained away almost as quickly, leaving him pale and clammy. The flask was only three feet from him. He looked around the room and while he was doing that his hand rose up toward the flask as if drawn by a force outside of his body. He jerked it back and staggered a step backward with the effort. With his chin lifted, he sucked air through his nose, trying to smell the whiskey, trying to draw a few atoms from the stoppered flask. A look of angry disputation, of inner war, came over his face and he began to pace back and forth. Then with great effort, he backed away. Each step seemed harder than the last one. Now he was whimpering, and tears were welling in his eyes. Somehow he got himself turned around and with his back turned to the object that was calling to him; like Circe on the rocks he broke through the inertia binding his legs and stumbled into a run. Out of the hall, down the passageway and into the kitchen, where he ducked his head under the pump in the sink and frantically worked the handle while the cold water gushed over his head. Finally his arm grew weary, slowed, and then stopped. After staring at the drain in the bottom of the sink for a while he raised his head and slicked back his hair. There were no towels in the kitchen, only tea towels on a rack by the sink.

He walked in the direction of the janitor's room, but before he could get there Eklund walked out of the room and started slightly at seeing Peter.

"Well — uh — there you are," Eklund said.

"That's my room."

"Is it? Sorry. Stupid of me. I didn't realize. Left a tape measure here on Thursday and I thought it might have made its way there."

"Not likely. I haven't seen one lying around." Peter tried to ignore the fact that he was dripping on the floor. "I'll ask Charles when he comes back."

"Thanks. It was a good one. I'd hate to lose it."

"You left your flask in the hall."

Eklund looked bashful. "Wouldn't do for that to be found lying around, would it? I'll pick it up and be off then. I'll drop by Monday to get things started."

"That's fine. I'll make sure things are set up for you."

Later, when Charles returned, they were making, or attempting to make, scrambled eggs and toast for supper in the kitchen.

"I could swear this was the way my mother made scrambled eggs." Charles stared at the watery curds of egg in the frying pan.

"Maybe the hot water was a mistake. Here, let's drain it off. We can pretend they're poached." Peter took the pan and carefully strained off the greasy liquid into the sink. "Once I lived for an entire year on sardine sandwiches, lunch, and supper."

Charles made a face. "How could you stand it?"

"It didn't seem to matter. It wasn't food I was after."

They spooned the egg onto plates already furnished with toast, only slightly burnt at the edges, and bacon lovingly supplied by Mrs. Armitage, whose husband owned a butcher's shop on Dagmar Street.

"That fellow — Eklund?" Peter said. "He delivered the new beam this afternoon. We carried it into the parish hall."

"That's good. Did he say when they can they start?"

"Monday morning, he said. Do you know Eklund at all?"

"Not really. We've chatted a few times."

"Yes, he is a bit of a talker. He didn't seem to know who I was."

"No, he does. When we were taking the beam out on Thursday he was asking about you. Morbid curiosity, I suppose."

Peter looked puzzled.

"What's the matter?" Charles said.

"He offered me a flask of whiskey. If he knew who I was, why would he do that?"

Charles was caught by this piece of information with his fork suspended between his plate and his mouth. It hung there for a moment and then he put it down.

"He offered you what?"

"A flask of whiskey. We were chatting. I think he was trying to find out if I know my way around saws and hammers."

"I take it you refused?"

Peter sighed and mopped up some egg with his toast. "This time. I honestly can't answer for the next time. It's almost as if ..."

"What?"

"As if he was deliberately doing it. Trying to get me to drink."

"Why would he do that?"

"Maybe he just doesn't like me. I seem to rub people the wrong way. Maybe he thinks I should be in jail."

"Eklund doesn't seem to be the vindictive type." Charles scratched his chin in a ruminative fashion. "He was asking a lot of questions about you the other day. But I recall that he was sort of sideways about it."

"'Sideways'? Well, then there's the other thing."

"What other thing?"

"He said he left something here a few days ago — a tape measure — and he had to go and find it. He left his flask on the platform and then later I saw him walking out of our room."

They looked at each other for a second. "Was anything missing?" Charles said.

"I don't know. I haven't had time to look."

They went to the room. At first it seemed to be as they had left it that morning. They looked through the drawers of the dresser and neither could see that anything was missing. Then Peter remembered that he had tossed his shaving things on the bed that morning. Now they were on the dresser. And Charles realized that there was something strange about his drawer. It was actually neater than he had left it that morning.

"I think everything's been taken out and then replaced. It's probably easier to replicate neatness than my particular kind of squalor."

"It's hard to imagine anyone wanting to steal something of mine," Peter said.

"Or of mine. I think Eklund probably earns twice as much as I do." They wandered back to the kitchen and Charles sat down to his rapidly cooling eggs. He started eating them in a distracted fashion and Peter followed suit.

"Naw mindidivna. Niversah!" Charles suddenly said, his mouth full.

"Pardon?"

Charles swallowed. "It wasn't vindictiveness; it was diversion. He knew he wanted to search the room so he needed to distract you somehow."

"Well, it certainly worked. But if there's nothing missing, what was he looking for?"

"I can't make that out either. Oh —" Charles suddenly

161

thought about the strange package in his desk drawer at Mrs. Gough's. With everything that had happened, he had hardly given it a thought.

"Oh?"

"I wonder," Charles said.

"What is it?"

Charles looked pained. "That's just it. I can't tell you."

"I see. I understand."

"No, really, Pete. I can't tell you. I promised someone I wouldn't. I haven't even told Maggie about it."

"Oh well, if you haven't told Maggie, it really must be a secret."

Charles ignored the teasing inflection. "But who knows if that's what Eklund was looking for. For all we know, he just likes to root through other people's belongings. I've heard of stranger hobbies." Charles sighed. "Things are getting very confusing."

"Well, what are we going to do about it?"

"Just keep an eye on him, I suppose. He didn't take anything. Next time he comes around tell him to stay out of our room."

"I don't trust him. I don't think he wishes me well," Peter said.

"But it might have nothing to do with you. More to do with him, if you see what I mean." Charles shook his head in frustration. "I don't really know what I mean, either. But I do know we're not going to solve this tonight. Let's do the dishes. I've got to get changed."

"Going out?"

"Yes. To the All Charities Appeal Dance. It's the first of a week of events to benefit the Appeal. We're part of it, so I promised to make an appearance. Want to come?"

"Oh, no. No, I don't think so."

"There won't be any liquor served."

Peter snorted. "That's what you think. Just don't look too closely at the men who say they're going out back for a smoke."

"Ah. Yes, I see your point. Wash or dry?"

"Wash. You never get the bits in the corners."

27.

Charles arrived at the Young Men's Christian Association rooms on McDermot Avenue and paused in the gentlemen's cloak room to brush the dust off his best suit. The wind had been gusting wildly and had virtually blown him in the front door. He had promised to do an hour of chaperoning in the tea room, which for tonight's festivities was lit by candles and decked out in potted palms and other assorted greenery laid out to make a winding path for people to stroll in. For the price of two five cent tickets, young people could walk through the make-believe jungle maze in relative privacy. This was especially useful for young ladies and gentlemen of the Methodist persuasion, whose elders frowned on the dancing taking place in the assembly hall next door. Charles knew the rules. A couple could disappear for a minute or so behind the largest palm trees. If they had not reappeared after two minutes, he was to — not too softly — clear his throat. If this didn't flush them out, he was to take a plate of sandwiches down the winding path and engage the lucky couple in conversation, at which point the young lady would excuse herself politely and ask her escort to take her back to the well-lit assembly hall.

Tonight it was early in the evening and he had no customers as yet. He was humming to himself as the orchestra tuned up and chatting with Mrs. Underwood, who was setting out the tea and coffee things, when he saw Rosetta Cliffe struggling through the front doors weighed down by camera case, tripod, and assorted photographic paraphernalia.

"Mrs. Cliffe, good evening." He hurried toward her. "Let me help you in with this."

She looked relieved and handed him the heavy camera case and the tripod, blowing an escaped strand of hair out of her eyes. "Thank you, Mr. Lauchlan. I'm all for charity but next time I think I'll have them come to me instead of lugging my whole studio here. Could you take these through while I get the rest from the cab?" She tucked a bolt of drapery under one of his arms and a rolled Turkish carpet under the other. "And careful with my bread and butter, please."

Charles carefully wound his way through the keyed up swarm of organizers with his load until he found the corner of the assembly hall reserved for Rosetta's temporary portrait studio: full portrait for ten dollars, of which five dollars went to the All Charities Appeal and five to Rosetta. He let the carpet and the drapery bolt fall softly to the floor then set down the camera case and tripod. He was putting up the sign for the booth when Rosetta appeared with more draperies, a cardboard backdrop painting of a gothic window, flash powder and flash lamp, and what appeared to be a genuine bear skin.

"Oh good — they've given me a couple of chairs. Mrs. Ormiston is a wonder at organizing. Yes, that one will do quite nicely for the portraits. I hope I won't have much time to sit in the other myself."

"I'm chaperoning the promenade for the first hour. I'll do my best to direct some traffic your way."

"Then I would be in your debt, Mr. Lauchlan. And not for the first time, either."

"I told you, Mrs. Cliffe. We're called to bear one another's burdens." He gestured at the heap of equipment. "The literal ones and the not so literal."

"Well, I'm not very good at saying it, but I haven't forgotten your kindness to me in the past," Rosetta said as she fussed with her draperies and backcloths.

"You're most welcome." He cast a glance back at the tearoom. "I haven't got much to do in the tearoom yet. Can I help you set up?"

"All right, yes. But you may regret this."

Charles began to take the camera out of its case but Rosetta elbowed him aside. "I'll set up the camera. You see to the chair and backdrops." She gave him precise instructions as to the angle of the chair in relation to the camera and sent him off to find something to drape the backdrops on. She was delighted when he came back with a folding Chinese screen. Charles unrolled the Turkish carpet and set the chair on it in front of the faux window with the Chinese screen slightly to one side of the chair. Then he looked on, bemused, as she threw various sheets of drapery onto the screen, stood back, adjusted this and that, stood back, pulled the draperies sideways and let them fall. Then she took the bear skin and tossed it on the floor, stood back, picked it up and tossed it down again from another angle.

"Texture," she said. "You can never have too much texture." In the end she decided the bear skin looked best when thrown rakishly over the chair.

Guests had begun to arrive at the dance in larger numbers. Charles saw Maggie come in with a number of other girls, all with wind-blown hair and flushed cheeks and voices pitched high. He watched the flurry of activity as they disappeared, then emerged from the ladies' cloak room, having hung up their wraps, straightened their hair, and done a final primping in front of the mirrors. Mrs. Heavysege was stationed at the entrance to the assembly room carrying a basket of dance cards with small beribboned pencils attached, her imposing bosom festooned with the sash and rosette of the All Charities Appeal. Maggie and her friends crowded around to get their cards and boys were already hovering, waiting to ask for the third waltz or the first quadrille after the refreshment break. Maggie made Trevor wait until Henry McAlistair had taken his choice. Though Henry had a bad stammer, he was an amazingly fluent dancer and especially adept at two-steps and cake walks. Maggie motioned for him to turn around so that she could use his back as a writing desk, which he did, and she wrote his name against the dances he had requested.

"I'll s-see you at number eight then, Miss S-S-Skene"

"No need to be so formal, Henry."

Henry smiled happily and blushed. "M-Maggie, then." He went off in pursuit of Ellen Farquarson.

Trevor asked for the dance card and the two of them laboured over it, Trevor's head with its fine light brown hair flopping over his forehead and almost touching Maggie's darker hair. Charles counted the number of times she entered his name. *One, two, three, four, five. Six.*

"Wait, leave that one blank," Maggie said. She had seen Charles at Rosetta's booth and waved to him. She excused herself from Trevor and came toward him. He took his leave of Rosetta.

"Well, have you changed your mind?"

"About what?"

"About dancing with me. And don't say that, 'a praying knee and a dancing foot never grew on the same leg,' because I know you don't believe it."

It was an old argument between them. Like most ministers

he knew, Charles had refrained from dancing since he had been ordained. He didn't really disapprove of dancing on the part of his parishioners or his own part for that matter, but they expected him to abstain and he saw no reason to distress them. Maggie argued that this was hypocritical.

"You have very modern ideas about my dancing, for instance, so long as I have the right attitude and observe decorum. You concede that the Psalms tell us to sing *and* dance during worship, therefore God does not disapprove of dancing, *per se*. So why will you not dance with me?"

"All right, I will."

"What? Wait, is this a trick?"

"We can dance in the gymnasium. We can hear the music fine in there. Do you have the first one free?"

Maggie covered her consternation by looking intently at her dance card. "Well, yes. But — I don't know. Goodness! You've certainly done an about face."

Charles was brisk. "Come on now. You've worn me down. At least we can lay to rest your claim that I refuse to dance because I don't know how."

"This is a trick, isn't it?"

He did not reply but walked over to the door of the darkened and empty gymnasium, opened it with a flourish, and beckoned her to enter.

"Prepare to be instructed."

"We'd be alone there. Isn't that a little unseemly?"

"Have you forgotten that I am an official chaperone?" He pointed to the red rosette with trailing ribbons on his lapel.

She had some colour in her cheeks now and a glint came into her eye. "Very well. Let tongues wag. I am a woman of my convictions." She sailed through the door in what she hoped was a regal fashion. "And we'll see who instructs who."

"Whom," Charles said as she passed him.

He walked down the shaft of light cast by the open door, stepping confidently across the basketball court markings. Having no windows, the room was otherwise dark and smelled faintly of sweat and paste wax. The wind was buffeting the building and the high ceiling, which they could not see, creaked and groaned in unexpected ways. The orchestra struck an opening chord. Charles raised his arms; Maggie moved into them and laid her left hand lightly on his shoulder while he settled his right hand at her back. She put her right hand into his outstretched left and tilted her chin up slightly, angling her face toward her raised left elbow. It was a waltz. They balanced back and forth to establish the rhythm.

"Here goes," Charles said and began to lead her into the turns, tentatively at first. They were fighting each other to maintain the rhythm. Away from the light of the door they could hardly see each other as they turned in the cool shadows.

"Not perfect quite yet," he said. "It's been a few years."

Maggie didn't reply as she was faintly surprised. She realized that it was not necessary to "help" him lead her as she was used to doing with many boys with whom she danced. Now they were turning quite easily and strongly with the music and she could concentrate on doing her part, leaning back and balancing her weight against the steadiness of his arms. *Pity no one can see us,* she thought. *We're dancing so well.*

They relaxed more into the turns and he tried a few balances in place to break up the turns. When Maggie had taken dance lessons, the students had been instructed to chat amiably with their partners once the rhythm of the waltz had been established. But now talking seemed superfluous. She was more intent on the dance, on the exhilarating pull of the turns, on floating outward then feeling him pull her strongly and confidently back. They whirled through the light of the doorway and she saw that he was smiling back at her. He quieted the turns a little, making them smaller. Why not a pirouette? He raised her arm and she twirled underneath it and they laughed. They had only just settled back into the waltz hold when the music ended. The turn they were in slowly subsided.

"Well," said Maggie, catching her breath. "I think all dances should be held in dark gymnasiums."

"Maggie? Maggie is that you?" It was Trevor. She dropped her arms to her sides, turning in the direction of the door, and left Charles holding only air.

"I'm here," Maggie said and both she and Charles walked quickly toward the door. "Charles was just giving me instructions on the latest waltz steps."

"Oh," Trevor said, surprised. "Oh," he said again. "Good evening, Charles. Maggie, I think the next one's mine. We'd better hurry."

"Hello, Trevor. Yes, yes, go ahead."

"I think I could probably use a little instruction in the two-step," Maggie called back to Charles while Trevor was leading her away on his arm.

"I'm a little out of my depth on the two-step, I'm afraid," Charles said. "Besides, I have to take up my watch in the tea-room." But she was already too far away to hear him distinctly, as Trevor and she threaded their way through the crowd at the entrance to the assembly room.

28.

Charles found his hour as gatekeeper at the promenade pleasant enough. He sold tickets to several of the boys and girls from his Young People's Society and watched them amble through the twin palms at the entrance, arm in arm. With a wry smile, Charles reflected that strolling arm in arm can take many forms. The younger ones maintained their distance, the girl placing her hand in the crook of the elbow offered by the boy. They walked stiffly in this position, giggling and pulling awkwardly apart if by accident they strayed too close or bumped a hip. But then there was Arthur Ledyard and Primrose Ormiston whose arms were entwined so snugly that there was no space between them at all and they walked in a kind of sideways embrace — not saying anything but occasionally looking into each other's eyes and smiling. As the couple had announced their engagement in May, Charles didn't feel the need to interrupt the innocent caresses that the two shared as they strolled along. Why should he be the policeman of love? He chewed his lip with annoyance. There are so many worse things in the world than the possibility of two young people touching each other in ways that ancient prudery deems inappropriate.

In the midst of these surly ruminations, he caught sight of Frank and Agnes Martland chatting with Mrs. Heavysege at the entrance to the assembly hall. Agnes was dressed beautifully in cream-coloured silk with accents of what he thought might be called coral. Charles could see how Martland was showing her off and how he enjoyed the impression she was making. At one point she saw someone she knew and made to cross the hall but Martland caught her hand as it disengaged from his arm and drew her back to greet a business associate and his wife. *Martland doesn't like her to venture out on her own*, Charles thought. *That's why I never run into her on the street or at the houses of mutual friends.* The knot of concern in the pit of his stomach gave an uncomfortable tug and with it some formless ideas he had been mulling crystallized into a plan.

"Mrs. Underwood, could you spare me for a few minutes?"

"Of course, Mr. Lauchlan. You're almost done your shift anyway. Off you go."

He grabbed a plate, put some sandwiches on it, and poured a cup of tea. With these in hand he made his way to the assembly room and over to Rosetta's booth. She was just finishing a sitting.

"Try not to jump when the flash lamp goes off, Miss Stiven," Rosetta said from underneath the black cloth. "Mr. Stiven, you can wiggle your ears or something to distract her." At this Miss Stiven looked at her father and the camera caught her with just the beginnings of an amused smile.

"Good. Just right." Rosetta emerged from under the cloth. "Hello, Mr. Lauchlan."

"I've brought you some sustenance, Mrs. Cliffe. Can you take a break?"

"Lovely. Thanks. Yes, I think there's a bit of a lull now." Rosetta finished writing a receipt for the Stivens. "You can call for the finished photographs on Wednesday, Mr. Stiven." The

Stivens took their leave and Rosetta took the plate of sandwiches and the cup of tea with a sigh of relief. She perched on the portrait chair and ignored the glass eyes of the bear skin.

Charles pulled up the other chair and said in a hushed voice, "I have a favour to ask you, Mrs. Cliffe. I have a friend who may be in need of help."

"What kind of help?" She was wary.

"She may need a place to stay for a while — on short notice. And I thought, since you have lots of room —"

"Well, now, Mr. Lauchlan, you know I run a photography studio downstairs and work all hours in the darkroom upstairs. I can't have someone hanging around just getting in the way —"

"I think you would understand why she needs this help. She needs an out-of-the-way place where she will not be known."

Rosetta looked at him. "A bolt hole, then?"

"Yes. I'm afraid I can't be more specific. My suspicions may be just that. But I would like to be able to tell her that there is a place where she will be welcome — and safe — if she needs one."

Rosetta pushed a sandwich around the plate, her brows drawn together.

"I know it's a lot to ask. You need your privacy; I understand that. But it would only be for a short time until she could make other arrangements."

"I'm set in my ways, I'm afraid. Used to just doing for myself — and Eleanor — when she's home from boarding school." She looked Charles straight in the eye. "But tell your friend she is welcome at my house, such as it is."

"You can tell her yourself. I'm going to persuade her to have her portrait taken."

Rosetta looked surprised.

"I know I can rely on your discretion, Mrs. Cliffe. To anyone looking on it must look as if you are simply taking a portrait. But it would be best if I could be your assistant for this one."

"Of course; when will she come?"

"Soon, that is, if I can manage it. And when I bring her over, could you put off anyone ahead of her till later?"

"People are used to me being a little high-handed. As long as I can fit them in later, there should be no difficulty."

Charles thanked Rosetta and began craning his neck to see through the crowd on the dance floor. The orchestra was playing a cake walk to the tune "Whistling Rufus" and the older members of the audience were tut-tutting behind their fans, complaining about this bumptious American dance invading decent Canadian ballrooms. Charles spotted Maggie strutting around happily with Henry McAlistair. The last chords sounded and they came to a halt in the final pose. Maggie hopped up and down and clapped with pleasure while Henry made her a sweeping bow.

"Oh, that was grand! Henry, you're a credit to Madame Edna's School of Dance. Thank you so much." Henry just beamed and kept holding her hand.

"Hello Henry. Could I borrow Maggie for a minute?"

"C-c-certainly, Mr. Lauchlan. I have the next one with M-M-Miss Farquarson anyway." Henry disappeared into the crowd with a final smile at Maggie, who waved at him.

"I thought you said two-steps were outside your ken," Maggie said.

"They are — though if you wanted to teach me, I wouldn't complain. No. I have a favour to ask you. It's important."

She caught the change in his voice. "What do you want me to do?"

"Could you occupy Frank Martland for about ten minutes? I want to spirit Mrs. Martland off for a short while."

"Well, I suppose Trevor and I could waylay him and talk his ear off."

He sensed that tiny bit of fear behind her bravado that made it all the more necessary for her to accept the challenge. "Good. That's just the ticket. But we'll have to work quickly — so that he's taken unawares and doesn't have much time to react."

They were formulating a plan when Trevor found them.

"Ready for the next one, Maggie?"

"Oh Trev, do you mind if we sit it out? I need to catch my breath. Oh look, there are your parents. We shouldn't ignore them."

Trevor looked a bit alarmed but Maggie had already taken his arm and was leading him, protesting, toward his parents with Charles right behind. The two-pronged approach worked, for before Frank Martland knew what had happened, he was being peppered with inquiries by Maggie about the dance, his health, his views on charity, and his prediction as to who would win the upcoming foot race.

"Mrs. Martland, could I have a quick word with you? Over here, if I may." Charles took Agnes's arm and gently but quickly led her out of Martland's viewing range.

"Yes, Mr. Lauchlan, what is it?"

"We're having trouble getting people over to Mrs. Cliffe's portrait booth. It would really help if you would sit for her."

"Well, I'm not sure —"

Charles began steering her toward the booth. "Wonderful. It's just over this way. I'll be glad to escort you." He made her walk ahead of him so that her way back was blocked. When they arrived at Rosetta's booth, Rosetta was just greeting another customer. Charles nodded at her.

"Oh, I'm sorry Mr. Hardisty. I forgot that this lady is next. I can slot you in at ten o'clock, during the refreshment break. Will that be all right?" Her determined smile made it clear that it had better be all right. Mr. Hardisty nodded to Charles, gave a little bow to Agnes, and rejoined the crowd.

"Mrs. Cliffe, I don't think you know Mrs. Martland. She's most interested in sitting for a portrait. It's a surprise for her husband."

"How do you do, Mrs. Martland. Well, then, we must make sure that Mr. Martland is surprised — pleasantly, of course."

"Mrs. Cliffe. I'm pleased to meet you." Agnes was a little off balance, but she was playing along. "I've heard such good things about your work."

"Mr. Lauchlan, would you mind moving the camera a foot to the left — very gently — while I get Mrs. Martland seated?"

Charles busied himself moving and fussing with the camera while Rosetta directed Agnes. "Yes, that's right, Mrs. Martland. And look at the camera. Would you mind if I just pull your hair a little off your face?" Rosetta put her hand up to draw aside the wispy curls hanging at Agnes's temple but Agnes immediately caught the hand in her own.

"I'm sorry —" For a moment their eyes met. "Yes," Rosetta said. "You're quite right; we'll turn the other side of your face to the camera." Agnes stood again while Rosetta changed the angle of the chair and then seated her again. "Now, let me just have a look."

Rosetta walked to the camera and disappeared underneath the black cloth. "No need to be apprehensive, Mrs. Martland. I've been at this long enough that the camera will see only what I want it to see. Mr. Lauchlan, would you mind rearranging our friend the bear so that his eyes face the wall over there?"

Charles knelt in front of the chair and began to adjust the bear skin. "Mrs. Martland." His voice was almost a whisper. "This lady can help you. I've told her nothing — I know nothing for certain myself — but she can offer you the safety of her home — a place where no one would think of looking for you."

Agnes looked at him, wounded. "Please," Charles said, "forgive my bluntness. If I've mistaken your situation, I'm sorry. We haven't got much time."

"I ... don't know what you're talking about, Mr. Lauchlan —" She began to get up from the chair. Charles prevented her.

"Don't — if you leave without having the portrait taken, it will only attract attention." She sat back down. He dropped his voice lower again. "I'll come and get you and take you to Mrs. Cliffe's. You only have to send for me, day or night. You're on the telephone?"

"Yes."

"Telephone to Mr. Krafstadt's Dry Goods Store on Dufferin — night or day. He lives above the store. He'll send his boy to me with a message." Charles went back to join Rosetta.

"I'll just arrange your skirt. If I may, Mrs. Martland." Rosetta knelt in front of Agnes and began to arrange the folds of her skirt. "You think he will change," Rosetta whispered, "but don't cling to that, Mrs. Martland. Your real hope lies in getting out. I know what I'm talking about." And then speaking louder, "There now; such a beautiful dress needs to be shown to best advantage."

Rosetta looked through the camera lens again and loaded more powder on the flash lamp. "Now, if you'll just relax, Mrs. Martland, and think of something pleasant — your children, perhaps — being with your children on a perfectly sunny day. You're going to go boating with them on the river and then have a picnic at Nugent's Point." Rosetta's voice seemed to echo the lazy yaw of an old skiff steering into the current, the dip and pull of the oars. Distress ebbed slowly from Agnes's face, leaving her looking grave but composed. "That's right. There isn't a cloud in the sky."

Rosetta took three photographs in succession, quickly reloading the flash lamp in between. When she declared the sitting concluded, Agnes stood and took the money out of her evening purse.

"Here's your receipt with the address of my studio. I live just upstairs. The photographs will be available Wednesday, Mrs. Martland. Perhaps you could call for them yourself? I have a good selection of frames."

"Yes. Yes, if I can find the time, I will call for them, Mrs. Cliffe. Goodbye." Agnes extended her hand and Rosetta took it, holding it just a fraction longer than usual.

"I'll take you back," Charles said and broke a path for her through the crowd to where Trevor was standing, looking forsaken. There was no sign of Frank Martland or Maggie.

29.

Maggie couldn't quite put her finger on the point during her conversation with Frank Martland when control of the situation had slipped from her grasp. Though she had been on her guard, he had deftly fielded her barrage of breathless questions while proving to be surprisingly charming and talkative on his own behalf. Before she knew it, she had agreed to take the promenade with him so that he could, "see what all the fuss is about."

"Well, Father, Maggie has the next dance with me. You could take your promenade with Mother." Trevor, standing beside Maggie, had been mostly silent and fidgety until this moment.

"You could sit this one out, couldn't you, Miss Skene. Trevor, take another dance after the break. Your mother and I are leaving before the refreshments and this will be my only chance to see the promenade — and get to know Miss Skene better, of course."

"Well, I've already sat out one dance —"

"He's impatient, Miss Skene. But these young men, they have so many dances in front of them; but old gents like me? A promenade is all we're good for. So if you would join me, I would be most obliged."

"I don't see how I can refuse, Mr. Martland," Maggie said and threw a conciliatory glance at Trevor, who frowned back at her. As she took Martland's arm, she resolved to be particularly nice to Trevor for the rest of the evening.

The sun had gone down, so that the greenery of the promenade was lit by only a few gaslights along the perimeter of the room and by candelabra placed at junctions of the pathways.

"This is when a promenade is best, Mr. Martland. The candles make it look quite magical — like the Forest of Arden."

"I've never been to Arden. Never travelled much of anywhere, in fact. Mrs. Martland would like to go to Paris, but pressure of work has kept us from seeing as much of the world as we'd like."

"Oh, but you must go! I can hardly wait to see Europe. Father isn't very keen on sending me, but I'm going to talk him around."

"But you have your studies here?"

"Yes. But I want to attend lectures at a German university. They're so much ahead of Canada; I know I can make the best of the experience."

"I'm not sure I see the sense in young ladies taking university studies. But I do admire your determination. Maybe it will rub off on Trevor."

"Trev is quite diligent at his law studies, sir. He just hides it well."

Martland laughed. "That he does, Miss Skene. Once we get through this disturbance with the murder of my partner, I hope to bring Trevor more closely into the business."

"Oh, I should have said before now how sorry I am for your loss, sir."

"Thank you. Yes, it's been very difficult. But sometimes tragedies can help get things clearer in your mind. Do you know what I mean?"

"Yes, I think I do."

"I had wanted to talk to Trevor about the future of the

business that very night — the night of the murder. But I gather he was with you all that evening, and then —"

"Actually, he wasn't with me, but I'm sure that Trevor wants very much to talk things over with you. He's just —"

"He wasn't with you?"

"No. I was visiting Mrs. Drever. She has the shingles and Aunt Jessie sent me over with a poultice."

"Well. Well. I must have heard Trevor wrong. Shall we go this way?" Martland steered Maggie down a path crowded on all sides by ferns. They walked on in silence for a few moments.

"Won't you miss your family — and friends — a great deal if you go to Europe?"

"Yes — terribly. It's the only thing that worries me about going. I hate leaving Father all on his own. And, well, everyone. I wish I could just wrap 'home' up and take it with me. But other times, I think I'll just explode if I can't get there." She grew suddenly self-conscious. "I suppose you think it's wrong of me to be so selfish."

"Maybe it is, but I understand it. I can see that you aren't content to be ordinary, Miss Skene. I've never been content to be ordinary either. But I must confess that I'm a little relieved."

"In what way?"

"Well, I can see that you're not ready to form a serious attachment to my son. And that's good, because Trevor has to take his time and make the right choice. He needs a wife who will put his concerns above her own."

The meaning behind his words, the glint of steel, was so at odds with the benign good will she expected from older men that she wasn't entirely sure that she had understood him.

"Forgive me for being so blunt. I think we understand each other, you and me. We might have to pretend things to other people but we can be straight with each other."

The wind buffeted the building and the gaslights dimmed momentarily, which lent a melodramatic air to the strange turn this conversation had taken. She felt hurt and at the same time aggrieved. The thought that they might be alike, might share some covert bond distressed her, yet she couldn't explain exactly why. Was that it? Or was this the straightforwardness of an enemy who has dispensed with the niceties of diplomacy?

"Mr. Martland, this has been very ... pleasant. Thank you so much for asking me. But now I think I had better get back for my next dance."

Charles looked on from the doorway of the YMCA as Trevor, dressed in a long duster coat, clambered over his carriage, raising its hood against the threatening rain. Trevor was taking Maggie home along with his friend Sidney Jackson and a girl Jackson was courting in a desultory fashion. Charles walked over to the carriage with the group and handed Maggie and the other girl up into it. They crammed into the carriage talking and laughing, and the wind, though it had quieted significantly since the beginning of the evening, still blew their words away and caused the girls to wrap themselves tighter in their evening shawls.

"Are you sure you don't want a ride? Jackson can ride in the seat well," Trevor said, arranging the skirts of his coat over his knees and a blanket over Maggie's. "It's going to come down at any minute."

Charles thought of the state of his good suit and the solitary walk home. But he knew he should leave the young people alone to share their post-dance gossip. "No, no. We'd all feel like sardines. Besides, I have to think of a ringing conclusion to my sermon — nothing like a walk in the rain for that."

"Will you come for lunch as usual, after church?" Maggie inquired, looking intently at him.

"I'll be there," he said, touching the brim of his hat to the girls. He started walking away just as the first drops, small but slanting, began to hit the pavement. He turned up his collar, shoved his hands in his pockets, and began to whistle with counterfeit jauntiness. Maggie watched his receding back until he turned the corner. The tune was a waltz but the wind blew it away.

30.

Trevor let the others do the talking while he drove the carriage slowly down the streets lined with young elms that were stirring in the wind. Most of the houses were already in darkness. He dropped off Jackson and his girl in a flurry of umbrellas, leaving Maggie for last.

As they walked up the front steps of the Skene house, he held an umbrella over her, though it wasn't much help in the wind. Maggie could see her father nodding off over a newspaper in the parlour. She made to knock on the window to show that she was home but Trevor caught her hand and motioned her into the screened-in portion of the verandah where they were not visible from the window. Across the street the Hedlins' house loomed at them, stark in the momentary brightness.

"Maggie —"

"Shh! — one hundred, two one hundred, three — There it is," she said, as the thunder cracked and then rumbled away.

"Don't shush me. I've been more than patient this evening."

She thought he was joking, but then she saw his face.

"I'm sorry, Trev. There was such a lot going on at the dance."

"My father was so keen on taking you through the

promenade. Surprising." He flicked rainwater off the sleeve of his coat. "What did you talk about?"

She felt her face flush. "Oh, you know. My studies and so on. He doesn't approve."

"Did you tell him anything about me?"

"I think he was more interested in telling me to steer clear of you. At least I think that's what he was saying. Apparently he wants to protect you from the bluestockings of the world."

"You didn't talk about me, then?"

"Don't you care what he said? Or do you share his opinions about educated women?" She punished her evening shawl by twisting it and throwing a fringed end over her shoulder. "And anyway, we hardly talked about you at all. After he asked if you were with me on the night of the murder he returned to the prospect of my eternal spinsterhood."

He took his hat off with a gesture of frustration and shook the rain off it. "You think I should defend you? Shouldn't it be the other way around? You abandon me all evening, and then you pick this moment to exchange confidences about me with my father —"

"Trev, what are you talking about? I didn't abandon you. It was your father who practically insisted I walk with him. Why are you so upset? —" But he had already stalked down the stairs and up the walk. The thunder rolled again and the crowns of the young elms swayed back and forth with each new gust.

She didn't understand why this was happening. Trevor reached the boulevard and stopped, hands on hips, thinking and pacing with his hat held uselessly in his hand and the wind whipping the rain against his face. He turned and ran back up the walk and up the stairs.

"Trev —"

He pushed her gently back into the screened verandah. The

kiss was both surprising and sweet — though his arms and shoulders and face were damp and his lips, as they pressed urgently into hers, felt cool. She wanted more of this but he went on to her eyes, her nose, her cheeks.

"I'm sorry," he said, wrapping his arms tighter around her and whispering into her hair. "I'm sorry. I'm sorry. You couldn't know. You didn't do anything wrong and I'm an ass for taking it out on you."

She broke away and searched his face for a long moment. She brushed the hair off his forehead. "I'd like to help you. Please let me."

"I can't ask that of you, Maggie. I want to, but I can't ask that of anyone right now. I have to go." He took the verandah stairs in one leap and the walk in three loose-limbed strides, pausing to run his hand down the horse's nose and steady it against the low rumbling of the thunder. Then he sprang up into the phaeton, shook the reins and the carriage moved off down the street.

Charles arrived back at the church with his suit damp but not soaked, having evaded the worst of the storm. So far the rain had been sparse enough that the wind had begun to dry it as soon as it hit the ground. There was worse not far off, as he could see by the undifferentiated flashes of brightness over to the west and by low grumbling, felt more than heard. There was no point in trying to settle in to sermon writing. Not yet, anyway. Too much had happened; half of his brain was still at the dance. He peeled off jacket, dickie, shirt, and undershirt and then reached for his work shirt, fresh from being laundered by the ever-faithful Mrs. Gough. As he pulled it over his head he savoured the feeling of it: soft, warm, and dry. Peter wasn't in their room. He had taken to working all hours and Charles would sometimes find him in the morning curled up in a blanket on the floor behind his drawing table. Charles walked down the hall in the direction of the sanctuary. When he opened it, there was Peter in his cocoon of light making templates for some mouldings.

"Must have been a good dance; you didn't leave after your chaperoning duties were finished."

"As to that, the less said the better, but yes, yes. A fine dance, it made lots of money. Would you like a cup of tea?" Peter nodded and started to get up. "No, no. Stay where you are. I'll bring it through when it's ready."

As Charles was waiting for the kettle to boil in the kitchen, he remembered his conversation with Setter. He put the tea things on a tray and backed through the sanctuary door with it. After they were a good way into the first cup, listening to the rain and watching the pointed windows pulsing with bluish light at long intervals, Charles stretched and sat back in his chair.

"I'd like to try something with you, if you'll let me. It's a technique for inducing a deep contemplative state. Very old. Used by some of the most ancient cloistered orders. It may even have been used by the desert fathers."

"What's this? Dabbling in the black arts? Wouldn't your father call this 'popish nonsense'?"

"My father long ago concluded that my soul is in peril, so leave him out of it. Think of this as a way inward. It might help you to recover some of your memories — you know — of that night."

"Oh, come on, Charles."

"Look, don't set your mind against it without giving it a chance. What harm can it do? If it doesn't work, you'll at least have a good sleep tonight."

Peter sat back and sighed. "I suppose it's worth a try.

Especially since you won't give me any peace until I say 'yes.'"

Charles drummed his fingers on the drawing table. "That's the spirit."

"Well then, what do I do?"

"Right. Are you comfortable? Good. Sit back in your chair. Close your eyes — now, tell your arms and legs to just be easy, easy and still." He kept repeating soothing phrases while Peter concentrated on talking to his various appendages. "Now, think about some words that mean something to you. A short phrase or a sentence."

"You mean, from the Bible?"

"That's what I use, but it could be something else. Something from a poem, say." Charles reached over and turned down the coal oil lamps until all were off except one, which he turned down low so that they had only its dim orange glow in the surrounding darkness.

"This is ridiculous."

"No it isn't. We're just trying to get into a contemplative state. Focus the mind by concentrating on a single thing. Clear out the rubbish."

"What are you going to do?"

"I'm going to be your guide. I'll play Virgil to your Dante."

Peter laughed. "Oh, no. Not encouraging. I hope we're not going anywhere warmish."

"Stop stalling. Lean back. Relax."

"Can I stop it whenever I want?" His face was suddenly that of a boy.

Charles leaned forward and brushed some saw dust off the table. "Yes. If you want to keep avoiding it."

Silence. And then Peter nodded. "Let's go ahead, then."

"Good. Good. Close your eyes again. Have you chosen your phrase?"

Peter thought for a moment. "Yes. All right." He cleared his throat. "By the waters of Babylon, where we sat down, we wept when we remembered Zion." He said it in a slight sing-song way, enjoying the rhythm in the phrases.

Charles was surprised, but pleased. "Yes, that will do nicely. Just keep repeating it to yourself slowly. Keep bringing it to mind. If it slips away just bring it gently back. And relax."

Peter sat with his eyes closed, erect in his chair but still, his hands resting on the tops of his thighs. After some moments his breathing slowed.

"All right, I'm going to talk to you for a bit. The phrase is going to be there in the background, repeating itself while you're listening to me. You can bring it back to the foreground whenever you want. Are you feeling calm?"

"Mn hmm."

"Good. Now, you're feeling perfectly calm and safe. Remember you used to tell me about lying beside the creek bed for hours on a summer day?"

"Uh huh."

"How you used to watch all the little creatures in the stream?"

Peter nodded and the ghost of a smile crept over his face. His chest rose and fell slowly.

"Now, you're going to go back to that night and you're going to watch yourself just as if that other self were a strider bug or a tadpole in the creek." Peter's mouth started working and his brows drew together. "Easy, easy now. Bring the phrase back and set it going again. That's right. You're safe here. Nothing can hurt you."

The signs of unease slowly left Peter's face. His fingers relaxed where they had gripped his thighs.

"Now, you're watching yourself walk down Main Street. You're quite apart from what you see. Curious, but calm. Now you're in front of the Martland and Asseltine building. Tell me what you see."

"Nothing much. More like feelings." Peter's voice was thick, as if coming from a well. "Vague feeling of walking up the stairs. Mouldings on the stairway — always liked those — running my hand over them as I walked up."

"What floor is the office on?"

"Third, I think, no — fourth."

"All right, you're at the top of the stairs on the fourth floor."

"No, nothing."

"You're at the door to the outer office of Martland and Asseltine. Open it."

"Nothing. I've been there before and I know the layout — but nothing from that night."

"Describe the outer office."

"A large open space behind a counter with desks and a big table for viewing blueprints. Wooden filing cabinets. A cabinet with cubbyholes to store rolled up blue prints and plans. Windows onto the street on the left. A fern that needs to be watered — dropping its leaves. But I wouldn't be able to see much of that."

"Why?"

"The other times I went to see Asseltine at night the outer office was dark. Only the lights in his office were on — at the back. Asseltine to the left and Martland to the right. Wait! Something!"

"What?"

"Martland's door. 'F.H. Martland'. I could see light inside through the etched glass."

"What about Asseltine's office?"

"Dark, I think. Only Martland's office was lit."

"Good. Good. Now, breathe easy. Just take a few deep breaths.

Bring the phrase back." Charles was trying to stay calm himself. He had to concentrate on making his voice even. "You're still safe here, remember. No. Keep your eyes closed. You're watching yourself, mildly curious, that's all. Nothing can harm you. You see the light on in Martland's office. Watch yourself walking toward the door."

"I — I don't want to go in."

"Why not?"

"I don't know. But I know I have to. I know I should." Peter furrowed his brow and squinted with concentration. "Sounds, voices —"

"Whose voices? What are they saying?"

"Can't make out. Grunts. Things getting knocked over."

"Are you in Martland's office now?"

"Um. I don't know. I don't think so. Still outside."

"Are you one of the ones making those sounds? Are you in the fight?"

Peter's eyes were open. He was staring into the darkened sanctuary. "I don't think so. Charlie! I don't think I was." He grabbed Charles's arm. "Damn. It's so vague. But I don't think I was!"

31.

"No, no, back up into the dining room. I have to get it around the corner."

"I can't back up any more. My back's as backed up as it can get."

Charles and Maggie were on opposite ends of the Skenes' parlour carpet, now rolled up and in a problematic transition between the hallway and the back door. Why Maggie had chosen this particular moment to beat the dust out of the carpet was still a mystery to Charles. Aunt Jessie had not said anything but he could tell she disapproved of such doings on the Sabbath. But the afternoon was fine after the storm, warm and sunny, and a person could do worse than spend a half hour beating the living daylights out of a carpet in the back yard where the honeysuckle bush was in full bloom. He had soothed Aunt Jessie by saying that he intended to discuss the texts for the vesper service with Maggie as they worked.

They laid the carpet down parallel to the clothesline and draped the first section over the line, which sagged noticeably but held. Charles took off his jacket and started rolling up his sleeves in a distracted fashion while Maggie began to fasten a long pinafore over her second-best Sunday dress. At lunch he had not said anything further to Maggie about what had happened at the dance but it became clear that she was not content to leave it at that.

"Why did you need to be so secretive about Mrs. Martland's portrait last night? It wasn't just to surprise Mr. Martland, was it?"

His first thought was to just palm her off with some vague story. But, somehow, when he looked at her straightening her pinafore, ready to do battle, he couldn't do that. He motioned her around to the other side of the carpet so that they were partly hidden from the house.

"The other day, when I was visiting Mrs. Martland?"

"Yes?"

"You remember I told you she seemed frightened. Well, there were some bruises on her face and I thought ..."

"What?"

"I wasn't sure. That is, I could see that she'd been hurt and I suspected how, but I wasn't sure." He dropped his voice slightly. "Now I'm sure."

She was quite still. "It was him then."

"Yes. And I suspect not for the first time, either."

He told her how Rosetta Cliffe would take Agnes in and how he had offered to pick her up and take her to Rosetta's if only she would take that first step. He looked over at Maggie, who wore a look he couldn't interpret.

"Maggie?"

"Funny that I wasn't surprised. Sickened, but not surprised."

"What do you mean?"

She sat down on the sun-bleached steps of the clothesline stoop and smoothed the folds of her pinafore.

"It was why I wanted particularly to talk to you. While you

were at Mrs. Cliffe's booth last night I walked the promenade with Mr. Martland."

"Yes, I was wondering about that."

"At first he seemed so charming — I've hardly talked to him before — he asked me about my studies and — you know me. Never at a loss for words on that subject."

"Yes?"

"He doesn't approve of girls taking higher education, but that wasn't it. That annoyed me, but I've certainly heard worse. It was more the way he said it ... a feeling —"

"Did he say something hurtful?" All his protective instincts were engaged.

"No, no. At least, not on the surface. In fact he said he admired my determination. But he ... he sneaked behind my defences. It wasn't fair. I thought we were having a pleasant conversation but all along — I realize now — he was just interested in whether I had serious designs on Trevor; he was just worming information out of me ..."

There was that door again. Charles was irresolute.

"And then Trevor was so strange after the dance."

"In what way?"

"He was angry with me. I didn't give him my full attention at the dance but there was so much going on. I thought he'd understand, but he was angry. And he didn't want me to go on the promenade with his father. Charles, there's something really troubling Trevor. I think it has to do with his father, but he won't talk about it."

"I don't wonder, with a father like Martland."

"We have to help him. You have to talk to Trevor. He looks up to you. Couldn't you take him off for a brotherly chat?"

Of course he would have a brotherly chat with Trevor. *Handsome, rich and now, mysteriously suffering, Trevor.* He pushed that small stone of resentment around peevishly, trying not to acknowledge where it came from. And then he was thinking how that silly pinafore accentuated the slenderness of her waist and how extraordinarily well she looked with the sun on her hair, and how he would like to bury his face in its dark luxury. And then he was reciting Psalm 100 to himself, starting at the last verse and working backwards to the beginning, punctuating the inward recitation with resounding blows to the carpet. "... It is he that hath made us, and not we ourselves ..."

Later, when he was walking to Mrs. Gough's, he tried to discover what had changed or when it had changed. Wasn't his life focused, vital, charged with purpose? Right now it looked isolated, irrelevant, even a little pathetic — and lonely; that more than anything.

Mrs. Gough greeted him like the returning prodigal son and made him a cup of tea with some biscuits and jam. He paid her his rent for the month, drawing the bills from the section of his bill fold where he always placed his rent money on pay day. Then he took his second cup of tea upstairs to his rooms and sat in his reading chair. Everything was as before except for a little dust. He traced a line on the table beside his chair and found himself thinking of Maggie. What if she were there writing a letter at the desk? Or sitting beside him on a chesterfield. His arm would be around her. Perhaps she would be turned toward him, folded against him and resting her head, comfortably, easily, in the space between his chin and his shoulder. A butterfly seemed to be flying around inside his chest. He smiled absurdly. He laughed out loud. For a few minutes more he managed to keep this dear fantasy alive. And then down to earth. *I've got to get a grip on myself. Face facts.* He surveyed the second- and third-hand furniture of his worldly estate. How could she not be in love with Trevor?

But then the implications started seeping coldly into his brain. Marriage to Trevor would mean binding herself to that family. With Trevor caught in his father's magnetic field? A recipe for misery; she might even be in danger herself. There was Martland's strange behaviour to Maggie on the promenade. Something in his manner was threatening, unpredictable. He should counsel her against marrying Trevor, surely. He sighed. He might counsel away, but on this subject how much was his advice worth? Whichever way he turned in search of his duty to Trevor or to Maggie he found his own desires hiding like a little red devil in the long grass. There, too, was Jeremiah the prophet, wielding his pen of iron, cutting with his point of diamond, and saying, "The heart is deceitful above all things, and desperately wicked; who can know it?"

No blasted use. So, think of something else. He looked at his desk, then wandered over and sat there, fingers drumming on the ink-stained blotter. When he tried to get something out of the centre drawer and found it locked, he remembered the mysterious package. *Yes, that's odd.* Charles backtracked mentally, reviewing the events of the last few days. First, he had received a package under mysterious circumstances and then shortly after that Eklund, a person he hardly knows, rummaged through his belongings and Peter's too. Just a coincidence? What if Eklund was the person who left the package for him? The figure that ran past him on Mrs. Gough's walk had been roughly Eklund's height and build. But no. If he had left the package, why didn't he just ask for it back? And why ever would Eklund choose him as its guardian? Perplexed, Charles fumbled for his keys in his pocket and unlocked the desk drawer. He took out the package, passing it back and forth from one hand to the other. Should he take it to the police? Was there a duty that overrode his duty to the unknown writer of the note? Should he open it? He fingered the abraded edge of the envelope where it had been scraped coming through the mail flap, then set the package down on the desk, took out his watch, looked at it, and hesitated one more time before returning the package to the drawer. It was almost time for him to meet Peter. He turned the key in the drawer lock and heard a metallic click as the small bolt shot home.

32.

The Globe Hotel on Princess Street was the hostelry of choice for commercial travellers who were down on their sales quotas for the third month in a row, or farm wives on a spree with the egg money. Setter was a regular in the dining room, where Mrs. Mueller held sway. It being Sunday, no liquor service was allowed in the Globe's long, narrow beverage room, but Setter was pretty sure that they were handing bottles out through a cubbyhole in the back lane. He liked Mrs. Mueller's rhubarb pie too much to investigate further; what he didn't see couldn't hurt the Globe. He sat at his usual table by the window and pulled out the latest number of the *Lancet*. After reading only two sentences on the workings of strychnine, he put the journal down by his cutlery and stared off at nothing. Something was niggling at him about his present conduct. An under-the-counter meeting with a man charged with murder was a new experience. True, he had been forced into unorthodox methods. But there was some excitement in that, a heady rush in being out on a limb. No. What he worried about most was losing his balance. Being here, hiding out, letting himself get caught up in the feelings of an accused man and his supporters. Could he do this and still see the whole case clearly? He was still circling around this question when Lauchlan and McEvoy appeared and seated themselves at his table, both with smiles threatening to break through a determined firmness about the mouth.

"Good, good. You found the place, I see."

"Oh yes, no trouble there at all," said Peter. "Of course, I know the room across the hall much better than this one."

Setter looked in the direction Peter was pointing and saw the end of the long walnut bar, with its brass railing. "Right, yes. Not much happening in there today."

"No, but there'll be lots going on at the back."

"Well, er, I'd prefer not to hear any more about that, if you don't mind, McEvoy." Setter cast a cautious eye at Mrs. Mueller bustling in and out of the kitchen.

"Never mind that, now," Charles said. "I think we hit on something important last night. It could break the case wide open."

Civilians, Setter thought. "Let's hear it, then."

"I wasn't there!" Peter burst out. "Isn't that incredible?"

"I beg your —"

"We went over it — in a methodical fashion. That is, what Pete remembers of that night. And it just popped out. I wouldn't have believed it, but there it is."

"What was it, this popping —"

"Peter remembered hearing the sounds of a struggle in Martland's office. It sounded so bad that he was afraid to go in. Don't you see? He wasn't even in the room when the struggle that killed Asseltine took place!"

Setter turned to Peter, suddenly intense.

"I was in the outer office," Peter said, "looking at the light coming through the etched glass of Martland's office door. There were sounds — grunting, furniture being knocked over — then a crash and things went quiet."

"Did you hear voices? Anything coherent?"

Peter shook his head. "No, no. Only grunts and the sounds of movement. No words. And that's all that came back."

"Then you don't remember going into the office?"

"I'm afraid not. Nothing until I was sitting there looking down at Asseltine. But this is something, isn't it? Something really important. It means that someone else was there in the office before I got there. And he was the one who killed Asseltine."

"And whoever it was, he would have had to walk right past you in order to get out of that room. You must have seen him, McEvoy." Setter leaned toward Peter over the table. "Do you remember anything about him? Anything at all?"

Peter looked pained and shook his head. "Nothing. I've been over it and over it — by myself and with Charles. Nothing — except those muffled sounds behind that door."

Setter sat back in his seat and said, "Hnnnnnn."

"You don't believe me."

"On the contrary. It's what I've suspected all along. It explains a lot — to me, at any rate. Unfortunately, it's a question of whether the jury and the judge will believe it and —"

"And all they'll see is a down-and-outer trying to save his neck by — what? — convenient recollection, I suppose." Peter looked down at the empty plate in front of him.

"It's not enough, then?" said Charles.

"Well, not on its own, perhaps. But it's given me a lot to work on. Damned interesting development, really. Now, this will have to be kept between us for now, understand? No loose talk to anyone else."

Peter made assenting noises but Setter saw Charles hanging back and gave him a questioning look.

"Sorry. I didn't know it was as confidential as all that. I told the Skenes at lunch. I thought Doctor Skene should know."

"All right. No great harm there. But no one else, agreed?" Charles nodded. "And tell Dr. Skene to keep it close to his vest. Now ..." Setter took out his notebook, flipped it open, and started firing questions at Peter.

33.

The possible outcomes of Peter's trial came all too clearly to Charles's mind as he watched Setter patiently questioning Peter. Death by hanging; something less for second-degree murder or manslaughter, but still a horrible calamity for someone who was fragile to begin with. That's why it wasn't enough just to prove Peter's innocence. They needed to find the person who really killed Asseltine.

But Setter appeared to have that in hand, at least, Charles hoped he did. In an effort to silence his uncertain thoughts, Charles picked up the menu and looked down the list of items without seeing them. That nagging little voice. *Why are we meeting away from the station? What is this need for secrecy about? Justice seems to be taking a rather devious route on its way to prevailing.* A thought occurred to him and was instantly banished. *No, I should stay out of it.* The insinuating toe slid around the door again. *Why so?* Because it would not be prudent. Caution. Prudence. Let the appointed authorities do their work. And yet these words smelled of cowardice. He appealed to the light born of reason. Is it beyond the realm of possibility that the appointed authorities sometimes require a little help? And hadn't Setter already asked him to help Peter get his memories back? Wasn't that a kind of deputizing?

Well, then. But where to start? Asseltine couldn't tell them how he had died. But what if he could learn more about Asseltine from the person who knew him most intimately?

But before he could put into action that as yet formless resolve, there was the matter of Trevor. Later that evening he was standing at the church door shaking hands with his congregation following the vesper service. He saw Trevor slipping past him while Mrs. Macleod was delivering her verdict on his sermon.

"Now I don't say it wasn't good, Mr. Lauchlan. No, I don't say that. But I had hoped to hear more downright talk about the consequences of falling into sin —"

"Would you excuse me for one moment, Mrs. Macleod? — Trevor? Just a moment —" He disengaged his hand from Mrs. Macleod and just caught up to Trevor as he was going out the door.

"Trevor, did you bring your rig tonight?"

"Yes, why? Do you need a ride somewhere?"

"I do, as a matter of fact. Samuel McCorrister is ailing and I promised to visit him tonight."

"Fine. Be happy to. He's on Smith isn't he? I'll wait for you outside."

After Charles had changed out of his gown and tabs and had a quick word with Peter to tell him to do the locking up for the night, he hopped up into Trevor's rig and they were away. Trevor was mostly silent while Charles made inconsequential small talk. *Just postponing the hard part,* Charles thought. *Get to it now; it has to be done.*

"Actually Trevor, I wasn't entirely truthful with you. I don't really have to visit the McCorristers this evening. I wanted to have a word with you. Is there someplace we can talk?"

Trevor reined in the horse, though they were in the middle of a block. "Well — I'm not sure —" He turned and looked behind and around before turning to Charles. "Is this about Mother?"

"Yes. At least partly. And about you."

Trevor gave the walk signal to his mare. "I see." He was quiet for a moment. "Well, if you don't mind helping me bed Daisy down for the night, we can go to my stable."

"Fine. That'll be fine. It's been a long time since I had to see to horses."

They went along in silence for awhile. Then Trevor said, "I'm glad you know."

"Well, you practically insisted that I see her. Almost as if you wanted me to find out."

Trevor let out a long sigh. "I might not always be around, you see."

Charles nodded. "Yes. I see. Has it ... has it been going on long?"

He made a curious, stiff, figure-eight movement with his head. "Coming back from university — and from school before that — I always hoped that it had stopped. He's always sorry afterwards. He always apologizes." He turned to Charles, incredulous. "To me, of all things! He hits Mother or Clare and even sometimes Louise. Not me, unless I try to stop him. But then he'll just wait till I go out and hit her harder. It was just so much easier to be away and not have to see it." Suddenly Trevor's chest caved in and his head bowed down until his face almost touched the reins. Charles took them out of his hands.

He never knew what to do at times like this. He had hoped that, somehow, the knowledge of what to say would have descended on him with the laying on of hands at his ordination.

All he could think of now was to lean in Trevor's direction, addressing the gentling sounds, the geeing and hawing, to both horse and man. After a while, Trevor straightened up and his breath came easier. Then Charles felt it was all right to tell him about his plan, about Mrs. Cliffe.

"If only she would," Trevor said. "But she can't seem to leave on her own. God knows I've tried to persuade her."

"I'll do my best. I think she's starting to trust me."

"There's the stable. Macpherson's. Just there, after the intersection. Here, I'll take them." He took the reins from Charles.

In the stable yard a boy came out and helped Trevor unhitch the horse from the carriage. The boy and Trevor towed the carriage into the cavernous stable and jack-knifed it into its parking space while Charles led the horse down to its stall.

"If you could just get her some fresh hay, I have to get my driving coat and hang it up."

Charles put Daisy in her stall, removed her harness and hung it up. He forked some hay into the manger, enjoying the smell of horse and liniment, leather, and manure. Trevor walked up the aisle shaking out his coat that was still damp from the previous evening. He draped it over two pegs at the side of the stall.

Charles watched Trevor carefully spreading the oiled canvas skirts of the coat, twitching and stretching it to flatten the wrinkles, and he was suddenly certain, so certain that he blurted out the conclusion before his brain was finished totting up the evidence.

"It wasn't Eklund; it was you."

"What? What do you mean?" Trevor stopped dead.

"You bowled me over on your way out of Mrs. Gough's. The night I was called to the police station. You were wearing that coat."

Trevor continued to fidget with the coat. There was silence between them and Charles's conviction started to ebb away.

"Of course, I could have been mistaken —"

"No. No. I suppose there's no harm in your knowing now."

"You left me that package. Why?"

"I was afraid he'd find it. It's the one thing I've got that will do it."

"Who? And do what?" They were whispering now.

"My father. It's the only way that's foolproof. I've got to make sure he goes somewhere where he won't be able to harm her anymore."

"Where? I don't —"

"Prison. God knows he's done some things that should put him there for a long time."

"You mean for the beatings?"

"Yes, but that's not good enough. It's too difficult to convict. And anyway, she won't press charges. It had to be the hotel project."

"The Imperial?"

"Yes. The Imperial project." Trevor moved into the stall and took a currycomb off a shelf. He murmured to Daisy and began to comb her.

Trevor's voice was so quiet that Charles had to stand right next to him at Daisy's flank to hear him. "My father cheated the investors by inflating the cost of the building and then substituting inferior materials when it was actually built. He and Asseltine pocketed the difference and invested the money in New York. I found out by accident while I was learning the business."

"Fraud, then."

"Yes. Fraud." Trevor gave a small smile of satisfaction. "I've made a special study of the criminal law in relation to fraud. He could get as much as fourteen years for it."

"Why didn't you just go to the police with the information?"

"I wanted to. But you don't know my father. He has a way of persuading people to his point of view. I had to make sure I had enough information to convict, enough that he couldn't possibly wiggle out of it. Then there was this horrible business with Asseltine. It put Father on his guard and he hid everything else that might implicate him and paid off or threatened everyone who knows something."

"Does that include Eklund?"

"Eklund's in on it; he has been from the first. He's the one who was in charge of the real specifications for the building, the ones they used on the site. He bought all the material that went into the hotel personally. The workmen have no idea that the investors saw a completely different set of specs."

"Haven't some of the investors toured the site?"

"That was the beauty of it. Asseltine made sure that none of the investors actually live in Winnipeg. And the architect is from Toronto, too. If one of them happened to be in town, Eklund and my father made sure they only saw the parts of the building that were built according to the specifications given to the investors. Most of the shoddy stuff is hidden in the foundation and behind walls anyway."

"Asseltine. Did his murder have anything to do with this?"

Trevor was giving a lot of attention to some tangles in Daisy's mane. "I don't know. But everybody in the office knew about his gambling, the kind of people he associated with — drinking and betting — anything could have happened."

"So the package contains some kind of evidence of the fraud?"

"Yes. The papers are pretty damning."

"Why did you give them to me?"

"You were the last person my father would think of. And,

well, I thought that — I hoped — that I could count on something like the privilege of the confessional."

"You were right about that, as it happens. I felt bound to keep your confidence; at least until I found out whose confidence it was I was keeping."

Trevor stroked Daisy's nose. "Funny. It's surprising how easy it is to talk about this, after all. So many secrets in my family; we hardly know how to tell the truth."

"But surely you see that you have to turn these papers in to the police."

"Yes. Yes, it's time. I had pretty much decided that already."

"Why not get a good sleep tonight and go to the police tomorrow?"

"Yes. But it can't be tomorrow. I promised to run in the All Charities foot race tomorrow evening. If I go to the police tomorrow, they'll likely need me for questioning and I might have to miss the race. So many people have sponsored me; I don't want to disappoint them."

"But, Trevor. There's something else you should know."

"Yes?"

"Yesterday Peter caught Eklund coming out of our room at the church. We're pretty sure he was searching through our things."

Trevor leaned against the railing of the stall. "Yes, I see." He thought for a moment, pulling hair off the currycomb. "Well, they know the papers are missing and they're desperate to get them back. They must think that McEvoy got them out of the office somehow before he was arrested." He ran his fingers down the tines of the currycomb. "And that maybe he had help."

"But doesn't that argue for your going to the police earlier, then, rather than later?"

"If I'm right, they still aren't completely convinced that I'm the one that has them. I should be all right for another day or so if I'm careful. Don't worry, Charles. If I'm the mouse, I know how to trick the cat for a while longer."

Charles was far from convinced of that. "I'm uneasy about this whole business, Trevor. But I suppose I can't make these decisions for you. Is there anything else I can do to help?"

"Yes. If Eklund comes around, don't let on that you know anything. Don't confront him about searching your room. Just act normally."

"I'll do my best."

Before going their separate ways they agreed that Charles would return the papers to Trevor in the locker room of the YMCA before the race. Trevor gave his solemn promise to go to the police with the papers on the day following the race.

34.

The next afternoon Charles found himself in a place he had never been before, yet there was a map of it in his head. There it was — the blueprint table — and there, the large fern in its dark oak stand, looking better tended than Peter had remembered. The mission Charles had embarked on was not sitting well with his conscience but he had armed himself with the text: "Behold, I send you forth as sheep in the midst of wolves: be ye therefore wise as serpents and harmless as doves." The stenographer sitting behind the counter was distinctly *un*wolflike. She was intent on her typewriting and only looked up after he cleared his throat.

"Excuse me, Miss. I understand that Mrs. Asseltine is here?"

"Er. Yes, sir." She looked back over her shoulder in the direction of an office door with J.P.T. ASSELTINE painted on the etched glass. "But she never told me to expect anyone."

"Yes. Of course, I'm sure she has many things to attend to. But could you give her my card and ask her if she would be kind enough to spare me a few minutes?"

The girl took his card and, smoothing down her skirt and patting her hair into place, she walked to the door of Asseltine's office, knocked and slipped in.

No, this is madness. Make some excuse and get out. But before he had time to fan the flames of his panic, the girl had returned and was looking quizzically at him.

"Mrs. Asseltine will see you, Reverend."

He just had time to paste on a look of earnest kindliness before striding quickly into the office. "Mrs. Asseltine. How good of you to see me on short notice."

She had been sitting at her husband's desk with papers neatly laid out. "No notice, as it happens, Mr. Lauchlan. Kind of you to call. I must say, I hadn't expected anyone to find me here." She rose from the desk and moved around it to extend her hand.

"Yes. That's understandable. But, fortunately, when I called at your home, the maid — Gertie, is it? — told me you were here." He took her hand in his and placed his other hand on top. "My heart was so full that I couldn't wait another moment to extend my sympathies to you. And to say to you what an extraordinarily generous man your husband was. Such a loss for you — and for the whole city."

"Yes, well, Thank you, Mr. Lauchlan. Naturally, the children and I are desolate." She attempted to extricate her hand. "I was not aware that you knew my husband. We go to Knox — though not as often as we would like —"

"True enough, dear lady." He held her fast. "It was not my good fortune to know your husband well. But we did have the 'roaring game' in common." He noted her puzzlement. "Curling? No, no, I didn't know him well and that was why it was such a surprise — a delightful surprise — that he would speak to me as he did the last time we met."

"Surprise, Mr. Lauchlan? I'm afraid I'm not following you."

"Why, the bequest, of course." He let go of her hand at last. "I need hardly tell you that there are members of my own congregation who have not been nearly so generous in their support. I want to assure you that the money is greatly needed and will help so many in my parish."

"Bequest? No, no. There must be some mistake." She squinted at him. "Did my husband give you something in writing?"

"Why, no. He said that he was making some changes to his will and that he would be inserting a clause — for a very gratifying sum — to the Dufferin Avenue Church Neighbourhood Fund."

"But — I am the co-executor of my husband's estate, Mr. Lauchlan. And I'm sorry to say that I found no bequest to you or to your church in his will."

"Oh. But surely that is not — he was quite specific — Oh, dear. Oh — are you sure you've read the whole —"

"Yes, quite sure. I have it here on the desk. There's nothing —"

"Oh. That's curious. What could have — this is very —"

"Are you all right, Mr. Lauchlan?"

"Yes. Yes, of course. Just a little light-headed. The shock —"

She swept around him and to the door. "Miss Haskins, a glass of water — no, — whiskey. Quickly." She came back and led Charles, who was holding a hand to his forehead, to a chair in front of the large mahogany desk. He was fanning himself with his handkerchief when the whisky decanter arrived, not borne by Miss Haskins, as he expected, but by Frank Martland. As he juggled the decanter and a small cut-glass tumbler, Martland seemed just as surprised.

"Lauchlan. What the — Oh. You're the one feeling poorly?"

"Yes, er … possibly the heat. I just came to pay my respects to Mrs. Asseltine. Such a sad occasion." She took the decanter and glass from Martland, carefully filled the glass with amber fluid and handed it to Charles.

"How true. Yes, very sad. We're only too happy to

accommodate Mrs. Asseltine here. Least we can do. Well, Millie? Getting along all right? Finding everything you need?"

"Well enough, thank you, Frank." She placed the decanter on the other side of the desk from where Martland was standing. "The staff have made me quite comfortable. As you can see."

"Good." He surveyed the papers on the desk. "Good. I'll leave you to it then." He turned to Charles. "You'd best be careful, Lauchlan. Of the heat, I mean." With a nod to her, he turned to go.

"Oh Frank?"

"Yes?"

"There are one or two more things I should see. Here's a list." She picked up a piece of paper from the desk and handed it to him."

Martland's lips must have been dry. He pressed them together as he read. "Well, yes, you have been hard at it." He looked up from the page and there was for the briefest moment a deeper chill to the blue of his eyes. "I'll get Collier to bring them."

Charles had been watching them, fascinated. So fascinated that, as Martland took his leave, Charles took a deeper swig from the heavy-bottomed tumbler than he had intended. "Thank you, Mrs. Asseltine." It was all he could rasp out as he set the glass down on the desk. "You're very kind. Whew!" The distilled vapours were curling the hair in his nose.

"You're feeling better, then?"

"Yes, much, thank you. Hem! Really, Mrs. Asseltine, I'm terribly embarrassed. You must think me a complete fool. Trooping in here, intruding on your grief." He looked up at her, all limpid innocence. "I'm not a worldly man. Perhaps I misunderstood your husband."

"Perhaps so, Mr. Lauchlan. Mind you, I was not privy to every financial decision Joe made — as I'm now learning." She

213

resumed her chair behind the desk and leaned back in it, stretching into the leather folds. "And my husband was under a certain amount of strain these last few months."

"I'm sorry to hear it. Was it his health?"

"No. Well — not exactly. Business life is not always harmonious, Mr. Lauchlan." She picked up a letter opener and ran her fingers down the edges. "Sometimes the hardest blows are not the ones that come from your adversaries."

Charles leaned toward her and met her eyes. "I've always understood that Mr. Martland and Mr. Asseltine were on good terms. Did something —"

She drove the point of the letter opener deep into the desk blotter with a force that caused a metallic springing sound from the blade. The whiskey glass jumped an inch into the air and slopped its contents onto the desk.

Charles opened his mouth but nothing came out. A trace of outraged fury remained on her face before it was replaced by the look of slightly detached concentration she had worn before. He covered his astonishment by mopping up the spilled whiskey with his handkerchief. "O–Of course, I know neither Mr. Martland nor your husband well. My dealings have been more with Eklund."

"Eklund." It was said with neither rancour nor approval. She seemed to roll the name around in her mind as she removed the letter opener from the blotter with deliberate care and smoothed over the hole with her finger. "Well, Eklund has always been Frank's man. Ever since Frank picked him out of a day labouring gang and gave him permanent work. Fourteen years old and half-starved. I suppose it's no wonder."

Then she seemed to remember his presence. "As co-executor, I have a duty to my children to ensure that the estate their father built up — the complete share to which Joe was entitled — is fully realized." She leaned back in the chair. "I'm sorry about the bequest, Mr. Lauchlan. But now I must return to that effort."

So much for fearing that his little deception would harm Millicent Asseltine; avenging goddesses need take no heed of such trifles as he represented. Yet there was a whiff of brimstone in the air. Did she really know what she was walking into?

"Mrs. Asseltine, I think it's best to tread warily. There are, perhaps, things you don't understand." Too late, he remembered his script.

There was just the slightest sign of recognition, of clarity after confusion, before she replied. "I'm sure that is true, Mr. Lauchlan. But I intend to understand all — in good time. And perhaps I should give you the same advice?"

He could feel his ears getting red. "I can see that you're a determined person. I hope you achieve what you are seeking." He got up from his chair, stuffing his handkerchief back into his breast pocket. "Thank you for letting me down so gently. And please keep my card. If you need my help — at any time — just call on me." He picked up his hat from the desk, put it on his head and gave her a little bow of farewell.

As he was walking home to the church, the implications of this extraordinary scene came clicking into place. There had been friction between Asseltine and Martland. Was it the drinking and the gambling? Yes, he could see that such a man would become increasingly unreliable. And Eklund was Frank's man — two against one. Charles knew for certain two scurrilous things of which Frank Martland was capable. Was there a third? And with Millicent Asseltine on the scent of unexplained things in the company books, what might Martland do next?

35.

Charles picked his way through the crowded locker room at the YMCA. Then he spotted Trevor, detached and silent amid the loud calls and raucous laughter of men not altogether sure they were up to the coming challenge. Trevor was pulling his racing singlet carefully over his chest, his eyes fixed on some imaginary horizon.

"Hello Trevor. All ready, I see." And then in a whisper. "Here. Can't say I'm sorry that my custodial duty is over."

Trevor took the package quickly and, shielding his actions with his body, put it in his locker. He closed and locked the locker and pinned the key to the inside of his waistband.

"Thanks, Charles. I'll see it through now." He looked determined, if a little drawn.

"Look," Charles whispered. "Don't leave it till tomorrow. Go to the police tonight — after the race. I'll go with you."

Trevor shifted his weight from foot to foot. "I've already made plans for after. But you can come with me tomorrow, if you like. I'll meet you tomorrow at nine at Dingwall's Jewellers. We can walk to the station from there."

"But — there's something I should tell you —"

"Shhh. Not here. Tell me after the race." Trevor extended his hand and said, louder, "Good luck."

"Same to you. Meet you here after —" Charles said, but Trevor was already halfway to the locker room door.

As the runners lined up at the starting line in front of the YMCA building, Archbishop Machray, chairman of the All Charities Appeal, was receiving instructions on how to fire the starter's pistol. Somehow, however, the gun had gotten tangled in his long silvery beard. A six-mile course had been laid out in a rough square from McDermot to Main Street, across the Main Street Bridge into Fort Rouge, west along River Avenue to the Crescent Drive, down the tree-lined crescent to the Maryland Bridge, across the bridge and north along Boundary Street on the western edge of the city to Portage Avenue, then east on Portage, bringing the runners back to the centre of the city, and to the starting line again.

Charles felt exposed in his faded navy blue running shorts and his pale blue singlet with "University Co lege" sewn on the front. The air played around his legs and arms in a quite unfamiliar way. Trevor was doing elaborate leg stretches and bouncing lightly up and down on his toes. Charles began some dimly remembered limbering routines of his own and wondered if there might be a graceful exit; a parishioner suddenly taken ill, say, or an emergency wedding. But no, His Grace had quit fumbling with the starting gun and looked ready for action now. Charles took his place at the line with about one hundred other runners and assumed the ready position with what he hoped was a look of casual confidence. *BANG!* He lurched ahead, engulfed in a tangle of churning legs and pumping elbows. Trevor's pale yellow singlet vibrated five yards in front of him. They turned onto Main Street and headed south and Charles, in spite of himself, was filled with a sense of exhilaration as they thundered down the street at a full gallop, not yet breathing so hard that the cheers of the spectators were muffled. Trevor had dropped back level with him.

"Too fast."

"What?"

"The pace. It's too fast. Those lads ahead will regret it if they keep it up."

Charles nodded agreement and resolved to stick with Trevor as runners around them started to pass them. He sensed rather than saw a jostling just behind his left elbow as someone pulled level with them from behind. *Eklund! Where had he come from?* Just in time Charles remembered the conversation of the previous evening. He nodded, radiating cordiality. Just three hardy fellows out for a friendly run. Eklund smiled an equally convivial smile and gave a slight wave back.

"Eklund. This is a surprise. Wonderful evening for a race," Trevor said, after the slightest hesitation.

"That it is, Mr. Martland. Some of the boys at the yard have money on me, so I have to give it my best."

"I'm sure you won't disappoint them."

By the time they reached the Main Street Bridge the field had spread out. The front runners had separated from the middle group where Trevor, Charles, and Eklund were running and this group had begun to fray as slower runners straggled and fell back. They pounded over the bridge and felt the iron girders vibrate in sympathy. The evening sun glinted off the river and when they were across and had turned west on River Avenue, the full force of it caused Charles to narrow his eyes to slits. The road, though unpaved, was lined with wooden sidewalks but they were effectively in the country with the river bottom forest that stretched back from the road on either side only occasionally punctuated by clearings in which piles of brick, sand, timber, and foundation stone littered the sites of what would soon be very substantial houses.

As they went past Fort Rouge Park, Charles started to wonder where his next breath was coming from. Despite being only a quarter of the way through the race, sweat had popped out on his forehead and drops rolled down and hung suspended from his nose. He was now two paces behind Trevor. His own breath seemed to roar in his ears crowding out all other sounds. It helped him to imagine a silver cord running from Trevor's elbow to his own, towing him along. Eklund was still level with Trevor but he was flushed to a high colour, his breathing loud and wheezy. They had to stop and wait at Osborne as two streetcars trundled by in opposite directions and the passengers cheered them and waved as they went by. The slight rest and the warmth of his fellow humans buoyed Charles up and as they turned onto the Crescent Drive he was again side by side with Trevor and Eklund.

This was the more scenic part of the route where there was less traffic. Still, carriages and bicycles threaded their way among the runners, bearing wives, children, and fiancées of the runners, all cheering on their men. There were not enough policemen to help in keeping the carriages and buggies out of the lane the runners were occupying and Charles found it a needless annoyance to have to think about keeping out of the way of vehicles. Irritably, he wondered why the throngs of people hadn't just stayed home.

He was now several paces behind Eklund, who was just behind Trevor. They began to pass runners who had started out ahead of them. What mental effort Charles could spare from willing his burning legs onward he spent fretting about Eklund.

What was his game? And how far would Eklund and Martland be willing to go to secure the return of those papers? Possible answers to that question made him dig harder to close the distance between himself and the two younger men ahead of him.

Can't. Just can't. Too winded. Cat and mouse. Has to be now. With a surge fuelled by desperation he drew level with Eklund. All that was needed was to swing his foot a little to the right. *There.* In a nightmare ballet, Eklund and he, legs intertwined, tumbled in a heap. They hit the packed mud and sand of the roadway — humph! Runners behind leaped over and to the side of them. Eklund extended his arm for support to get up but Charles, also rising, knocked the arm away and re-entangled himself.

"Watch out, damn you!"

"Sorry! Sorry Eklund. Can't think what happened."

Eklund made no reply but strained to see ahead as he brushed mud off his thigh. Trevor was striding out confidently and smoothly with no wasted effort. Eklund set his teeth and trundled off. Charles started to run again after dusting off his knees. He did what he could as Trevor's yellow singlet grew smaller and smaller and the imaginary silver cord lengthened and grew exquisitely thin. It snapped and disappeared into the ether as Trevor receded into the distance. Eklund, too, was ahead of Charles but now it was clear that he would not catch up to Trevor.

That left Charles with only his bottomless fatigue and an undercurrent of alarm for company. Two more miles. As they approached the Maryland Bridge, one or two runners beside him fell back and slowed to a walk, hands dejectedly on hips. Charles concentrated on putting one foot in front of the other and trying to ignore his rapidly stiffening calf muscles.

He turned east on Portage Avenue on the homeward stretch

back to the starting line. *Stop. Just want to stop. No harm done. Had a good crack at it.*

"Charles! Hurray! Only one more mile. You're almost there." She was just ahead at the corner of Balmoral and Portage — about a hundred yards away opposite Wesley College. Quitting now out of the question. *Quit? Not for me, the coward's way.* He straightened up, willed the knotted sinews in his legs to stride out, lifted his chest and pushed his belly out for the deepest and most sustaining breaths. He forced his arms to pull forward stronger and his feet to hit the ground quicker, causing him to move up through the group of shambling laggards he'd been sharing the road with. As he ran by he managed a wave and a smile, his expanded chest straining against the damp singlet. Maggie jumped up and down and whistled in quite an unladylike manner. He laughed. Well! He seemed to have caught a bizarre kind of second wind. The pain was excruciating but he was somehow apart from it. Two blocks from the end the crowds were heavier and they bore him along. He crossed the finish line feeling as wonderful and as awful as he had ever felt in his life.

As Charles came into the locker room there was no sign of Trevor but it was clear that the front runners had already changed and cleared out. After using the shower bath and changing as quickly as he could, he reappeared outside for the prize giving ceremony. The slowest runners were still jogging and walking across the finish line. He found Maggie in the crowd and basked in her praise.

"Charles! You're full of surprises these days. No need to pick you up off the pavement after all. And in the top half of finishers, too."

"It did go rather well, didn't it? Have you seen —"

"Oh, shush. They're starting …"

They turned to the dais, where the dignitaries had gathered. Charles assumed that Trevor was among the faster runners and he was not surprised in due course to hear the archbishop calling out, through a megaphone, "Second place, Mr. Trevor Martland." They clapped and cheered and Charles was warmed by an inner satisfaction in having kept up with Trevor for more than half the race.

The archbishop was looking over the crowd. "Trevor Martland? Don't tell me he's going to disappoint the ladies?" General laughter. "Come now, Mr. Martland. We want to salute your achievement. No? Will someone accept the trophy on his behalf?" The crowd murmured and looked around. Eventually more than a few people picked out Maggie. Charles could tell that some teasing was forthcoming and when he turned to Maggie, she looked flustered and reached out to put her hand on his arm.

"Shall I get it?" Charles said. She sighed with relief and nodded.

"Ah, here's the Reverend Mr. Lauchlan fresh from the race course. Thank you, Mr. Lauchlan."

Charles did not feel fresh, but he took Trevor's trophy nonetheless. He wasn't sure how to feel about the fact that Trevor seemed to have left already. Depended on who he left with, really.

"Maybe he misunderstood and went to my house," she said. "I'd better go and see if he's there. If I run I can catch the Broadway tram." He just had a chance to hand her the trophy before she was off in a flurry of hiked skirts, galloping to the streetcar stop on Main Street. He looked after her, suddenly at loose ends. Maybe she was right and Trevor would be there, sitting on the verandah, as usual. Or maybe not. Better take one last look around. He took a final reconnoitre around the edge of

222

the crowd and bumped into Eklund, hair uncombed and necktie thrown loosely around his collar. Charles adjusted his face into the right planes for backslapping commiseration and tried not to show the relief he felt.

"Eklund. Fine race. But I guess neither of us could keep up with Trevor, eh?"

"What? Oh. No. Right enough. Got away from me. Yes, quite a race. Congratulations." He continued looking through the crowd. "Well, excuse me. Mr. Lauchlan. I've got to get off home now." He rushed off at a pace that made Charles wince just to look at him.

36.

The hands on the large clock at Dingwall's Jewellers said 8:59 a.m. Charles took out his own watch and noted that it was a little fast. He had left himself time to walk a little slower than normal on the aching stumps that had once been his legs. But the walk had proved beneficial and after ten minutes or so, he had been able to move quite freely. Dingwall's was a good place for watching the world go by and Charles was taking full advantage when, out of the crowd, a familiar figure emerged.

"Mr. Lauchlan. Good morning. Still no sign of young Martland yet?"

"Jessup, Good to see you." They shook hands. "What brings you here?"

"I'm not exactly sure. Truth to tell, I'm a bit puzzled by the whole thing."

"What do you mean?"

"Well, I got a visit from Trevor Martland last night at my apartment. Turned up at about ten. Most peculiar. It wasn't a social call, though. He wanted to retain me."

"For himself, you mean?"

"Apparently so. He instructed me to meet him — and you

— here this morning and that the three of us would go to the police station together."

"Oh. Well, that's interesting. I suppose he's just being cautious. He is an officer of the company, after all."

"You know what this is all about then?"

Charles grew suddenly wary. "Didn't he tell you?"

"No. He wouldn't tell me a blessed thing except that he needed the services of a lawyer urgently. Said he would have to brief me at the station — for my own safety, no less!"

"I see. Well." Charles took his hat off and rubbed his forehead, trying to think what to do. "This is a bit awkward, Jessup. I suppose I do know more than you at this point, but we'll have to wait for Trevor to show up, I'm afraid. I can't tell you without his say so."

"It's damnably puzzling, if you ask me. Oh, excuse me, Mr. Lauchlan. No offence meant."

"None taken; I'm sure Trevor will make everything clear when he gets here."

"He did say that you might need my help in relation to a family matter of his and that I was to give you whatever assistance you needed."

"Oh? Well. Now we're both mystified."

"I'm not too keen on mystification. Clarity is more in my line."

At this they waited, exchanging awkward pleasantries and checking the time. Nine-ten a.m. went by and no Trevor. At 9:15 a.m. they were both getting frustrated and Charles was becoming concerned.

"I'm sure he said nine, sharp. I hope nothing untoward has happened."

Jessup started pacing up and down, holding his hat in one hand and tapping the brim against his leg. Charles tapped his foot and chewed his bottom lip.

Jessup took his watch out of his vest pocket and checked it against the clock. "All right. Nine twenty-five. It's clear he's not coming, Lauchlan. Well, he wouldn't be the first client I've had that lost his nerve."

"Look — I'm absolutely convinced that he intended to meet us here. I just hope nothing has happened to him."

"Well, we're not going to solve anything by standing here. I've got to get to the office. You're in his confidence. Maybe you can find him and sort this out. Tell him I'm ready to act for him but I've got to know the facts."

"I will. I'll let you know as soon as I find him."

They shook hands again and Jessup started up the street, stopped and turned. "Oh. There was one other thing. Also very strange. There's a coat that he wants to give to you. He asked me to be sure to tell you. Said you've been such a help that he wants to give you this coat. He said you'd know the one he meant. No idea what I have to do with it. You don't need a lawyer to convey a coat."

"Oh, well. Thanks. Yes, it is peculiar, isn't it?" They exchanged bemused glances and then Jessup turned on his heel.

Charles began to walk toward the church. Maybe Trevor had lost his nerve. Or maybe he just needed more time to think. And the coat. How strange that with so many other things on his mind, he should be thinking about a silly coat. *You've been such a help that he wants to give you this coat.* Charles stopped in his tracks. That sounds just like an item from a will. He saw the race again and Trevor's yellow singlet receding in the distance. He had started running again himself, not even feeling the groaning in his legs.

He went first to Stobbart and Long. No one had seen Trevor since the end of the business day last evening. He hopped on the perimeter streetcar and got out at Broadway and Carlton. He was sweating now and his apprehension was growing. He rapped the door knocker at the Martland House and the emphatic sound surprised him.

"Yes, sir?"

"Oh, Hello. Ethel, isn't it?"

"Yes, sir."

"Ethel, is Trevor at home?"

"No, sir. Mr. Trevor went on a fishing holiday to the Winnipeg River."

"Really? When did he leave?"

"Early this morning, sir."

"Hmnn. Funny. Is Mrs. Martland at home?"

"No, sir. She's gone to visit friends in Portage la Prairie for a few days."

"Ah. Yes. I see. You know, Ethel. There's just one other thing that I need to see about myself." He swept confidently past her.

"Sir. I can't let you in! Wait — you can't come in, sir. Please!"

"Don't worry, Ethel. I'm sure I can find what I'm looking for." Charles was going from room to room with Ethel trailing after him, complaining piteously.

"Please, sir. I don't want to get in trouble with Mr. Martland. I need this job, sir."

"Don't you worry, Ethel. I'll find you another and that's a promise." He started taking the stairs up two at a time. In the upstairs drawing room? No. How about down this hall. He rounded the corner and found her in a pretty, screened-in sunroom. She was startled and then looked ashamed, as if she did not belong in her own house.

"Mrs. Martland. Are you all right?"

"I'm sorry, madam. I couldn't stop him."

"Never mind, Ethel. It's not your fault."

"She said you were out of town?"

"Yes. A small lie. Frank told me not to see anybody."

"Do you know where Trevor is?"

"Yes. He's gone on a fishing holiday. To the Winnipeg River. He loves fishing; it always settles his mind."

"Did you see him go? Did he say goodbye to you?"

"No. He left too early. I was still asleep. Frank told him not to wake me."

"It was Frank who told you where he went?"

"Yes. Mr. Lauchlan, what is this about? What are you trying to say?"

"Do you know where Trevor keeps his fishing gear?"

"Yes, but —"

"I want to see if it's gone. Where should I look?" He looked from Agnes to Ethel and back. Agnes paused, puzzled.

"Ethel, would you go to the basement storage cupboard and see if Mr. Trevor's fishing rod and bait box are gone?" Ethel bobbed and left.

"Thank you." Charles drew a deep breath. "I've no intention of causing distress. I just need some answers. Trevor was supposed to meet me at nine this morning. Don't you think that's a little strange? To suddenly leave like that?"

"Well, yes. It was sudden. If you must know, Frank and Trevor had an argument about the business. It was quite heated. Frank told me that he wants Trevor to go to Chicago to learn the real estate business after he joins the bar. Trevor doesn't want to go. I think it may have something to do with that girl, the Skene girl. Frank thought he needed to go somewhere to cool off, have some time to think."

"And you believe this story?"

"Of course. Why shouldn't I?"

"Look, Mrs. Martland — Agnes — I don't believe that Trevor has gone fishing and I'm concerned for your safety. Come with me now. I'll take you to Mrs. Cliffe's. You can have a bag packed in five minutes —"

There was sudden heat in her face. "Mr. Lauchlan, my husband is not a perfect man, far from it. But he would never lie to me about Trevor. He adores Trevor. He doesn't care what he does to me but he loves that boy. It's been the only thing keeping me sane. I know that he would never harm Trevor. Please go away now."

"Madam?" Ethel had returned.

"Yes, Ethel?"

"I looked where you said. Mr. Trevor's fishing rod and his bait box and his oilskins and boots are all gone — and the old jacket that used to be Mr. Martland's."

Agnes could not help but show her relief. "Thank you, Ethel. You can go now. You see? I'm sure that Trevor will be back in a few days and he'll work things out with his father. Trevor knows how to handle Frank. I've never found the knack."

Charles was momentarily flummoxed. "There's something not right about this. I don't know what's happening but I do know it's dangerous for you to stay here."

"I know you only want to help me. But please go now. It only complicates things when I have to explain to Frank."

"Explain what to Frank, my dear?" He was standing in the entrance to the sun-room. Neither of them had heard him coming. "Explain how I found you and Lauchlan together. How he barged into this house on false pretences? How I found the two of you, practically in my own bedroom?" His voice was level; he could have been describing what he'd had for breakfast.

But Charles was not calm. "Mr. Martland, suppose you explain something to me. Where is Trevor?"

Martland gave him a look, as if he were a horse fly. "Everywhere I go, Lauchlan, there you are. Poking into my business and now poking my wife."

"That is an outrageous accusation —" Before he could finish he was suddenly bent double, clutching his belly and wondering why his lungs had suddenly lost the knack of breathing.

"No, Frank, please —"

"Stay out of it." Martland grabbed hold of Charles's coat collar and dragged him out into the hallway and toward the stairway. Charles made to catch one of Martland's legs and upend him but he missed and Martland dragged him down the stairs on his knees. At the bottom of the stairs, Martland slammed him against the wall and forced Charles to look him in the eye. The mask of detachment had slipped; leaving a face filled with such a venomous mix of cruelty and exultation that Charles shut his eyes rather than see it.

"Go to the police if you like, Lauchlan. Caught you making love to my wife. Gave you a Goddamned thrashing. Threw you out of my house as any righteous husband would. A reputation for interfering with married women might pose certain difficulties for you, wouldn't you say?" Each of these sentences had been punctuated by slamming Charles against the wall.

"You'll find the police a little doubtful about your story. *Slam.* My word against yours. *Slam.* And I can back up my words. *Slam.* My wife will say what I tell her to say if she knows what's good for her. *Slam.* Here. I'm going to throw you out the back door — for the sake of my wife's reputation, not yours." This time he concluded with the kind of left upper-cut and right cross that nothing in Charles's career as an instructor in the Boy's Boxing Club had prepared him for. The hallway lamp shattered into a thousand, million pieces, all brightly coloured; a crazed hurdy-gurdy played fast and then very slow. Happily, he was not quite conscious for the final ignominious heave down the back yard steps.

37.

"Are you saying that Martland would kidnap his own son in order to prevent him revealing details of a fraud?" The chief got up from behind his desk and began to pace.

"Yes." Charles was holding a piece of ice wrapped in a tea towel against his jaw.

"And that the younger Martland was going to, in effect, turn his father in?"

"Yes, that's pretty much it. And this adultery story is a bit of blackmail to prevent me from coming to you."

Sergeant Setter sat hunched over beside Charles, taking notes in a tiny hand while Inspector Crossin, seated on the other side of Charles, frowned and tapped his right foot to an erratic rhythm only he could hear.

"Have you seen proof of this? Did you read the papers in that package?" The chief had narrowed his eyes.

"Well, no. I had no right to read them. I gave the package back unopened." More frowns.

"Will Mrs. Martland corroborate your story?"

Now it was Charles's turn to frown and shift uncomfortably. "No. She believes that Trevor is off fishing. And as for the … the other, Martland will force her to lie about it."

"And you were there with her when Martland came in."

"Yes, but —"

"And the maid found that young Martland's fishing gear was gone."

"Yes, but it's not hard to —"

There was a knock at the door. "Come in," the chief said, and Constable Smithers poked his head around the door.

"Yes?"

"I've just talked to the ticket office at the railway station, sir."

"And?"

"The girl on duty in the booth this morning said that a man matching the description of Trevor Martland and carrying fishing tackle bought a ticket to Rat Portage — for the seven-thirty train."

The chief thanked Smithers, who cast a questioning look at Setter. Setter shook his head without speaking; his lips in a firm line, and Smithers withdrew. Charles felt the sand under his feet percolating away.

"Now look, Chief. Trevor Martland has evidence of a serious defalcation of funds and he was going to present that evidence to you this morning. I'm convinced that his father or someone in Martland's pay prevented him from coming here. Quite apart from anything else, I'm afraid for Trevor's safety."

The chief walked to the window and stood looking out while the clock on the mantelpiece tick-tocked into the silence.

Finally he turned around. "It comes down to this, Lauchlan. I can't order a fraud and kidnapping investigation against one of the most prominent men in town without something more solid than what you've just told me. It's as flimsy as a grass hut in a hurricane. You can see that, can't you?"

Setter, who was hunched even lower over his notes now,

jerked his head up as if it were pulled by a string and opened his mouth. And then closed it when he saw Crossin scowling at him.

"I don't have proof in my hands," said Charles, "but if you'll only look into it, a young man's life may —"

"Well, as for young Martland, I don't doubt he's had some differences with his father. Most sons do. But his father said he's gone fishing to cool off and that's apparently where he's gone. I don't think we want police mixing in a family matter."

"Look, I agree that from your point of view this may seem preposterous —"

"I think, with time, it will seem that way to you, too." The chief came around his desk and sat down on it in front of Charles. "You've taken quite a beating. I feel sore just looking at you. It's hard to think clearly at those times. But we're all men here and Agnes Martland is a beautiful woman. Easy to lose your head. Go home. Soak your bruises in Epsom salts. And as for the assault, I can't allow you to risk your reputation in open court. In these things we have some — *ahem* — discretion." He held out his hand and Charles realized that the interview was now over.

He said nothing but rose stiffly from his chair and handed the towel, now dripping, to Setter and thanked him for it. The way things had gone, he hadn't even had a chance to talk about his suspicions about what really happened to Asseltine. Why hadn't Setter said anything about that? Surely he of all people could see that there might well be a connection between the fraud and Asseltine's death. He tried to catch the sergeant's eye, but Setter was looking down at the sodden towel and doing something funny with his jaw muscles. No help from that quarter. Charles mumbled a farewell and left the office.

The chief returned to the window, scratching the back of his head. Crossin shambled to his feet and Setter followed suit.

"Poor man took quite a hiding. He certainly didn't make that part of it up," said Crossin.

"Damn it, Crossin! I can't open an investigation into every lunatic story that walks in this door. I won't expose this department to ridicule. Martland may cut it a little fine sometimes — what man of business doesn't from time to time? — but he's done good things in this city and I won't meddle with him on the word of someone who may just be smearing him to save his own neck."

"Quite agree, sir. But somehow Lauchlan doesn't strike me as that type."

"And — for God's sake, sir!" Setter burst out, "shouldn't we at least do some —"

"Some further work on the Bank of Hamilton robbery," Crossin cut in, grabbing Setter by the arm and pulling him toward the door. "Yes, indeed, Sergeant. That's just what we'll do, and let the chief get back to more pressing matters."

He shoved Setter out the door in front of him, strode through it himself and with an acknowledgement to the chief pulled the door shut.

"The man's a —" But before Setter could finish, Crossin propelled him into the bathroom across the hall. Constable Hickley was just buttoning his fly at the urinal.

"Out!" said Crossin and Hickley, grabbing his helmet, ran for the door.

Crossin bolted the door and turned back to Setter. "Now," he said, straining to keep his voice low. "Don't be so hard on the chief because he's being over cautious."

"Over cautious! He's blind! Or worse."

"Chief's got to answer to the mayor same as I have to answer to the chief. It's a damn ticklish dance we're doing —"

"But —"

"And the last thing we need is to provoke him into giving us a direct order not to investigate further."

"But, don't you see, we have to look into what Lauchlan said today —"

"I didn't hear that."

"I said —"

"No, you see. I've got this hearing problem. Comes and goes. Damndest thing."

Setter couldn't figure out why Crossin was poking him in the chest insistently while he was saying this. "What are you —"

"Really. Mrs. Crossin wants me to have it seen to. So you'd best not say anything else that I'm not going to hear." Crossin raised his eyebrows in an interrogative fashion and gave a final poke to Setter's chest.

"Oh, I see," Setter said, exhaling with relief. "I think I understand. About your hearing problem, that is."

Crossin nodded and smiled.

38.

It was a relief to Charles that it was Maggie who opened the door. The smile died on her face when she saw his swollen jaw.

"Charles! What happened?"

"Shhsh. I'm all right." He covered her mouth, moved her and himself into the hallway and shut the door.

"I'm all right." He took his hand away. "Where is everyone?"

She placed her hand on his face. "Father's still at the college and Aunt Jessie is at her knitting circle. Oh, it looks sore."

He placed his own hand over hers for just a moment, then pulled her hand gently away. "Good. No one else home. As for this —" pointing at the livid bruise and swelling on his jaw. "The story — for now — is that I fell off the scaffolding at the church."

"But that's not what really happened?"

"No. Look, there may be some rumours — ugly ones, I warn you. But they're not true, I swear."

"Tell me. Come and sit down."

"No. It might be best if we moved out to the verandah where people can see us." When they got to the verandah, he settled on the step below hers with some difficulty and tilted his hat so that his face wouldn't be so visible from the street. "Try to look as if I'm telling you about the ice cream social."

"Are fisticuffs now part of the fun at the ice cream social?"

"No jokes. Hurts my face."

She made cooing sympathy noises that threatened to undo him. Until this moment he had been able to keep a lid on the caustic anger and humiliation over what Martland had done to him. Now all he wanted was to crush her in his arms and take refuge in the sweet comfort she offered. That could not happen so, under cover of fumbling with his handkerchief and wiping his brow, he mounted a struggle to compose himself.

Then he told her everything: about the fraud, about the race, about Trevor not turning up to meet him that morning, about the run-in with Martland. He had to swallow a few times before he spit out the part about Agnes, the thing that Martland had said.

"Promise you won't go anywhere near him again. Promise!"

"I can't —"

"And Trevor …"

Everything in that sharp intake of breath told him that there were fearful images in her mind.

"Where is he?"

"I don't know," he said. "I hoped you might. Has he talked to you since the race last night? Did he mention anything about going on a fishing holiday?"

"No. Nothing. I was expecting him to be at the prize giving but he wasn't there. And then he wasn't here when I got home, either."

"I think he left before the prize giving to shake Eklund off his trail. Then he must have gone to Jessup's apartment."

"Jessup?"

"Yes. He told Jessup he needed a lawyer and that Jessup

was to meet us at Dingwall's this morning and go with us to the police station."

"But if his father committed the crime, why would Trevor need a lawyer?"

"Trevor is an officer in the company so he may be implicated, I suppose. But he wouldn't tell Jessup any of the particulars. It was all very odd. Jessup told me another funny thing."

"What?"

"Trevor said that Jessup was to make sure I got that old driving coat. He was apparently very insistent that I should have that coat."

"That's a strange thing to be arranging when his whole world is crumbling about his ears."

"That's what I thought, too." Charles furrowed his brow and absently ran his hand over his misshapen jaw. Their eyes met.

"Charles?"

"I'm going to get that coat."

"I'm coming with you."

She was ready to insist on the point but he only looked at her for an instant and said, "Then hurry."

She ran in to scrawl a note to her aunt to tell her not to wait supper for her. When she reappeared she was dressed in her second best hat, a cream coloured straw boater with a trailing blue ribbon, and a paisley-patterned cotton shawl in case the evening should turn cool.

It didn't take them long to walk through the late afternoon light to the Macpherson Stables. The stable hand recognized Charles from two nights before and accepted his story readily enough about having dropped something in Daisy's stall. Charles and Maggie walked down the centre aisle of the stables, trying to adjust their eyes to the lower light. When they got to the stall, Maggie ran her hand down Daisy's nose and produced some sugar cubes from her bag. Charles looked the coat over as it hung from its pegs, and stood back.

"All right. What is it about this coat?" He began to search through the pockets.

"Anything there?"

Charles enumerated the items as he put them into her hands. "Three tooth picks ... a pair of collar studs ... a handkerchief ... stub end of a pencil ... candy wrapper ... and a golf tee."

"Are there any inside pockets?"

"Yes. Wait. Here's something."

"A key?"

"That's funny. It looks like — Ah!" He waved it in front of her eyes. "Come on. We have to get there before they close."

They took the streetcar on Broadway for more speed and arrived at the door of the YMCA building just as the janitor was turning the key in the lock. They rapped on the door and called to him but he looked dubiously at Charles and began walking away.

Maggie rapped frantically. "Sir? Sir, please! Just a moment."

The janitor returned and squinted at her. She smiled winningly. He unlocked the door.

"Thank you! Thank you so much. My brother here was just refereeing the junior boy's lacrosse match, as you can see. No. He can't talk, poor man, but there is some liniment in his locker, if he could just go in and fetch it? Oh, thank you. That's very kind of you."

Charles tipped his hat to the janitor and disappeared into the locker room while Maggie entertained the janitor with the highlights of the lacrosse match. After a short while Charles reappeared, took Maggie's arm, tipped his hat again to the janitor and steered her out the door.

"Was it there?"

Charles answered by patting a bulge in his jacket.

"What now?"

He looked furtively up and down the street. "I need to put it somewhere less obvious. Put on your shawl."

"What? Oh, I see." She untied her shawl from the handle of her handbag and made a great swirling to-do about putting it around her shoulders. Under cover of this manoeuvre, Charles took the package and stuffed it down the back of his trousers.

"We're really quite good at this," she said. "Maybe we should become professional footpads."

"Yes, and why not? If Martland has his way I'll be out of a job anyway. Now, if I'm right, Trevor wouldn't have left me the key if he didn't intend me to read the contents. Where can we go that's quiet, where we won't be noticed?"

Maggie thought and looked around. "What about the chemistry laboratory?" She looked at her watch. "It'll be quiet. The afternoon classes are over and the evening classes don't start till seven."

The building housing the university laboratories was a short walk away. The chemistry laboratory was deserted and the assembled apparatus burped and dripped without an audience. Charles installed himself at Maggie's section of the bench while she stood at the open door surveying the hallway in case someone should come in their direction. If that happened, Charles was to dump the contents of the package into the drawer under the bench and pretend to be mesmerized by Maggie's explanation of her current experiment. But luck was with them and Charles had a stretch of over twenty minutes to sift through what looked like a wide assortment of papers. Maggie grew restless after ten.

"Well?"

"In a minute. I'll tell you in a minute."

After ten more agonizing minutes passed. "Well?"

"Right." He gave one last look at a sheet of onion-skin paper and started stuffing the material back in its envelope. "There are records of investments from several New York brokerage houses. Copies of telegrams with buy and sell orders. Also invoices from suppliers related to the hotel project. And an account book. The invoices are posted to the accounts in the book and there's a section for the investments, too. What we've got here, I think, is a separate set of accounts from the regular Martland and Asseltine books."

"So you think Trevor was right?"

"I'm no accountant, but that's the way it looks to me. Now we have to decide what to do next."

Maggie decided that such decisions should not be made on an empty stomach. They chose a small café run by a German family tucked away on a short street near the market. As they settled in at a table with a rough linen tablecloth, Charles kept an eye on the door of the café while Maggie bantered away in German with the waiter, who seemed quite charmed at these halting attempts and went off to give their orders to the cook.

Maggie took off her hat and sat with it on her lap, spearing it with her hat pins while she talked.

"I think I'd better take the papers to the police after supper," Charles said.

"I suppose so. They'll have to believe you now that we have proof. But what about Trevor? We have to look for him. We can't just leave it to the police."

"We'll work out a plan. And we'll find him." He tried to sound reassuring.

"But I don't even know where to begin. How are we going to find him if they took him to Rat Portage?" She fretted at the ribbons on her hat. "I suppose we should start at the last place someone saw him."

"The station, you mean? Yes. I wish we knew who was with him. I can't think that he went on that train willingly."

"Wait! Mrs. Morosnick."

Charles looked around. "Is she here?"

"No, silly. Mrs. Morosnick works nights as a cleaner at the railway station. And she would recognize Trevor because he came to pick me up at the church last month when we were sorting clothes and she teased him. Maybe she can tell us who was with Trevor when he boarded the train."

"Do you know where she lives?"

"Yes, on Gertie Street next to the dairy."

"Right, soon as we finish here, I'll take the papers to the police and you can visit Mrs. Morosnick."

It was all settled and they tucked into their bratwurst and red cabbage with a will. He was glad she was going off on this errand. Martland seemed to be capable of anything and Charles didn't want her to be too closely associated with what he was about to do. He saw Maggie onto the streetcar to Mrs. Morosnick's with strict instructions to stick to well-lit streets where other people were walking. She agreed to meet him at the church at 9:30 p.m. and he would walk her home. Then he set out for the Central Police station.

He wasn't looking forward much to the return visit and so he took the long route in order to think out the best way to present this new information. Would the contents of the manila envelope be enough to overcome the chief's skepticism? While stewing over this he came to the Willow Book Shop. He could never pass by a bookstore without at least looking at the display in the window. Here were the latest in romance novels and a handsome edition of Browning's poems. He was mentally working out whether he could afford the Browning when out of the corner of his eye he noticed that a man in a grey cloth cap some distance behind him had also stopped and was now lighting a cigar. Charles began walking again and so did the man. Glancing over his shoulder, Charles rationalized that it must be just a coincidence, that he was simply feeling skittish. He decided to turn at the next corner just for reassurance.

Grey Cap turned as well and seemed to be closing the distance between them. Charles saw a back alley, turned into it sharply and quickened his pace to a trot. Grey Cap followed. Now absolute, white hot, searing rage banished thoughts of evading capture. Charles broke into a full run and pulled ahead of his pursuer. Then he turned a corner and lunged into a narrow space between buildings. Grey Cap ran by and immediately Charles hurtled off after him propelled by all the venom he had stored up to direct at Frank Martland. *Now how do you like it?* Grey Cap, caught off balance, reached the mouth of the alley and looked around to see a demented clergyman with bared teeth in his grotesque face coming at him like a rocket. He bolted.

Charles chased him toward the next intersection. The small part of his mind not consumed with bloody revenge registered first, the sound of brass instruments, then the tune: "Stand up! Stand up for Jesus." As he followed Grey Cap around a corner the sound exploded. Grey Cap darted across the street inches in front of the tambourines. Charles tried to follow but was immediately caught up in a confused welter of marching navy serge, tubas, euphoniums and stiff-visored bonnets trimmed with red. A trombone slide grazed his nose and tweaked it on the pull-back, then the bass drum loomed in front of him and he lost sight of Grey Cap entirely.

"Sing with us, brother! You look as if you could use it."

Someone pressed a hymn sheet into his hand and then what hearing he retained was blown out by the stentorian baritone beside him. He was borne along, unwillingly part of this raucous centipede, until it spit him out on the other side half a block from where he had last seen Grey Cap. As he looked frantically to right and left, someone bumped into him from the back, shoving him forward.

"Sorry! Did you see where he went?" Setter said, gasping for air. "Oh, hang it! No point now. Gone down some rat hole."

Charles bent forward, winded himself, sucking great lungfuls with his hands on his knees.

"All right, Lauchlan?" Setter was fanning himself with his hat. "Quite the turnaround. When I first saw him he was chasing you."

"I'd have caught the blasted fellow, too. Except for divine intervention." He saw Setter's wry smile. "Yes, all right. Lost my temper. But I would at least like to have gotten some information out of him."

"Recognize him? Any idea what he wanted?"

"Never saw him before. But — hold on, I think this may have something to do with it." He was trying to extricate the papers, which with all the exertion had worked their way some distance down the back of his trousers. "Where'd you come from, anyway?" He inspected the package for damage.

"Been trying to find you. Conscience bothering me. What's that you've got?"

"This — believe it or not — is the package Trevor was going to show you this morning."

"Well, I'll be damned. Where did you get it?"

Charles explained about the key and described the contents of the envelope.

"If we can go to your office, you can look them over."

"No."

"No? No! I just risked life and limb to get these to you, you know. The least you could do is look at them, for pity's sake."

"I know, I know. That was what I wanted to explain to you — why it was I couldn't lend you a hand with the chief today."

"Well, I certainly could have used one. But I thought you didn't believe me — like the others."

"Not at all. We — the inspector and I — thought there was definitely something to your story."

"Well, why the devil didn't either of you speak up?"

Setter pushed his fingers slowly through his hair, pulling it off his forehead, and looked past Charles to a point down the street. "The thing is, it's pretty clear the chief is seeing this case from a particular point of view — and he seems blind to any other view."

"What do you mean?"

"Just before you arrived at the police station this afternoon, I saw Frank Martland leaving the chief's office."

39.

Smithers was taking his turn on the night desk, something he didn't mind since it allowed him time to catch up on his assignments. At Sergeant Setter's suggestion, he was taking classes two nights a week to gain his senior matriculation certificate. Nellie was proud of him but it meant he was only able to see her on Sundays. Just as he was counting out the scansion on *Horatius at the Bridge*, the front door of the station flew open and banged against the door stop. Rosetta Cliffe appeared in the doorway and called back to someone as yet unseen.

"Don't hang back, Mr. Fescue. This will only take a minute." She held the door open.

"But — Mrs. Cliffe — it's the police station. Would it be too much trouble to tell me what in hell we're doing here?"

"Everything will become clear very soon, Mr. Fescue. Now please just come in. We haven't a moment to lose."

A young man with dark curls falling into his eyes stalked through the door and followed Rosetta up the steps to the night desk looking equal parts exasperated and wary.

"Mrs. Cliffe? Good evening. What brings you here?"

Smithers took in the thin young man outfitted in a floppy bow tie and a vest in a contrasting colour to his jacket. The whole effect was pleasing though it became apparent that the clothes had not been intended to be worn together and that his shirt was on the edge of threadbare.

"Good evening, Constable," Rosetta said. "Is Sergeant Setter here?"

"He was, but I'm afraid he's gone out. Can I help?"

"I hope so. This is Desmond Fescue. He does artwork for me when I need it. Lettering, background painting, and layouts — that sort of thing."

"I am a professional artist, Constable," Fescue said. "A painter."

"You mean — like, painting pictures?"

"Yes. I mean painting pictures, though in this miserable backwater no one would know a good painting from a sack of flour and I've had no commissions — unless you count the portrait I made of Homer Allison's prize sow." He swept his hand toward Rosetta. "Hence my resorting to Mrs. Cliffe's soul-destroying piece work." He added, with a sigh, after Rosetta had glowered at him. "Which, nevertheless, has been most welcome."

"Pleased to meet you, Mr. Fescue. Has there been some difficulty? Do you want to report a crime?"

"Not in the least, Constable," said Rosetta. "Look at his jacket."

"What, oh! My lord. Where? — Just a minute. Mrs. Cliffe, take him into Sergeant Setter's office, just there, around the corner — and don't let him get away."

"Now, wait a minute. I've done nothing wrong. I protest this violation of my rights as a British subject —"

"Oh, for heaven's sake, Fescue. We're not arresting you. Just your jacket. Now come along." Rosetta took Fescue by the arm and led him, still protesting, down the hall to the small office Smithers shared with Sergeant Setter.

Smithers ran around the end of the counter, shouting, "Archie? Archie! Come up here and take the desk for a minute, will you?" There was a faint acknowledgement from the basement and Smithers joined Fescue and Rosetta in the cramped office.

"Right. Let me see them up close." Smithers sat on the edge of Setter's desk and grabbed the front of Fescue's jacket, pulling him forward in his chair. Smithers stared intently at the buttons. "Mrs. Cliffe — centre drawer of the sergeant's desk — could you fetch me the picture?"

Rosetta pulled open the desk drawer, scrabbled around briefly, and came back with her own photograph. Smithers held the photograph up against one of the buttons on the jacket.

"It's perfect, isn't it?" Rosetta said. "It's a perfect match. And see, there's one missing on the cuff. Imagine my luck. He just came walking into my shop."

"Look. I didn't steal it, if that's what you're implying."

"Mr. Fescue. This is very important." Smithers still had him by the lapels. "When did you come by this jacket?"

"Whose bloody business is it of yours when I got it? And while you're at it, let go of my damn lapels!" Smithers let go and Fescue sat back in his chair, pulling his jacket back into shape.

"Mr. Fescue," Smithers said. "Your answers to these questions may make the difference between a man hanging or going free. Now, what do you say? Tell us when, how and where you came by this jacket."

"Well, why didn't you say that in the first place, Constable." He gave a final tug to the sleeves of his jacket and adjusted his bow tie. He looked around the office. "I just hope my old mother in Lincolnshire never has to hear about how I was forced to admit to wearing another man's cast-off clothes."

"Come to the point!" Rosetta cast her eyes to the ceiling.

"Very well. Just because a man is down on his luck doesn't mean he can't present a dashing figure to the world. I've made it my business to know where the finest second-hand apparel can be found. On Mondays, they always have fresh things at the church and on my regular pass through there yesterday, I found this — if I may say — very stylish coat there."

"Which church?"

"Dufferin Avenue Presbyterian," Rosetta said, in triumph. "It's Mr. Lauchlan's church."

"Well, what do you know!" Smithers rose from Setter's desk with a small, excited, hop. "I wonder if they keep track of where their used clothing comes from?"

"The only way to find out is to go to the church," Rosetta said. "Pity it's so late. I suppose it will have to keep until the morning."

"No it won't. Mr. Lauchlan is living at the church while he's minding McEvoy. I'll go right away." He grabbed Rosetta's hand and shook it vigorously. "Mrs. Cliffe — on behalf of Sergeant Setter and myself — you've been a great help and I thank you most sincerely. And Mr. Fescue. My thanks as well."

Fescue gave a bemused smile, which faded when Smithers began to strip him of the jacket. "Hey!"

"Sorry, sir. But I'll need to take this with me."

40.

Charles and Peter busied themselves making tea and toast, trying to create as little noise as possible in the high-ceilinged church kitchen while Setter sat at the kitchen table, engrossed in the contents of the manila envelope. Occasionally Setter made a slight "ah" noise or a "ha" and a brief nod to himself as he turned the pages of the account book and ran his finger down them, matching the loose sheets to the small, neat entries. Then he closed the account book, arranged the papers into a tidy sheaf and stuffed them back into the envelope.

Charles and Peter sat down with their mugs and waited for Setter to speak.

"Yes, well." He patted the envelope. "Looks genuine — and if an accountant confirms our suspicions — definitely incriminating. Martland would have every reason to try to prevent us from seeing this."

"And every reason to get rid of his partner, too," Charles said.

Setter sat back in his chair, tilted his head to one side and looked at Charles through half-closed eyes. "Now. What makes you say that?"

"Well, put two and two together," Charles said, pulling his

chair closer. "Asseltine and Martland hadn't been on the best of terms for some time. Add to that the fact that Asseltine was drinking and gambling more. What if he inadvertently disclosed something about the fraud?"

"Well, yes, Asseltine was probably worrying Martland, but — how do you know all that?"

"Well, um. I made a — sort of — condolence call on Mrs. Asseltine — while she was at her husband's office," Charles tried not to blush, but that made it worse, " — and it just came out that there was some kind of friction between Asseltine and Martland. I think Asseltine was afraid Martland was trying to force him out."

"This came out during a condolence call?" said Setter. "You might have told me, you know."

"I was busy being beaten to a pulp. And your attitude in the chief's office was not encouraging of further disclosures."

"All right, all right." Setter put up his hands. "You have a point. I wish I knew what the woman is playing at, that's all. You say she was at the office? What was she doing there?"

"Checking through the books of Martland and Asseltine with the finest of tooth combs, apparently. And I can tell you, Martland doesn't like it one bit."

"You saw him, too?" Setter ground his teeth.

"But wait a minute," Peter said. "If Martland was trying to force Asseltine out of the company wouldn't Asseltine go right to the police with evidence of the fraud?"

"That's what I've been wondering about," said Setter. "But Asseltine would have to incriminate himself in the process. Maybe that was Martland's little insurance policy. Maybe he was just trying to force Asseltine into a more minor role — you know — trying to limit his ability to give the game away. Asseltine wouldn't have much leverage to prevent it."

"But it would be so much tidier and surer to kill Asseltine

outright, don't you think?" Charles gave a flourish with his hands, setting the scene. "I can see how he did it. He has Asseltine watched. Martland knows the drill; he knows that Asseltine needs to get into the safe in his office to pay off some card sharpie. All Martland has to do is get to Asseltine before said sharpie arrives. Bob's your uncle, Pete turns up right on schedule to take the blame."

"Yes, that's right. It makes perfect sense," Peter said.

"And after what Martland did to me — and other things he's done — why would he stop at murder, if the stakes were high enough?" Charles said.

"Well, yes, but ..." Setter sat back in his chair and pulled at his collar where it irritated the skin of his neck. "The problem is, I don't think that Asseltine was deliberately killed. I didn't think so that night when I saw his body. And I don't think so now. It just doesn't —"

Before Setter could finish, there was the sound of a door slamming and footsteps in the hall.

"Charles? Where are you?"

"We're in the kitchen."

Her voice preceded her into the room. "Wait till you hear. It wasn't Trevor! He wasn't on that train — oh? Sergeant?"

Setter got up and nodded in her direction. "Miss Skene, hello."

"Setter's been reading the papers — and we've figured it all out. Pete's off the hook for sure!" Charles was giddy and swept her off her feet, twirling her around. Peter and Setter watched them, Peter with a small, nervous smile. It didn't take long for the larger view of things to settle back in like a chilling mist. Charles spun out his theory for her.

"Then it was Mr. Martland that Peter heard before he went into the office?" Maggie said.

"I think so," said Charles. "Asseltine must have put up quite a struggle."

Setter started to say something but Charles cut him off. "What did you say when you came in? What did Mrs. Morosnick say?"

"She said that a man got on the train for Rat Portage with fishing gear but it wasn't Trevor."

"Would she recognize him? Was she sure?" Setter piped up.

"Yes. Completely sure. She's met Trevor."

"Then he's likely still here in town."

"Oh, Charles." Maggie put her hand to her mouth. "On the promenade. Mr. Martland must have suspected that Trevor knew something about the murder! That's why he was interested in whether Trevor was with me that night. We have to find Trevor right now!"

"What did you tell him?" It was Setter.

"What? Who?"

"Martland. Was Trevor with you that night?"

"No. At first Mr. Martland thought that he was, but I told him he wasn't."

"And that was the truth?"

"Of course! Don't you see that we have to find Trevor right away!"

Charles grabbed her hand. "We'll find him. Won't we, Setter?"

Setter did not answer right away. He had pulled out his watch and was cleaning imaginary dirt off its face with his thumb.

"Setter?"

Setter suddenly came to life and shoved the watch back into his vest pocket. "I've got to go back to the station and organize a search party. Chief be damned. You three will stay out of it and leave it to me. This is still police business." He put his hat firmly on his head and as he was walking by Maggie, he paused and said, quietly. "Try not to worry. We'll find him. I was never so sure of anything in my life." He marched down the hallway with the envelope under his arm and called back, "I'll send word when I know something."

The three left in the kitchen felt suddenly like actors dressed for a performance that have just been told the production is cancelled.

"Look, there's nothing more we can do tonight. You heard Setter. It's for the best that the police are taking over now," Charles said.

"But suppose he can't manage a proper search?" said Maggie. "Suppose he can't get enough men? The police have other things to do besides this case. I still think we should be doing something."

"But they know how to do these things and they've got warrants to give them legal access. They'll find him faster than we would."

"I have to hope so," said Peter. "Imagine. Me urging the police on." He made a face. "But it's my only chance, isn't it? If they find Trevor and make Martland talk, I could be in the clear."

"I think Setter's going to be able to make a case against Martland, Pete. We've got a lot of hope tonight that we didn't have yesterday." He patted Peter on the shoulder. "Could you lock up, while I walk Maggie home?"

"Right. Of course."

Maggie was not totally convinced but she put on her shawl and seemed resigned to being walked home. Just as Charles was putting on his jacket, there was a pounding noise, insistent, echoing throughout the wooden building.

They hurried down the hall and through the door to the sanctuary. The noise was coming from the front doors of the church. Charles threw the bolt on the middle door and opened it cautiously.

"Yes? Who's there? Can I help you?"

He saw a solitary woman in a plain dress, carrying a small leather valise. She was in shadow.

"Mr. Lauchlan. You've got to help me. Please."

"Mrs. Martland!"

"Please, you have to help me find him."

"Come in. Come in and sit down." He took her arm and gently pulled her through the door, and led her through the narthex and into the sanctuary. She sank down on a pew. Charles lit one of the gaslights. As he adjusted the flame, her face was revealed.

"Oh!" Maggie said and came to sit by her.

"Mrs. Martland, what's happened?"

Whatever fury had possessed her outside the church now seemed to die away. She seemed wary of the light. One of her eyes was blackened and there was a fresh cut on her lip.

Her voice was flat. "I'm sure he's there. I know Frank is holding him there."

"Trevor?"

"How could I have believed him? I've been living in a fool's paradise, I'll never forgive myself."

"'Believed him'? Mrs. Martland, do you know where Trevor is?"

"I offered up my suffering to God as a sacrifice. But He turned away from me." She hid her face with her hands.

Charles grabbed her by the shoulders, turned her toward him and gave her a shake. "Agnes! Look at me. Tell me where Trevor is."

She looked at Charles as if from a long distance away, and tried to focus on him. "At the millwork shops — Bainbridge Millworks. Frank's company owns it."

"Are you sure that Trevor is there?"

"Yes. Tonight after dinner I heard Frank asking cook to pack up some food. For a sick friend, he said." She gave a small sniff of derision. "Frank has no real friends let alone sick ones. I knew right then. So many lies I've swallowed. I'm choking on them."

Charles had to turn her face toward him again. "But how did you find out where Trevor was?"

"After that I listened outside the library door. Frank was having a telephone conversation with one of his men. He said, 'Make sure that Bainbridge stays down in his office.' So I knew it had to be the millwork factory. I waited until Frank left the house. Then I packed a bag and came straight here."

"I'm taking you to Mrs. Cliffe's."

"No! You have to go and help Trevor!" She was suddenly fierce again.

"We'll get word to the police —"

"There's no time. You — please! You have to go right away."

"All right, Agnes. All right. I'll go."

She grabbed his hand. "Please. Please go now. Frank is not himself. I don't know what he may do."

"Maggie can you take Mrs. Martland to Rosetta's?"

"I'll get her settled at Mrs. Cliffe's. We can send over for her things in the morning," Maggie said.

"No," Agnes said flatly. "No. I will not take one more thing of his."

They did not argue with her. "I'll hire a cab for you and Mrs. Martland from Krafştadt's. You can fix her a cup of tea while you wait." Maggie helped Agnes out to the kitchen.

Charles called after her. "Make the cabman wait for you at Mrs. Cliffe's. When she's settled, take the cab home. I'll send word to both of you the moment I know something."

"You promise? No matter how late?"

"No matter how late."

Peter turned to Charles and said in a hushed voice, "We should get word to Setter somehow. He only left ten minutes ago. I can find him if I go right away."

"No. You'll break your curfew. I'll telephone the police station from Krafstadt's."

"Waiting till you can get to Kraftstadt's just wastes time. If I run, I can catch up to Setter. And as for my bail conditions, they may not matter now."

Charles hesitated, and then nodded. "All right. When you find Setter, tell him to come to the Bainbridge Millworks with some extra men as soon as he possibly can." Their eyes met and each found on the other's face the same jumble of emotions: fear mixed up with a kind of boyish elation.

41.

The Red River is in no hurry to reach its outlet at Lake Winnipeg; it winds across the plains, cutting sweeping loops as it goes. The Bainbridge Millworks factory was built on just such a loop, a meander called Point Douglas in the very centre of the city where the land is surrounded on three sides by the river. It was close to midnight when Charles arrived at Sutherland Avenue and surveyed the Bainbridge factory from across the street. Feeling that he would be very noticeable in his clerical collar, he had changed into his work shirt, an old vest and corduroy trousers before leaving the church. He still felt rather conspicuous but there was a new building under construction behind him and he found that he could slip behind its wooden hoarding. Once there, he was hidden from the street but still able to watch the entry to the Bainbridge Millworks. The factory itself was an elongated building three storeys high made of buff-coloured brick and set back from the street by a gravelled yard. Along the ridge line of its roof there was a raised section that accommodated the steel beam on which the hoists and pulleys travelled the length of the building. If Trevor was in there, where exactly would he be? And how would he look for him without attracting a lot of notice?

He needed a plan. But something that Setter had said to Maggie was playing around in his head. Why was Setter so interested in what Martland had asked Maggie in the promenade? Martland thought Trevor was with her on the night of the murder and she said he wasn't. Martland must have gotten that idea from somewhere. From Trevor, he supposed. Well, so why would Trevor tell his father he was with Maggie if he wasn't?

Suddenly Charles said out loud. "Oh Lord! I never asked him how he got the papers!" He clamped his hand over his mouth and stayed perfectly still. With luck he was far enough away from the factory that nobody could have heard him. An abrupt hand had just scattered all the little dominoes that had been so neatly lined up in his mind. Now he had to arrange them into a new pattern, a pattern he liked much less than the first. But before he could work out all of the implications, there were sounds of men's voices across the street. He peeked out. It was a shift change at the factory.

It's a chance; I have to take it. He edged out from behind the hoarding and walked as casually as he could across the street and toward the group of about thirty men walking through the factory gate in groups of twos and threes. He attached himself to a rag tag group and walked through into the yard and then through the factory doors. Once inside he was struck by a wall of ear-shattering noise from the belt-driven lathes and planers and a fine mist of sawdust hung in the air. The men ahead of him lined up in front of the timekeeper's cage. He stopped and pretended to be reading some notices on a board by the entrance. The men who had signed in were walking into another room. He slipped past the ones still signing in and followed the others into what turned out to be a cloak room where men were changing into overalls and putting masks over their faces to protect them from the sawdust. Charles walked through that room and into an adjoining room in which there were toilets and wash basins. He went into a stall, sat down and waited. The smell made his eyes water. He tossed several scoops of red clay down the hole but that didn't help much. Soon the sounds in the room grew less as the men filed out to work. When he hadn't heard anything for about two minutes, he came out of his stall gingerly, and peeked around the corner into the change room. *Empty. Good.* He walked back into the changing area. There were overalls and masks on pegs. He grabbed a pair of overalls, stepped into them, and pulled them up over his trousers and shirt, hiking the straps over his shoulders. The mask smelled musty when he pushed it tight against his face and tightened the canvas strap at the back of his head. A pair of canvas and rubber work gloves completed the ensemble. When he looked in the mirror over the sinks, the mask with its cylindrical metal snout gave him a distinctly piglike appearance.

He took a deep breath and walked out of the cloakroom. Under cover of adjusting his mask and gloves, he tried to get his bearings. Behind the timekeeper's cage there was a counter and behind the counter an enclosed area of offices with a large window that looked out onto the factory floor. Through the window Charles could see a couple of desks, one bearing a large typewriter. There was a door marked F.C. BAINBRIDGE. High above the floor he saw hoists attached to the steel beam and pulleys hanging and a series of catwalks suspended from the roof to service the hoists. There was a kind of high mezzanine at the level of the catwalks and on this mezzanine an enclosed room with a door. An open metal stairway led up to this mezzanine.

"You!"

Charles almost leapt out of his skin. He looked around to see a burly figure with mask at half mast.

"Are you deaf? Get over there and load those balusters!"

He kept his own mask in place but nodded to the foreman, walking over to a pallet of turned balusters destined for some stairway or verandah railing farther west. The balusters were in rectangular bundles and bound by metal straps. Two other men were loading large flat dollies and Charles joined them. After his dolly was loaded he helped another man to roll it out to a loading dock at the back of the factory. This route took him past the bottom of the stairway. After two more trips all the balusters were out on the loading dock. Charles hung back as the other men returned to the floor. It was going to be hard to get up those stairs without being noticed. When he was sure the foreman wasn't looking, he sprinted up to the first landing and dropped onto his stomach. He wasn't so worried about the other men. There was solidarity in putting one over on a fore-man. There. The foreman had gone out of view behind a large lathe. Charles bounded all the way to the top of the stairs and flattened himself against the outside wall of the factory, away from the edge of the mezzanine and out of sight from the floor. He moved behind a huge spool of greasy block and tackle chain and from that vantage point was able to observe the layout of the mezzanine.

He knew that the place where Trevor was being kept was higher up than Bainbridge's office. This room seemed to fit the bill and he couldn't see any other alternatives. For fifteen min-utes he kept watch trying to think of what to do next. Suddenly the door opened and Charles had to duck down. Peeping around the side of the spool, he had to look twice to be sure. Yes. Grey Cap closed the door, and, after rolling the tobacco between fingers and thumbs he licked the cigarette paper and stuck the cigarette into the corner of his mouth. In defiance of numer-ous "No Smoking" signs posted around the factory, Grey Cap took a wooden match out of his pocket and flicked it with his thumbnail. It popped into flame and momentarily lit up his face as he turned and headed down the metal staircase.

It was then that Charles noticed that the walls of the room didn't rise all the way to the roof of the factory. He wanted a better look. By going up a metal ladder, he got onto the highest catwalk, the one up in the rafters, and from there he could easily step over onto a beam that, at the end of its span, ran along one wall of the room at ceiling height. He took his mask off, stepped over onto the beam and then lay down on top of it. The beam was coated with sawdust which made it easier to slide along. He tried not to think about the other things it was coated with. Now he was getting close. "Yes!" he whispered under his breath. The room was actually open to the factory roof. If he was careful, he would be able to look down into it. He was suddenly conscious of the fact that he could now hear himself sliding along and he stopped cold. He looked down over the edge of the mezzanine to the factory floor. All of the lathes and planers had been shut down and the men were evidently breaking them down and rubbing assorted parts with oily rags. He took a deep breath and inched closer to the wall of the room trying to make as little noise as possible. He was close enough now to lean over the edge, just far enough to see down into the interior of the room. *Oh Lord.*

42.

Trevor was sitting on a chair, his hands bound behind him and his legs tied — one to an iron pole beside the chair and the other to the chair leg. He had apparently been gagged but the gag was now loosened and hung around his neck. There was a table in front of him and Martland sat opposite him, the remains of a meal and its packaging were on the table. Charles was shocked at the change in Martland's appearance. He looked as if he had slept in his clothes. His face was flushed and the rims of his eyes were red. As Charles watched, Martland ran his hands slowly through his hair where the sawdust had settled on it like snow on straw.

"Sorry we have to keep you tied up. If I could be sure of you, I'd let you go in a minute. You know that. Don't want to make you any more uncomfortable than necessary." Martland toyed idly with the plate on the table.

Trevor opened his mouth, hesitated, but then Martland cut him off. "You know, for the life of me I can't think how you got that safe open. Did you get the combination from Joe?"

"No, no. Don't you remember? I was six or seven. You showed me how to open it when it was just new. I could have played with it for hours if you'd let me."

"You surely didn't remember the combination?"

"No. But I did remember where you hid it. The same place after more than fifteen years."

Martland looked sheepish. "That's right. That's right. I'm a man of habits. I had forgotten that. You used to visit me at the office quite often when you were a boy."

"I used to bother the staff. I knew they couldn't box my ears for it."

They both laughed.

"If I could have that night back again ..." Trevor was suddenly serious again. "I never thought Joe would be in the office at that time of night. He tried to grab the papers back from me. He had his hand around my throat. I swear, I only meant to push him off me."

"Don't trouble yourself, boy. Don't trouble yourself over the likes of Joe Asseltine. We're better off without him."

"Trouble myself? He's dead! He was your partner for twenty years for God's sake!"

"Hah! Of course." Martland was triumphant. "That's why you paid for McEvoy's lawyer, isn't it? Guilt money."

"When he walked into the office and saw me, I panicked and ran like a fool. But if you hadn't stopped me I'd have done what I should have done in the first place."

"Do you hate me so much? To ruin everything I've built for you?"

Trevor shook his head. "It would have been so much easier if I did hate you. I found a way to get you away from us, that's all. But I botched it. Too much of you in me, Father."

Martland seemed to have no answer to this. He got up from the table and used a handkerchief to wipe off his forehead. "Damned sawdust. Why Bainbridge doesn't install better vacuum catchers on those bloody machines, I don't know." He walked over and checked the knots on the ropes. "Too tight?"

Trevor said, "Yes. Why don't you untie them?"

Martland looked pained. "Not yet."

He arched his back in a stretch and Charles, looking down, caught sight of something metallic on a belt under Martland's jacket. A pistol, a revolver, in what looked like an old army-issue holster on a belt over Martland's shoulder.

"Funny, I can always think of something but now, every way I turn, I see the way barred." Martland said. "Thought I could buy some time — while you were on your fishing trip." He gave Trevor a half-hearted smile. "Persuade you to give me the papers. We could maybe have brazened it out together then. But you put paid to that, didn't you?" He rubbed his eyes. "Well. I expect the police have them by now."

"I certainly hope so."

"Now there'll be a scandal and you'll be held up to ridicule. And we'll both go to jail or worse." He screwed up his face and shook his head. "I can't let that happen. No, no. That's not for us. We need to make a clean break, you and me. I won't let them gabble at you and hurt you. It's better this way."

"What do you mean? What are you talking about? This is craziness, Father!"

But Martland didn't seem to hear that. He reached under his jacket in a distracted fashion and adjusted the holster. "Strange for there to be nothing to look forward to. I've lived all my life for the future. For your future." His face contorted, tears and sweat mixing in its knotted folds. He waged a visible struggle to hang on. After a long exhalation of air through gritted teeth, he said, "Is there anything you want? Whiskey? Maybe some brandy?"

Charles wanted to cry out. He willed Trevor to think of something, anything.

"Cigars. Those little Cuban ones." Trevor's voice shook slightly. "That's what I'd like."

Charles held his breath.

"Oh, yes. Yes. I like those, too. I've got a box at the office." Martland took out his handkerchief once more and mopped his face. "I'll just go and get Kobler to fetch them." He opened the door, closed and locked it again and Charles heard the sound of his boots on the metal staircase going down.

Charles swung off the beam and over the side of the wall in one motion. He dropped and landed nine feet below, giving at the knees and then falling over at Trevor's feet.

"Charles! God! How did you — can you untie me! Quick — he won't be gone long."

Charles worked ferociously at the knots tying Trevor's hands.

"I can't believe it. I think he's going to —"

"No, he isn't." The knots were finally loosened on Trevor's hands. He dove at the rope tying Trevor's leg to the pole while Trevor attacked the other leg. Sweat and sawdust stung his eyes. The knots were rock hard and his hands kept slipping on them.

Charles turned toward the door. "Hurry! He's —" Then everything happened at once. Martland was in the open doorway. Charles hurled himself at Martland's solar plexus and with perfect fullback technique brought him down outside the doorway of the room. They wrestled around on the floor and Charles was once again in the grip of Martland's powerful arms and shoulders. Somehow, Martland got his hand on the gun which, though Charles held the arm that held the gun, Martland began to turn, by trembling inches, in Charles's direction. With a mighty heave, Charles whipped his legs around and caught the older man by surprise. He was knocked over sideways. That momentum allowed Charles to get to his feet. He kicked at the gun and sent it skittering out of Martland's hand over toward the edge of the mezzanine where a gangway, barred by a flimsy metal gate, led out to a platform where the large roof hoist was serviced. Both men ran over to the gun but as Charles bent down to grab it, Martland kicked him in the ribs, sending him crashing through the gate and out onto the platform. Martland lumbered after him and kicked again. This blow propelled Charles right off the platform. Only his instinctive clutching at the edge saved him from falling. He hung suspended over the factory floor, kicking his leg upwards toward the edge of the platform, trying desperately to get a purchase.

Martland seemed to hesitate for a moment. He levelled the gun at Charles and their eyes met in complete wordless understanding. Charles thought, *The next thing I will feel is the bullet ripping into my brain.* He closed his eyes, *Lord, Lord, Lord ...* There was a sound above him, as of a wounded animal.

Charles unscrewed his eyes and opened them to see Trevor and his father struggling, both men red faced, groaning and heaving with the effort. Now Trevor had the gun and threw it in one perfect arc over Charles's head and into space. The force of this gesture caused Martland to overbalance backwards. There was a moment. It was just a moment when father and son hung, it seemed, perfectly counterbalancing, hanging onto each other still. And then they pitched over Charles's head, Martland first and Trevor falling after. Charles covered his ears with his extended arms.

With almost his last strength, he swung his leg up to the platform. His ankle hooked it at last. With this solid anchor, he pulled himself up enough to grab onto a metal post with his left hand and with one final effort, heave himself up onto the platform, where he lay face down and breathing hard. There was someone thundering up the stairs.

"Lauchlan! Are you all right?"

"Think so. Need to rest for a sec."

"Good, I've got to —" Setter began to get to his feet again but Charles had reached out and grabbed one of his lapels.

"Something you need to know. It was Trevor — the Asseltine thing, I mean."

"I know. Just stay here and I'll get help."

But Charles would not let him go. "It was an accident. Heard him say so. Understand?"

"Understood. That will help to clarify things." He gently detached Charles's hand.

Then he heard Setter yelling as he ran back down the stairs. "Smithers! Get to a telephone and call the hospital. Gillies, clear the van. Are there stretchers here?"

Amid shouts and counter shouts, Charles was lying still, trying to catch his breath. He could feel that place in his ribcage where Martland had kicked him and knew that feeling would soon turn into pain. His hands throbbed and his body trembled but he inched slowly forward on his belly to the edge of the platform and forced himself to look down. And then he saw her. Maggie. Her arms reached upward toward the press of men trying to extricate the bodies from the chaos of the machinery and lift them down onto some blankets laid out on the floor. She was hatless and had tied the paisley shawl around her waist. Charles got to his feet by pulling hand over hand on the guard-rail. He took a shuddering breath and then launched himself down the stairs.

43.

There was a crispness to the air when he awoke that chilled his legs where they had kicked free of the covers. When he looked out the window, Mrs. Gough's back yard looked as green and mellow in the long shadows of early morning as it had yesterday. But he knew that no matter how quickly the heavy dew burned off under the August sun, no matter how fast the return to the overripe smell of midday heat, fall had given its notice. When he walked into the dining room for breakfast, Mrs. Gough's children were full of talk about their return to school the following week. Bertie peppered Mr. Krause with questions and he, in his methodical way, was answering each in turn and ignoring interruptions. Hilda and Dottie were arguing about who had the nicest pinafore. Charles wolfed down a bowl of porridge and a mug of tea, and braving Mrs. Gough's disapproving look, wrapped a piece of toast in a napkin and put it into his pocket. As he walked down Edmonton toward Portage Avenue he tried to somehow hold on to it all: a fat bee nuzzling into the last of the roses; the pungent spice of the marigolds bruised by his heel; Chickadees pecking at seeds among the cosmos.

He no longer needed to brace himself and walk slowly to

protect the cracked ribs. They had knitted and his bruises had faded. Not so the dreams. Days would pass and sometimes a week and he would think he was over it. But then he was in that room again. The din of Martland's returning steps horribly loud and himself in a swirl of sawdust fumbling as if underwater at the rope around Trevor's leg. Or they were running through a field of longish grass, the two of them in racing singlets, and cackling like crows having left Martland far behind. Then he would wake up and it was not so.

This morning he had an appointment that he had been putting off for some time and he lingered on the sidewalk, conning the shop windows in the shade of striped awnings while the clerks in long aprons put out boxes of their wares and swept their allotted expanse of pavement. He unwrapped and ate his toast, then consulted his watch before crossing to the median to wait for the St. Boniface tram. It rumbled to a stop, took up its human cargo and rolled off down the wide, dusty avenue and then across the Red River onto the main street of the French town. He had never had much cause to come over to this side of the river and had sketched a map, which he now pulled from his pocket, in order to find which stop to ring for. His map told him that he had already gone one stop too far. He descended and walked down the busy avenue. The shop fronts bore mostly French names — Senez et Fils, Marcoux & Cie — but there was also the occasional interloper — Wong Siu Laundry. He passed two nuns in grey, pleated habits with black shoulder capes, their eyes veiled behind the jutting edges of black bonnets. A priest at the next corner with a large crucifix stuck into his sash, like a sword, hung onto his shapeless hat when a sudden gust whipped at the skirts of his cassock. The workers installing new curb stones called out to each other in French that was almost impenetrable to Charles. Then he recognized a word and smiled to himself. They knew he must be a priest of some sort — but how strange to see his legs.

Up ahead the new hospital building loomed, its solid mass balancing off against the green expanse of park and convent grounds on the opposite side of the street. Then at the end of a cul-de-sac he came to a large brick house with a mansard roof screened from the street by a tall lilac hedge and a grove of elm trees. It could have housed a large family but something about it betrayed an institutional quality. He checked the address on his map, and then made his way up the driveway to the front door. He turned the knob of a mechanical door bell under a small crucifix and heard a shrill ring echoing far back into the house.

Presently the door opened and a diminutive nun in the same brownish grey habit, black shoulder cape and black bonnet as he had seen on the street ushered him in with a murmured, *"Entrez, s'il-vous-plait. Entrez."*

"Thank you. Very kind. Do you speak English?"

The little nun looked flustered and motioned him over to a cage-like wooden screen set into the high wainscoting of the entry hall. Charles looked through the screen to see another nun of more generous proportions sitting at a desk in front of an enormous typewriting machine. She looked up from her work and squinted at him.

"Oui, monsieur? Puis-je vous aider?"

"Oui. Um. *Je veux* — ach, sorry. My French is not good."

She pushed herself up from the desk and approached the screen. "I was born in Ottawa, Father. But my English, it's not much better." She had thawed slightly but he was still an object of suspicion.

"I'm sure you're too modest, sister. And I'm not a priest." He introduced himself and stated his business. She knitted her brows for a while and then went over to a board behind her desk where several rope pulls with silk tassels were installed. She pulled one twice in rapid succession. Then she returned to the grill and spoke a few words in French to the diminutive nun.

"Sister St-Placide will take you to the parlour, Reverend. Please attend there."

When the door of the parlour closed behind Sister St-Placide, he found himself in a large, cool room where, it was soon apparent, few of the sisters were allowed to tarry. The floor had been aggressively waxed. Heavy, dark chairs of an older vintage were set opposite straight-backed settees arranged more with an appreciation for geometry than sociability. The doilies covering the chair backs were impossibly clean. There was a fireplace surrounded with green tile and above that a mahogany mantle. In the place of honour above the mantle there was an etching of Christ looking down on the room with large, liquid eyes. The figure was devoid of colour except for a red object in the middle of the chest that Charles initially took for a misshapen apple but on closer inspection turned out to be Christ's heart disconcertingly on display. Charles perched on the edge of a petit-point covered settee.

He had been there for quite a while and his mind had gone off somewhere else when the door opened and suddenly she was there.

"Mr. Lauchlan, I'm so sorry to have kept you waiting. There were the breakfast dishes to finish and then Sister Bernier needed help gathering the bed linens for the laundry."

"Mrs. Martland, good to see you." He jumped up to greet her, knocking his hat to the floor.

"It's kind of you to come all this way." She extended her hand, which almost clipped his nose as he retrieved his hat.

"Not so far, really. Just over the river." He was surprised at how red and chapped her hand was.

"I suppose it only seems far," she said, trying to decide which of the uninviting chairs to sit on.

The obligation to see her had weighed so heavily on him that he had taken any pretext to avoid it. Yet now that she was here, he didn't know quite what to say to her. He hadn't seen her since Trevor's funeral, and was surprised at her appearance: the long linen apron with fresh stains covering her simple cotton print dress, sleeves hiked and fastened above the elbow; the flat, serviceable shoes.

"Did you say you were helping out?"

"I asked Reverend Mother for some work to do. She was reluctant at first but I was quite determined. Now I work in the kitchen and help out on the wards upstairs when there are patients. Anything, really, that needs doing."

"But surely you don't need —"

"I had to, you see. I had to."

"I see. Stupid of me. Yes, under the circumstance I might do the same thing."

She seemed only just contained, running the thumb of one hand over the reddened knuckles of the other hand. "It's good that you've come," she said, looking down at the carpet. "There's something else, something you deserve to know. After all you've done for us, it would be cowardly to send a note ..."

"Yes?"

"I have returned to the Church. To my faith, I mean."

Of course; it made perfect sense. And given the surroundings it wasn't surprise he felt but recognition — that and a slight dent to his vanity. Surely if he had been a better pastor he could have held onto her. And this was followed immediately by another thought. *Idiot. Don't exaggerate your own importance in this.*

"Please don't try to persuade me otherwise, Mr. Lauchlan.

Now that Frank is ... gone, I think, perhaps —" She lifted her chin and met his eyes. "That is, I mean to go my own way."

"Mrs. Martland — Agnes — I hope you don't think I'm here to save you from error. I'm here as a friend. And if your heart is in this, I'm happy for you." It wasn't quite true but he hoped to get there in the end.

"Oh, that's a relief." She almost laughed. "It's been on my mind. But I want you to know that I won't forget everything you've done for me."

It was the second time she had said it and again he felt the stab. "But I didn't do the one thing that mattered most, did I?"

She just looked at him, surprised. "What? —"

"I keep going over it in my mind. If I'd gotten to Trevor sooner. If I'd kept Martland on the floor longer. If I'd just managed to get the gun —" He bent toward her. "If I'd insisted that Trevor go to the police immediately, that night, when he first told me, then maybe —"

"Or if I had taken the children and left Frank ten years ago, or if I'd insisted that Trevor stay on in the east after university, or if I'd paid more attention six months ago when I knew something was troubling him." Now tears began to roll down her cheeks and off her chin onto the bib of her apron. She rustled through the pockets of her skirt.

He took out his handkerchief and handed it to her. He hadn't told her how afraid he was that in some truly black corner of his soul, some hidden place of which he was only dimly aware, he had wanted Trevor out of the way. *The heart is deceitful above all things*. How could he tell her that? Was he offering her a little guilt on account, a small amount down against that darker matter?

"I shouldn't have added to your burdens. It was selfishness, pure and simple. I suppose it's just that you're probably the only person I can talk to about this."

"Yes. It's a great relief," she said, dabbing at her eyes. "After everything that's happened, I don't have to pretend anything to you." She handed him back his handkerchief. "But I would like to do something for you. If you'll allow me, I will say a novena for you, starting tonight."

There was a sudden pricking in his throat that made him swallow. "That means a great deal to me, Agnes."

"Now tell me about Miss Skene. She was so kind to me that night. And then she was there for that horror. How is she?"

"Oh, well, she's going away to study — to Germany. Her father thought it best. A complete change of scene. New interests to draw her mind away from that." He flicked a non-existent piece of dust off his trouser leg. "I suppose it's what she needs."

She tried to see his eyes but he was still looking down. "You know, part of the penance in the case of sins of omission is to resolve to act in the future, when opportunities present themselves."

Somehow he knew that there was no use denying it. "It's too soon. It would only confuse her."

She smiled and the sun caught a line in her face that had once been a dimple. For just a moment he saw the unshadowed gaiety she must have felt when she was a girl.

"I don't think you know much about young ladies, Charles."

He arrived back at the church in time to meet Peter and take him to lunch. They were off to the Clarendon Hotel to raise a glass of Mrs. Rotheney's finest rhubarb punch to the completion of the chancel. Since the charges had been dropped, Peter had been working like a demon in order to finish by the end of August. Charles stopped just inside the narthex doors to get the long view down the aisle toward the new chancel. There was a lustre to the choir pews and casings that seemed to come from deep within the wood and owe nothing to the sun streaming through the pointed windows. The aroma of fresh shavings, varnish and pine resin, entirely pleasant, still hung in the air.

Charles and Peter had done most of the staining and varnishing themselves, though Peter had insisted they get a professional painter in to teach them how to apply the stains properly. Charles had loved the process of removing the stain, leaning his body into the wide swipes of the staining rag, watching the grain come up.

The pulpit was set on a slight projection of the platform so that the preacher would be wrapped around by the congregation. The new brass reading lamp had come all the way from Chicago, a rare extravagance insisted upon by Mr. Arbuthnot and paid for by him.

They had not talked much about what Peter would do next but Charles had a plan. There was a congregation in the west end ready to build a new church. And after that he was sure that between his other brethren and the Methodists they could keep Peter busy for several years. He looked at his watch. Where was Pete? He went out the side door and walked down the hall to the janitor's room. At first he thought he must have taken a wrong turn. In place of the general mayhem of shirts and towels and newspapers and plates with toast crusts and stained mugs full of half-drunk tea, there was order and cleanliness. The cleanliness of absence. Peter's iron bedstead now sat with its disreputable mattress rolled up to match the one that Charles had left two months earlier. He checked the drawers of the chipped dresser. Empty. Strange how easily a room can be stripped of the personality that has inhabited it.

There was a package wrapped neatly in brown paper and tied with string beside the basin and ewer on the wooden china barrel. He picked it up and found a white card stuck to the paper. It read, CHARLES, OPEN ME.

He cut the string with his penknife and pulled the brown paper off. In his hand was a small carved wooden statue, a curious figure with a large head and smaller body, rather comical. It was a man in a monk's gown with a clerical tonsure and large feet enclosed in sandals peeking out from underneath the gown. All the details were beautifully carved and the whole stained with the same colour Charles had so lovingly applied to the choir pews. The little monk was clutching something — yes, a square like the one that Peter had kept on his drawing desk, a carpenter's square. There was another white card attached to the statue by a piece of red string. Charles opened it.

> Charlie,
> Here is St. Thomas — doubting Thomas — who also happens to be the patron saint of carpenters and builders. I'm leaving him as a token of the work we did together.
> So much to say that I can't. Forgive me.
> Pete

Charles sat down heavily on the bedstead, which protested with a metallic groan. He looked closer at the face of the little monk, who clutched the large carpenter's square to his chest with an intense expression. There was something familiar about the rapt features. Then Charles laughed out loud.

44.

"Mr. Lauchlan! Won't Maggie be glad — and Miss Jessie. Shall I set another place for dinner?" Lizzie dried her hands on her apron and closed the door behind him.

"Yes, thank you, Lizzie. Is Dr. Skene at home?"

"No, sir. Still at the college, but expected any moment. I'll tell Miss Jessie you're here."

There was no need for at that precise moment Aunt Jessie came barrelling through the swinging door, face alive with all the doings of the kitchen. Also at that precise moment a voice came down the stairwell from the second floor.

"Charles?"

"Charles, how good to see you," Aunt Jessie said. "Pork pie for dinner. You'll stay?"

"Of course he'll stay. He can't avoid us forever." Now Maggie was standing on the landing and looking down on him rather coolly.

"Maggie, don't abuse Charles. I'm sure he's been busy."

"Well he can make himself useful while waiting for his pork pie by helping me pack my trunk. Somehow I have to get under the two hundred pound limit."

"Up you go, Charles." Aunt Jessie dropped her voice and spoke out of the side of her mouth. "But I hope you're good at walking on eggshells; she's been that hard to deal with."

Charles dutifully ascended the stairs and followed Maggie to the second floor sitting room. The open trunk was in the middle of the pleasant, book-lined room with all manner of shoes, umbrellas, parasols, sporting equipment and assorted personal oddments in piles on the overstuffed chesterfield and chairs.

Until now he had somehow managed to evade thinking about the enormity of her leaving. He looked at the trunk, gaping open like a foreshortened coffin. "Should you be taking so many books? They have libraries in Germany, you know." Blast. That wasn't what he felt like saying at all.

"You can go back downstairs if all you're going to do is criticize."

"I thought you wanted some help."

"Help, yes. Carping, no. We don't see you for weeks and when you come around, it's just to find fault."

"It hasn't been weeks. I had to help Peter finish up in the sanctuary."

"But I'm going to be gone for a year, maybe more. Didn't you — I thought you would want —" She faltered but her eyes held his.

The air crackled orange and yellow. Suns exploded into sparking showers and her hair, her clothing, rippled with a dangerous energy. His resolve was crumbling, smashing to powder and along with it any thought of suffering in noble silence. The floor heaved and gave way underneath him as he crossed toward her.

"Stay!"

Her arms slipped under the back of his jacket just as their lips collided. The walls of the room bowed outward in a rush of air. Former points of reference vaporized; bridges burned merrily but all unheeded. Even gravity worked on them in strange new ways. The open trunk, though, remained stolidly itself. All wrapped up together and oblivious, they bumped into it. She overbalanced and, to avoid falling into it, fell backwards onto the chesterfield, dragging him down on top of her.

He should get up immediately. And he would. As soon as he could splice together the shredded connection between his doing and his thinking selves. The sensation of her body beneath him was not helping, especially when she moved like that. With Herculean effort, he pulled away and landed flat on the floor next to the chesterfield, facing up. From there all he could hear was his own breathing. Up above he could only just see her diaphragm rising and falling under the fine, starched linen of her shirtwaist, now sweetly disarrayed.

She raised herself on one elbow, looking down at him, strands of hair escaping their pins and falling down around her face.

"Stay?" she said, reaching for his hand. "And do what?"

He removed a pair of galoshes and a tennis racket from his chest with his free hand and raised himself to a kneeling position. "Marry me, of course. Look, it's a lot to take in, I know. So soon after Trevor —"

"But I wasn't in love with Trevor."

"Uh — What? You weren't?"

"No." There was a sadness in that finality. She let go of his hand, slipped off the chesterfield, and walked over to the window where a glass paperweight set on the sash was catching the late afternoon sun. She captured the wayward strands of hair and pinned them up again, a gesture of such unselfconscious beauty that he wanted to see it again a thousand times.

"I kept expecting to fall in love with him at any moment.

We were such grand friends. But it didn't happen." She turned back to face him. "And I can't pretend that it did just because he's dead. That sounds awfully cold doesn't it?"

After he had scrambled to his feet and put his arms around her again, she buried her face against his chest.

"*Shssh* now, *shssh*. Breathe. It's just the truth, that's all — that's better, breathe. You can't love someone because they want you to."

She pulled back, leaving tears blotted on his lapels. "But it's horribly unfair, isn't it?" She found a handkerchief in the pocket of her skirt. "When I should have been thinking about Trevor, when he needed me to love him, I was actually thinking about you."

"Darling girl. Don't ask me to feel sorry about that." He saw the crease in her forehead. "About everything else, but not that." He tried to pull her gently back.

"Now what will we do?" The crease was still there.

"Well for a start, we'll have to cancel your train ticket," he said, "And we'll have to cable the steamship company to return your passage money. Oh, and I suppose you'll have to write and cancel your —"

"But Charles, I'm still going."

"Still? But I thought —"

The train jolted and groaned, straining to be gone. He detached her from the huddled group on the platform and, taking her arm, led her to the foot of the metal steps going up to the car next to the sleeping car where she had a berth. She was juggling the small bouquet of flowers he had given her, and the basket of fruit. He handed her up the steps and she turned back at the top as the train began to move. He walked along with it. She said she wished she could explain why she had to go. He said she had to have this chance; it was what he loved about her.

The train began to move faster. He jumped onto the bottom step to give her one last thing, a small white cotton bag of humbugs from Mrs. Gough, tied with a blue ribbon. Then he kissed her quickly and jumped off onto the platform. As the space grew between them, the conductor appeared behind her and shooed her into the car.

He crammed his hat back on and walked slowly back toward the others. Dr. Skene looked stoical but he had his arm around his sister. Lizzie was dabbing at her eyes with the corners of her apron. Without speaking, they walked back into the station.

On the way to the streetcar stop, Dr. Skene said, "I've a plan to send a few of our theology students to Germany next summer. You know, our top men. Can't let Queen's and Knox steal the march on us. We'll send a few of the better arts men, too."

Charles, whose mind was still on that train, answered in a distracted fashion, "Well, you'd better send someone older with the arts men, or the parents won't pay to send them." He heard what he had just said, and halted, mid-step. "Sir? Can you arrange it? Can you pull it off?"

"You should have some study leave coming, shouldn't you?" said Dr. Skene. "You haven't taken a real holiday in six years."

When the tram rolled up, Aunt Jessie had to tug at their sleeves, so deeply were they immersed in the details of the scheme.

Afterword

I would like to thank Dave Margoshes and Doug Whiteway, both of whom read excerpts from an early draft of this book and offered much encouragement. I owe a debt of gratitude to Sylvia McConnell, who read the manuscript at a later stage, dealt sensitively with my jitters, and suggested changes which made this a much better book. It may interest readers to know that there was a real life model for Rosetta Cliffe, the photographer in my story. My thanks are due to Elizabeth Blight, former Head of Still Images at the Archives of Manitoba, for sharing with me her research on Rosetta Carr, who plied her craft bravely in the male-dominated commercial photography business of 1890s Winnipeg.

Of Related Interest

A Siege of Bitterns
A Birder Murder Mystery
by Steve Burrows

Inspector Domenic Jejeune's success has made him a poster boy for the U.K. police service. The problem is Jejeune doesn't really want to be a detective at all; he much prefers watching birds.

Recently reassigned to the small Norfolk town of Saltmarsh, located in the heart of Britain's premier birding country, Jejeune's two worlds collide when he investigates the grisly murder of a prominent ecological activist. His ambitious police superintendent foresees a blaze of welcome publicity, but she begins to have her doubts when Jejeune's most promising theory involves a feud over birdwatching lists. A second murder only complicates matters.

To unravel this mystery, Jejeune must deal with unwelcome public acclaim, the mistrust of colleagues, and his own insecurities. In the case of the Saltmarsh birder murders, the victims may not be the only casualties.

Local Customs
by Audrey Thomas

Letitia Landon, "Letty" to her friends, is an intelligent, witty, successful writer, much sought after for dinner parties and soirées in the London of the 1830s. But, still single at thirty-six, she fears ending up as a wizened crone in a dilapidated country cottage, a cat her only companion. Just as she is beginning to believe she will never marry, she meets George Maclean, home on leave from his position as the governor of Cape Coast Castle on the Gold Coast of West Africa. George and Letty marry quietly and set sail for Cape Coast. Eight weeks later she is dead — not from malaria or dysentery or any of the multitude of dangers in her new home, but by her own hand. Or so it would seem. *Local Customs* examines, in poetic detail, a way of life that has faded into history. It was a time when religious and cultural assimilation in the British colonies gave rise to a new, strange social order. Letty speaks from beyond the grave to let the reader see the world through her eyes and explore the mystery of her death. Was she disturbed enough to kill herself, or was someone — or something — else involved?

The Resurrection of Mary Mabel McTavish
by Allan Stratton

It's the Great Depression and Mary Mabel McTavish is suicidal. A drudge at the Bentwhistle Academy for Young Ladies (aka Wealthy Juvenile Delinquents), she is at London General Hospital when little Timmy Beeford is carried into emergency and pronounced dead. He was electrocuted at an evangelical road show when the metal cross on top of the revival tent was struck by lightning. Believing she's guided by her late mother, Mary Mabel lays on hands. Timmy promptly returns to life.

William Randolph Hearst gets wind of the story and soon the Miracle Maid is rocketing from the Canadian backwoods to '30s Hollywood. Jack Warner, J. Edgar Hoover, and the Rockettes round out a cast of Ponzi promoters, Bolshevik hoboes, and double-dealing social climbers in a fast-paced tale that satirizes the religious right, media manipulation, celebrity, and greed.

Mary Janeway
The Legacy of a Home Child
Mary Pettit

Mary Janeway is the story of a little girl's childhood while living on a farm as a domestic servant in the late 1800s. Based on extensive historical research, Mary's story begins in Scotland where family circumstances lead to her being sent to Canada as a home child. Separated from her siblings, Mary, at age eight, is sent to a farm near Innerkip, Ontario, where the Jacques family "needed a girl." Her story brings into focus the intimate details of hardship and deprivation experienced by the many of the thousands of young people sent to Canada between 1869 and 1939.

Available at your favourite bookseller

DUNDURN

Visit us at
Dundurn.com
@dundurnpress
Facebook.com/dundurnpress
Pinterest.com/dundurnpress